BIRTHING PAINS

A STORY OF TRANSFORMATION

DENISE RAYNOR

To my children

Derek, Shelley and Keith, who I try to make proud.

CONTENTS

been years since I've seen a presence, but I know this house holds someone new.

Something moves outside the door, but when I look, it's gone. For now.

Lynn hasn't come around the corner to check on me yet. I like that about Lynn. This is our third house tour together, and the elf-like cheer grows on you after a while. Newport seems pretty quiet so far, and her smiles aren't so hard-won – genuine or not.

I feel comfortable in here, almost too comfortable. George hates when I get excited about a house too quickly. Sliding open the top drawer reveals several thick papers, each folded in squares, jumbled together. I'm about to open one when there's a knock at the exterior door.

Looking up, I see the mirror reverberating with the knock like a small fairy flying across the entryway. That would be George, finally. He had a photography shoot in Philly, and the blue route is always backed up from three to seven. Rush hour is much longer in the City of Brotherly Love.

Closing the drawer, I stand and go to him, giving him a hug and a kiss on the cheek. The tiredness from driving leaves his face as he smiles back at me. He hangs his brown leather jacket next to mine. He's taller than me, blocking the light from the window beside the front door. I rub my hands on his arms, taking him in: his light wash jeans, baseball tee. His smile radiates against his copper-brown skin, making me reach up and kiss him again.

"Good shots today?" I asked, slipping my hand in his and leading him into the study.

"Always. Philly's got character," he grins at me, then waves at Lynn, who smiles and returns a small wave, clasping the folder again in that same position. George takes in the room, exhaling a "wow" over some titles on the bookshelf. He drops my hand, moving toward the bay window and sitting down on the bench in front of it. "I can already see you reading here and writing at the desk. I can bring you lunch," he muses.

I raise an eyebrow at him, crossing my arms as I sit back down in the desk chair. "You've been here five minutes," I say. "And you scold *me* about getting attached quickly." I roll my eyes good-naturedly, smirking.

He shrugs then pats the bench with both hands, raising himself. "It's true, I can see it. Doesn't mean it's the right house, but I can see it."

"Any remarks on the town so far? What did you think, driving in?"

George shrugs again, fiddling with the frayed edges of the aging bench cushion. "I think I'll be the only Black guy here," he feigns a laugh. "But I dig the small-town vibe."

I smile at him, and he meets my eyes. "It seems like the fall here is just as beautiful as upstate New York."

He nods and returns my smile. "You're right about that. It really reminds me of Maybrook. And this house seems like it'll have room for my parents to come down for the holidays. Maybe even Alicia, too."

I stand up and walk around the desk towards the door. "Your sister hates small-town life, but maybe your parents could convince her to visit."

"She just likes to be contrary. Like someone else I know." He nudges my shoulder with his. "Have you seen the upstairs yet?" He bounds out of the room in a slow-motion mock-run. I follow him, laughing.

As we go through the atrium to the foyer, Lynn takes her cue. "This is the foyer, of course, and the staircase is just behind me, here. This is the original balustrade," Lynn enunciates the last word in a way that makes me think she has to use that word for railing "per company policy" or something. But it is beautiful, much more of a balustrade than a railing, orna-mented with flowers. I walk up a couple of steps – "a glis-tening natural hardwood," says Lynn as I run my hand up the wood. It has been polished smooth. Elegant. Good move, Lynn.

George follows me up the stairs. I feel the railing's little flowers and leaves on vines snaking up and around the balustrade – even the columns are decorated. Stunningly origi-nal. I feel like Kate Middleton at Buckingham looking down at that foyer.

"Hmm," intones George behind me, his hand on my waist. He raises his eyebrows approvingly, touching the vine work.

"It's got history," I say.

He nods. "My parents would love that this whole house is built with antiques."

I smirk. "And you know my dad will be obsessed with the details of this woodworking. Even he hasn't made something like this before."

The wallpaper along the stairway is a damask of flowers – definitely gardenias. The flowers on the balustrade are, too, with greenery and small cornflower buds for effect. Before we round the stairs and make it to the landing, I'm in love. I can feel George rolling his eyes internally; he knows all this history will pull me in even if there's black mold or asbestos.

"You'll see that this is just the first of the upper floors," Lynn swings her arm gently through the air in a gesture of invi-tation to explore. The first floor opens to a massive living area, with four rooms and a bathroom, nearly symmetrical on either side.

At the far end between two windows is a brick wall – no, a fireplace. "There's a fireplace on the bottom floor in this loca-tion as well," Lynn puts in, tracing my gaze. "It's a very effec-tive heating method. This house runs on a wood stove system, in fact. It's great for the environment overall when the wood is locally sourced." Lynn really had us pegged.

"Can we go upstairs?" I ask, peering up. The stairs continued to another floor, at least.

"Absolutely," says Lynn. She comes forward up onto her toes again. "You go on ahead, I'll wait downstairs while you two look around."

I realize then that she hasn't left the top stair. "Lynn, is..." I begin, and then pause before saying, "is this in the Newport School District?"

Lynn doesn't respond, as if she doesn't hear me. "Hmm? Oh, yes, it's a small district in number but encompasses nearly thirty square miles out here. It's a tight community really." She smiles without showing her teeth. "I'll be downstairs!" She repeats as she leaves.

"Is she okay?" George asks as he checks the windows for cracks or looseness.

"I hope so." I step onto the stair and switch on the light, illuminating our climb. "Come on, then."

"Don't you want to see the bedrooms?" George asks, his hand on the doorknob of the room nearest the stairs.

I shake my head. "No sense getting attached if there's holes in the roof or a bat infestation."

"You love bats." George smirks and comes toward me on the stairs.

"I love bats in nature," I correct him, beginning the climb up the steps. "Not my own house."

The stairs turn upward again, but this time, the balustrade really is just a railing. The wallpaper stops, and the wall is painted a dull blue – or at least it's dull now. The ceiling seems to be undamaged by water or humidity. The white trim is yellowing but unscuffed. The whole space feels forgotten.

"I don't think people go up here much, but I guess it *is* a large house. Maybe they didn't have kids either and just used it for storage."

George shrugs and wipes a finger along the wall. It comes away dusty, and he rubs his fingers together. He wipes them on his jeans. "Nasty," he mumbles.

I turn on the light switch at the top of the stairs and see a rectangular, flat hallway with room for no more than a small table against the back wall. No windows, and a room on either side. I go to the left side room and peer in. It's dark, but I can make out a small window on the opposite wall, square but eaved in a perfect triangle. I put my hand to the wall on the right and feel for a switch. Nothing but more dust. I wipe my hand on my jeans and take out my phone, shining the flashlight into the room in a wide sweep. When the light lands on the right side, I see an old medical-looking chair, reclined. But no light switch.

"What's in the room over there?" I call as I turn with my flashlight. It illuminates the hallway and a bit of the room in front of us. "George?" Peering into the room with the flashlight, I see that it's identical to the other but with no furniture.

"Kendra, in here!" I jump at George's voice, turning my head to see he's right behind me. For such a simple space, the attic is disorienting.

"Right here, baby," he puts his hand on my shoulder and squeezes. "Didn't mean to scare you. Let's go downstairs. We haven't seen the kitchen yet or the living room. And I'm sure there's a basement."

I nod and head down the stairs, shaking off the unease of the attic.

When we get to the bottom, Lynn is waiting in the foyer like a statue unmoved. "Would you like to see the kitchen?" She gestures to the right.

George and I exchange looks and nod. She is definitely

acting weird. Usually, she peppers us with questions, offering pennies for our thoughts on each room we see. In the shed at that last place, she had to know what we thought of the rack shelving. But today... nothing.

At the bottom of the stairs, we turn left to enter the kitchen. George and I look around as we open the cabinets and the fridge. I slide open the drawers, checking for rat droppings or bugs. I catch George's eye, and he gives me a brief, slanting nod: *Not bad.* He sits down at the head of the kitchen table, his back to the fridge. I follow his lead, sitting across from him, the back door beside me admitting the leaden light of twilight.

Looking at her in the doorframe, I watch Lynn worry her lip in her front teeth, the folder in front of her in that shield-like grip. I heave a deep sigh and ask her point-blank. "Lynn, is this house haunted?"

CHAPTER TWO

I couldn't *not* ask. She stares at me for a dragging millisecond, her eyes wide. And then that toothless, tight-lipped smile snaps to attention. Her foot starts tapping then stops as I try again.

"Because if it is haunted, that's okay." I lower and raise my hands softly in the calming movements of a zookeeper or a kindergarten teacher. "We're not the type of people that run from a ghost. Seriously, we can handle it." I smile encouragingly and pat the table, beckoning for her to sit down. She hesitates, nods, then sits. The sink behind her reflects sunlight from the window above, her face dark in the contrast.

Lynn sighs, her eyes unfocusing as she looks toward the center of the table. "The couple who lived here weren't here for long. They didn't have any kids. I'm not even sure they were trying," Lynn stops and puts her folder down slowly, returning her hands to her lap. She breathes deeply, in and then out. Then, leaning back from the table, she crosses her legs. She reaches into the inside pocket of her vest and removes a vape, taking a few hits.

Okay, Lynn.

"They would hear things." She puffs again, exhaling. "They would hear laughter or feet running, sometimes crying at night as if someone was waking from a nightmare. Eventually, the wife thought she could just treat them kindly, respect their space, and they could coexist. Or, maybe, help them to cross over by listening to them. It never resulted in anything except more engagement. The girl –" Lynn stopped. She twirls her vape like a pen a few times, thinking. She carefully stands it upright on the table before starting again. "The *sounds* became more persistent. Like kids, I guess, more excited the more you got them wound up. The couple felt too heartbroken and unsettled about the whole thing and just, kind of gave up. Moved away. He worked online, and I think she was a crafter or an MLM girl or something. That's a lot of time to be home with... *that*."

I grin and laugh shortly. "We aren't part of any multi-level marketing schemes – I have no protein powder or makeup to sell you. But I'm a writer, and he's a photographer. We're always home!" The look on her face makes me laugh more genuinely. "Seriously, it's fine. This sounds very manageable."

George chimes in, "You have no idea: Kendra can manage. She'll get the sage and the palo santo, and we'll be spic and span here," he says merrily, giving Lynn a game show host smile and a wink. "She might even enjoy herself."

Despite myself, I blush, and George reaches over and places a hand on mine in quiet apology.

Lynn doesn't look completely convinced, but her smile, which had gradually become a grimace as she told the ghost story, is reviving bit by bit.

"Can you give me a minute in here?" I ask Lynn, "I want to feel the energies alone." I blush again. Why am I embarrassed because I'm *not* afraid of ghosts, energies, or spirits? Lynn nods and stands, taking the folder and pausing before exiting. It's hard to know what she's thinking.

George stands as well, kissing me on the head. "See you out there. I know you love this place already, but be objective," he smirks, then follows Lynn out.

Alone, I look around the kitchen. Dark wood cabinets, deep-set farmhouse sink. Yellowed curtains but charming. I always like yellowed things; antique books, vintage clothing. New things don't have a story to them like the old and yellowed do.

Leaning back in my chair, I place my hands on the table. The wood is solid, a dark wood like the cabinets, with more to show for its age and use. I take three deep breaths and close my eyes, grounding myself.

Inhaling, I smell the must of the place. It feels like it's been empty for much longer than a few weeks. It's amazing how old houses settle back in like that.

Opening my eyes, I take a pendulum from my jeans pocket. Rose quartz – I learned after my first attempts with clear quartz that rose is much quicker at setting a calm tone for communication. Resting my elbow comfortably, sitting on the edge of my seat, I hold the pendulum still, the rose point slowing to a stop in a straight arrow toward the dark wood.

"Spirits of this home," I start, "any who dwell in this space, speak with me here today." Talking to spirits is like opening a window – the energy and air around me shifts like a breeze through the curtains. It's refreshing, energizing. I always feel a rush when I address a spirit, whether there's answers to come or not.

Slowly, I move the pendulum in a clockwise motion. A slight move of my wrist gets it going. "Move the pendulum thusly to indicate a yes," I say to the room, the emptiness feeling acute.

Changing directions with another twist of my wrist, I tell whoever may be listening, "Move the pendulum counterclockwise, in a circle to the left, to tell me no."

I change directions once more, going up and down, out and in, toward me with the pendulum: still, slow, and subtle. "If you don't know the answer, swing the pendulum out and back toward me."

I let the pendulum swing a few more times in this direction to show them the difference. "If you prefer not to answer, swing the pendulum side to side." The last instruction. I go through each direction one more time and then allow the pendulum to settle again, unmoving in a straight point downward. I always ask the same question first.

"Is there anyone here with me?" I speak clearly, kindly. I never want to feel demanding or authoritative. This may have been their home – they might still see it as such.

There's no response. I try again.

"Is anyone living here?" This phrasing gets a response. The pendulum swings in a confident clockwise circle: yes.

"Do you live here alone?" I ask as the pendulum slows and settles again.

A hesitation this time, then a few decided anticlockwise swings. There's more than one person.

"Do you like living here?"

Almost before the question is asked, the pendulum moves side to side quickly. They prefer not to answer; interesting.

"Are your parents home?" I ask softly, gently.

The pendulum remains still. Maybe they are afraid of their parents hearing this conversation.

Next, I'll ask the obvious, important one, "Are you children?"

I should have started with this perhaps. The pendulum

waits again, then swings clockwise three times, before switching directions, anticlockwise. Yes and no?

"Is there more than one person talking to me right now?"

The pendulum doesn't move. I wait several seconds, almost a minute.

"Is there more than one person here?" I ask again. The yes-or-no-questions restriction is annoying at times like this.

I wait again, and no answer.

"Would you mind if someone new came to live here?"

The pendulum swings up and down, away and back toward me. They're not sure. That's promising.

"Would you mind if I came to live here?"

Perhaps a little too personal, but we've broken the ice. The pendulum swings again – up and down, up and down. They're not sure.

"Thank you for speaking with me today and welcoming me into your home." I smile, gently pull up the pendulum, and return it to my pocket, standing and walking to the sink as my fingers trail along the table. I notice it's not completely flat, as if years of food prepped and meals shared have lovingly diminished its surface.

Suddenly I feel a chill at my neck, at the back of my arms, down my back.

I turn toward the back door. I go over and touch the handle; it's securely closed. I bend down, looking to see if the draft is coming from underneath. A dark reflection crosses the window. A black mass recedes beneath the table just as I turn to look.

CHAPTER THREE

"Well?" George asks as I come out of the kitchen and into the wide foyer again. Lynn is standing with her back to the stairs, arms over that folder, of course. George offers me his hand and walks me through to the living room. Sitting on the couch, I unfurrow my brow. Why my face has to show exactly what I'm thinking is beyond me.

Still processing, I muster a smile. "Not good, not bad," I say to him. Turning toward Lynn, who hasn't moved – her respect for privacy is admirable – I continue. "We'll have to come back another time, to be sure. I want to see more of the bedrooms. But it is getting late." It takes it out of me, the channeling and focus.

"Of course! I'll set that up with you this week," Lynn replies, moving toward the door. "Can I ask you something?"

My heart is in my throat as I smile and nod.

"Did you find anything in there?" She asks the question casually, grabbing her coat.

I do my best to maintain my smile. "Yes and no." I laugh

internally at my little inside joke. I swear I almost hear a light, quiet laugh coming from behind me.

"Hmm. Well, give me a call anytime." That tight-lipped smile again. I thought we were lightening up, here, Lynn. I notice her folder seems to have grown since we arrived here. I watch her as she goes outside, giving us a moment inside alone. I turn my back to the fireplace in the living room, looking out across to the foyer and toward the kitchen. The kitchen is brighter than the foyer, the uncurtained window illuminating the scarred kitchen table and the white-tiled floor beneath it.

Then, beneath the stairs, I notice a solid, oaken basement door. It's easy to miss. As I start to approach it, I feel that same presence I felt in the kitchen. Like I'm being followed. I turn back to George, and we follow Lynn to the front door.

Slipping on his jacket, George peeks into the study. "That is a great writing room, Ken." He rubs my back as I shrug into my coat. Following me out, Lynn pulls the door shut behind us. I notice the doorknob, tarnished silver or iron. Another gardenia.

"Hey, Lynn, could you look something up for me before we come back next time?" Lynn's retreating back stops. She turns as I add, "Can you find out the history of the owners back to the year it was built if that's possible?"

"Sure thing, I'll see what the township has on it and call you this week." Lynn's hands are stark in her pockets. She must have put the folder in the car. Even in the twilight, I see she's tense. She must really need this sale.

George walks me to my car. Holding open the door as I sit, he asks, "Chinese or pizza?"

"Surprise me." I pull the car door shut and turn the key. I hope it's both. I'm starving.

Backing out of the gravel drive, I look up at the house in its full frame. The symmetry is striking. Two eaved windows at the top for each of the attic rooms, two windows on the middle floor, the ground floor's wide living room window on the left. The balance is only disturbed by the lack of windows in the study from this angle; the bay window faces the alley to the right. A corner property: I wonder if it looked out on fields or a garden in the past.

I smile up at the dark windows. It feels like home, somehow. Like it could be my home. Like it was meant to be my home.

It makes me want to write.

As I PULL up in front of our apartment building nearly an hour later, exhaustion sets in. I take a minute in the car, rolling my shoulders and turning my neck from side to side. George'll be a few minutes behind at least with the food.

I grab the mail from the box on the wall by the front door, then head upstairs. I won't miss hiking to my own doorstep. Unlocking the front door, I walk through the living room, heading to the kitchen to take care of some dishes. I can't wait to move out of Harrisburg; there are too many stairs, steps, and locks. I'm thinking about packing, writing, and ordering Chinese food as I turn on the kitchen light in the window above the sink.

I see my reflection, darker than it should be. My appetite vanishes as an unsettling chill teases at the back of my neck, getting stronger the longer I look at the shadow where my face should be.

It's wrong.

It's my face, but not my face. A shadow is over my face, like a black veil. I peer closer, then stop. I don't know why: logically, I know it's just glass on a window. But I feel like I'm making eye contact with something sinister. I try to swallow, but there's a sudden dryness in my throat.

I look away, turning to open the fridge and grab the water pitcher. When I close the fridge, I look apprehensively at the window.

My reflection is clear. Too clear – the bags under my eyes stare at me as my mess of brown waves remind me to wash my hair tonight. Pouring a glass of water, I drink deeply, eyes closed.

When I open them again, I catch my reflection in the window, a sense of deja vu washing over me as I drink. The chill on my neck returns, stronger, spreading goosebumps down my arms.

The lights haven't changed.

I haven't moved.

But my entire reflection is completely dark.

I feel another presence here with me, but I resist the urge to turn around and look behind me. As I stare into the window, the shadow across my face shifts to the right.

I choke on my water, backing up, scrabbling against the stove. I catch my breath, placing the cup on the counter. Slowly, taking measured breaths, I approach the sink again, forcing myself to look at the window.

My reflection appears normal this time, no shadow, no darkness. I feel a sense of victory even though the goosebumps haven't left my arms, and my neck is still tingling with anxiety.

I get two plates from the cupboard, carefully avoiding the window.

I'm on the couch ready for dinner when George comes home.

"I got both. I hope you're hungry," he announces like a town crier holding a pizza box and a bag of Chinese food in either hand, high in the air.

I fold my legs under me and open my arms to him – and the food. "My hero. You always read my mind!" George puts the food down on the table, the box resting on top of some books I'm in the middle of reading, and then he falls into my arms.

His head on my shoulder, he looks up at me. That boyish 'what are you thinking' look he's given me since we were first dating eight years ago. Those brown eyes kill me every time. "So…" he intones musically.

"So, I really like that house," I say, brushing an errant curl of dark hair from his forehead. Unfolding my legs from under me, I reach for the Chinese. "It's got a lot of history. Did you feel how heavy it is? The energy I mean?"

"You know I never do," he says, sitting up and putting two pieces of pizza on his plate. Pineapple and mushroom. We both love it. When we first realized our odd, shared tastes, we joked that it was proof we'd get married. Five years later, we did. "But I could see you in that study every day. Writing away at that desk. The bay window cluttered with notes; if you don't get distracted by the books, that is." He adjusts his shirt over his tummy, presses his glasses into his face and sits back, pizza in hand.

"But what did you think? I mean, rural PA is definitely not rural New York."

George swallows his bite of pizza before answering. "I went to college in Philly because I thought I wanted big city life, but I feel like I haven't had a good night's sleep outside of visits home. Even when we moved to Harrisburg, it was just too noisy and crowded. Maybrook was boring, but I like boring."

I hesitate on my next question, not sure how to bring it up. "Would you feel like, I don't know… would you fit in enough? You're probably right about being the only Black person. I looked it up before you got home: Newport is ninety-seven percent white."

"And I'm fifty percent," George says, finishing his first slice of pizza. "The world is full of people waiting to judge me for the color of my skin. I can't let it control my life."

Scooping lo mein onto my plate, I grab a dumpling and change the subject. "I felt like I could see us there, like we had lived there for years in some ways. The study, of course, but the attic rooms, the giant sitting room by the fireplace in the hallway upstairs, the farmhouse sink in the kitchen..." I take a bite of my dumpling. "It's huge for us, but it's so charming."

"It's just us and the cats. Don't you think we should look for something cheaper? It's just at the limit of our budget."

I chew meditatively. "I know. But we'd each have an office, and we'd still have another guest room, not to mention the attic if we can find a way to get lights in there. It's a forever home."

He's finishing off the lo mein, shaking the container out onto his plate now. When he doesn't respond, I continue. "I know it's a lot. Every penny we've saved. All of it."

"And what if we need a new roof? Or appliances? Or there's flooding? We're sinking it all, Ken."

I look at him and put my fork down. "But it's perfect." I see a smile tease at his dimple.

"I think this is our house," he pauses, placing the lo mein container back in the takeout bag before continuing, "but there's something you're not telling me, and it's not about the lack of diversity."

"Well," I start, swallowing my bite of noodles. "I saw something. Something under the table. The pendulum reading wasn't as helpful as I'd hoped. There's definitely ghosts, at least two; one or more of them is young, maybe a child. They were nervous, whoever I was talking to. Then I felt a draft. I checked the door, but that wasn't where it was coming from. And then, under the table..." I put my fork down on my plate. "I saw, like, a shadowy person. They were hiding under the table and backing away from me." I meet his eyes. "Do you think it was the setting sun or a car passing or something like that?"

Instantly, George is shaking his head. The glare of his glasses masks his eyes, but I know he's looking at me. "I know you, Kendra, and I trust your intuition. When we went to Gettysburg you used that pendulum to figure out exactly how many soldiers were in that clearing, that they were from Georgia, and how old they were. We verified it with the historical records. I don't know what you do, but I believe it."

I give him a wan smile. "I'm surprised I didn't scare you away then with my witchy ways."

He smirks. "I know by now that you only use your powers for good. In that house, there's something or someone –"

"Definitely 'someone'. It didn't feel scary, just... intense. Nervous," I explain.

"Then you can talk with them again and hopefully learn more before we agree to the house. Good idea asking for the history of the home. Newport is so old. I'm sure there's a story of someone who needs help."

"That feeling of nerves could even just be a residual haunting. Maybe they didn't know why a stranger was in their home. They might not know they've passed on. Or maybe they're just tired and wanted me to leave. Or maybe I reminded them of someone. Maybe –"

"Don't worry about it now. We'll be back there this week to feel it out after reading the research. Let's eat and watch some TV," George says. He's already opening Netflix on his phone to cast something to the TV.

"You're right," I say, grabbing a slice of pizza. "Do you need a drink?"

George nods between bites.

Getting up, I go to the kitchen, taking the pitcher from the counter. I fill two glasses of water. My reflection looks back at me, clearly; my white cardigan visible over my gray shirt. What was that shadow earlier? Hearing the TV switch on, I turn to bring the water back to the table.

A dark mass flurries across my ankles.

"Shadow!" I mock-scold our little black furball. She loves drinking out of water glasses. Placing the glasses down on the coffee table in front of George, I ask her, "Where's your sister?"

Peeking into the guest room off the living room, I see a curled-up mass on the pillow of the bed – Sherry is always the sleepiest.

"Hey sweet girl," I call to her, her beacon eyes opening and reflecting in the darkness. She narrows her eyes slowly, feline language for *I love you*. I narrow my eyes slowly back: *I love you too, Sherry*.

I turn on the guest room light and walk past my altar, sitting on the bed next to her. I have my ritual space in here, away from the more populated areas of the house. A low table with a purple altar cloth, symmetrical taper candles for the God and Goddess next to statues of each, and four colored chime candles in a circle in the middle for each element, it's a bit imposing; I don't always want to have to explain when guests come over.

Sherry stretches and gives a short *mew*, yawning and pressing her paws against my leg. Scratching her behind her ears, I reach over to my tarot cards on my altar table. I think they'll have some advice on this.

I take the cards and return to George. He's scrolling on his phone. "I think the client is excited for our shoot tomorrow," he says. "They're doing an engagement shoot at Laurel Hill Cemetery. I bet you'd like them," he laughs.

"Yeah because all witches love cemeteries," I sarcastically roll my eyes. I do love cemeteries. The first thing I did when we moved to Harrisburg was walk through the cemeteries here.

Harrisburg Cemetery is my favorite fall excursion when I need a breath of fresh air. The apartment has no other nature nearby, so the cemetery is the closest I can get to connecting with something larger than myself.

"Ken, can I ask you something?" George sits up.

"Sure," I say, shuffling my cards.

"Was your mom a witch, too?"

I feel my ears go red with frustration. "No," I say, blushing deeper. "That's not how witchcraft works." When George looks at me questioningly, I pause. I guess I've never really opened up much about this. "Witchcraft is like a religion. It's a personal path," I start. When he doesn't drop his eyes from mine, I continue. "You don't have to be born into anything or have any special powers or childhood moments – although you might. But you don't have to. It's something active. You decide to do it and so you do. You believe in the Goddess. You worship," I pause, rephrasing. "We respect nature. It's different for everyone, but we all believe in magic."

George nods. "I get that, I guess."

"Magic, like the idea that we can manifest changes in our lives with our thoughts and actions. Spells, rituals, prayers on the full moon or equinoxes. It's about tapping into the energy of the universe and manifesting change in accordance with our will." I blush. I've never talked this much about my magic. I keep my eyes focused on my tarot cards.

George is quiet for a minute before responding. "That sounds empowering. When we would go to church, it was always, 'let Jesus take the wheel'. I think it's nice you take your life into your own hands that way."

I look up, smiling. "That's it! That's exactly it." I put down the cards. "Mom liked magic, too, in her own way. I think she'd like the empowerment of it. She always wanted me to be whoever I wanted to be." I think back on that day in the kitchen, my last clear memory of her before she got sicker. "Maybe she would've liked witchcraft, who knows? It's not like we were a good churchgoing family." I chuckle. "Nature was important to her, I think. I remember going to the park for picnics as a kid."

One of the main reasons we're fixed on Newport for our new home is the nature. It's by the river, it has a small-town feel, and it's got history. It'll be nice to have that atmosphere around.

I like the feel of that small-town energy. It's inspiring. I don't know when I'll finish my book, but I feel like a change of scenery is the key. At least I hope it is.

I've been writing for years, but ever since moving to Harrisburg, it just feels... off. Boring, somehow. After we visited 117 North Front Street, however, my creative mind is already buzzing. And Newport has a bank location I can transfer to. If I get the branch I applied through, I can walk to work. I don't want to be a teller forever, but it's what I can do with limited hours and a chance at snagging a few moments for writing here and there throughout the day. Fingers crossed, the bank will be even quieter in little Newport.

George puts on a horror miniseries, our obsession in recent years. The latest Mike Flanagan is more monologues than usual but great acting. Before long, he's dozing against my shoulder. I gently shift him to a pillow on the other side and reach over to the remote on the coffee table, switching off the TV. Gathering up our trash in the takeout bag and piling our dishes onto the pizza box, I clear a space and prepare for a reading.

I'll do three cards:

First card – What is the spirit of this house? No pun intended.

Second card – What fears or obstacles are in my way?

Third card – What can I do to overcome this?

I shuffle, focusing on the house, the way it felt, the strange happenings and the difficult pendulum conversation. Placing three piles, the middle one calls to me. I draw the first card from the top of the pile.

The first card symbolizing the house: the Three of Pentacles. Two men in a religious building, looking up at the pentacle stars on the ceiling overhead. Growth, recognition, mastery over challenges. Teamwork. Focus. George and I are a great team, and maybe the spirits there are, too. I can work with this.

The second card is accurate from the first glance. The obstacles: the Seven of Swords. A man stealing swords, looking over his shoulder for witnesses. Manipulation, deceit, cunning, chaos – the fears I have for the real estate process in general, much less a house that won't move. Am I projecting my fears onto the house? Were the energies nervous and reluctant to talk, or was it just me? Buying a house in this market makes anyone distrustful. This card also means ego – is it my ego I'm worried for? Or does the house's ego intimidate me?

The third card – the Empress. Seated on her throne, she is awesomely regal, yet her body language speaks to kindness. Motherly intuition, actions of love. Maybe it's that simple: nurture these spirits. I wonder if that's what the last couple thought if Lynn was right in her account. But the Empress is also creativity, the fertility of progress – I can't help feeling that I'm going to finish my book while in that house. Because of that house. Maybe it's because of those spirits.

Looking at the cards spread in a line before me, I place my hands on the Empress. *Bring me her strength*, I ask silently of the universe. *Come what may.*

CHAPTER FOUR

The bank is slow today, even for a Tuesday. Maybe it's this weather. The clouds have been threatening rain all day, the gray October heaviness that you feel in your joints as you open the door in the morning.

Unlocking the apartment door, I can hear mewing on the other side before I swing it open. Sherry is the chattiest girl. Giving her a scratch behind her ears, I walk around, tidying up side tables, taking a few books to shelves. I'm feeling that nervous energy of the need to move. Our lease is up in December, which means we have until next week to give notice. I'm ready, trepidacious. If it's not this house it'll have to be a different one, but even as I think those words, I feel a heavy resolve. I feel so drawn to Front Street.

I push aside the niggling anxiety of writing. I haven't written in a week at least, and I've submitted sample chapters. If I hear back with a manuscript request without a finished ending... But somehow, packing feels more pressing. When I meditate on it, I get the same feeling I did with my card reading: there's something at this house that will help me. Packing feels like a step toward it. Maybe today I'll start on the guest room – not my altar yet, but I feel good about us moving soon, so the shelves can be cleared. George might not understand the deep trust I have in my tarot deck, but I do. For whatever else it told me, that card reading last night at least gave me confidence about this move. Come what may.

Going into our bedroom, I find Shadow nestled between our pillows. George made the bed, a good sign. He's been booked lately, so his mood is good. His favorite hoodie isn't on its peg on the back of the door, so he is definitely having a comfortable, energized day. Maybe he's as excited as I am about this house. I open the top drawer of his wardrobe and pull out another hoodie of his, one from Virginia Beach, a million years ago before we met. It's perfectly stretched out, like wearing a blanket.

He hasn't texted, but he never does. I love that about him, actually, that he's living in the moment and never on his phone. The crazy dude doesn't even have social media. His strength is astonishing.

Assembling a box, I decide I'll begin with the DVD collection. We haven't even owned a DVD player in years, so I plan to mark this one 'donate' and see if I can get away with it. George is a bit of a sentimentalist about outdated tech.

Shadow follows me in, jumping on the bed and curling up. Of course, right where I want to put the box; but that's cats for you.

My phone rings as I'm placing a stack of *Lost: Season 3* DVDs in the box.

It's Lynn.

"Good afternoon, Mrs. Levy," says Lynn, chipper as ever. She never remembers that I didn't take my husband's last name.

"Hi, Lynn. Kendra's fine," I'll find a way to mention I'm still Kendra Hill another time.

"Right. Sorry, Kendra. I have an availability tomorrow at one-thirty or Friday at four o'clock. Let me know what works for you," she chirps.

"Tomorrow, I think – let me ask George and get back to you."

"I'll put you down for now. I'll also hold the time slot for Friday until I hear from you."

I can hear her toothless smile from here. "Will you have the history and building records?"

"Oh, yes, I am working on that. So far, I have records dating back to 1919. And the build date, 1860... no, 1865." I hear her shuffle papers. She's good – it's only been 24 hours. She must need this sale.

"That's great. Thank you so much, Lynn. You're on it," I smile genuinely. Whatever her motives, I'm tingling at the chance to peruse those files. "I have off tomorrow, so if George's shoot is later in the day we'll definitely be there. Thank you again."

"Thank you, Mrs.– Kendra," Lynn says, and the call drops.

1865. The Civil War ends, and a booming railroad town is free to grow. I close my eyes, painting a picture of an era on my eyelids – I can see Front Street in its heyday already in my mind's eye.

Turning off the guest room light and leaving the door open for a sleeping Shadow, I go out to the living room and grab my laptop. Going to Google, I type, "Newport PA, 1865".

Incredibly, there are some photos of the late 1800s.

I recognize Front Street in a photo with a caption that reads: The Great Flood of 1889. I've heard of it before. Probably in school. Google tells me that it even affected where I grew up in Philadelphia.

The big town hall is the same today, minus the festive bunting in some photos from 1918, celebrating homecoming veterans at the end of World War I. The pharmacy on the corner of Front is still there today, but with vinyl instead of that lovely wood awning. I think that hotel is a restaurant now.

The oldest photo of a stagecoach from 1840 in front of a nondescript dirt lot could be taken anywhere. Now looking at 'newer' photos from 1920, I see that even at that time, Market Street wasn't even paved. It was just a dirt road.

I'm clicking through when my phone buzzes. It's almost seven already – George says he's on his way. He won't be here until nine with traffic, but it's dinner-cooking time.

On a whim, I check for podcasts on Newport. No results, but not too surprising. YouTube videos yield minimal results, too – except I learn of another flood in the 1970s. I think we'll be getting some flood insurance, for sure. I put on one of my go-to playlists and get cooking.

DINNER IS READY, keeping warm on the stove. Book in hand, my feet are curled up under me on the couch with Sherry at the other end when George comes in.

"Awesome day at the cemetery," he says cheerily.

"Was the drive terrible?" I ask, getting up, kissing him, welcoming him home.

"Always," he laughs. "I think Newport will be better." I smile at his quick mention of the house. He walks past me, leaning over the couch to pet Sherry. "Where's Shadow?"

"Sleeping in the guest room," I answer, nodding towards the open guest room door.

"Did you hear from Lynn?" He asks, smiling at me. He can always tell when I have something exciting to report.

"Yes!" I say, clasping my hands together loudly. "Tomorrow at one-thirty, does that work for you?" I hold my hands together in a childish gesture, begging silently. "She has the documents on the history of the house; you know I can't wait to see them."

"Lucky for you, I don't have anything tomorrow. You're off too, right? We should make a day of it, see the town, get to know the community." He puts his hands around my waist, pulling me toward him. His sweatshirt needs a wash.

"I'm in," I smile, our brown eyes meeting. "I did some research today – we will need flood insurance, whichever house we go with in Perry County. There's been at least two floods in Newport, 1889 and 1972."

"With that gorgeous river, I'm not surprised." He sighs longingly like a cartoon character. "Can you believe this might be happening? We can own a house?" He pulls me closer, hugging my face into his shoulder.

"I know, I've had this nervous excitement all day." Drawing back from the hug, I pull my hands into my sleeves, and then slip them in his, leading him to the kitchen. "A small town, nature, a backyard?"

He leans back on the counter, "Room for you to write, room for me to work?" He lifts a pot lid, inhaling the curry scent. He loves spicy food. "We are really doing this, baby." Putting the lid back on, he leans against the counter again. "I know you've never lived in a small town, but it's amazing. Really. Everyone knows each other. You can leave your windows and doors open and no one will come rob you," he chuckles. "When Alicia and I were growing up, we would go trick-or-treating every year. You know those bowls people left out with notes saying 'please only take one'? She'd always want to take more, but I always thought of the next kids and how sad they'd be if the bowl was empty."

I smile. That sounds like George: thoughtful, even when no one was looking. "I believe that wholeheartedly, baby." I kiss him on the cheek, leaning next to him on the counter.

"It's different, Ken," George continues. "The local community events, and maybe even town meetings. And they decorate for the holidays, and..."

I put my hand on his arm. "I'm glad I'll get to experience what you did growing up."

"We might even, I don't know, feel like having kids."

I feel my heart jump into my throat as he continues. "Once we've been there, you know, and gotten used to the community."

When I don't answer George adds, "It's probably a swell place to raise them." He blushes a bit, visible even beneath his copper skin.

I give him a thin smile. "'Swell', eh? Hold your horses, Ricky Ricardo." He knows I don't want kids. But this is the first time I don't feel queasy at the thought.

"It could be nice, that's all. You never know. You know I'm fine without having kids." He says, smiling. "We've got cats, what could be better?"

I reach up to the cabinet to the right of the stove and grab two bowls. "You've got that right."

Suddenly, he steps over me to the sink. He's looking at the window. "What is that?"

I go behind him on tiptoe, looking over his shoulder. "I can't see, what do you –"

He backs up abruptly, elbowing the dishes out of my hand.

They drop to the floor, one cracking, the other shattering. I stoop and pick up the large pieces, grabbing a towel from the oven door and covering the shards.

"What is that?" George's voice is low, almost a whisper. "It's dark, like a..."

Crouched on the floor, I look up at his profile, only his open mouth and the white corners of his eyes visible from this angle.

I wait for him to finish for what feels like an eternity. "Like a what?"

"It's gone now. Maybe it was just my reflection." He's visibly shaken but shakes his head, ready to forget the whole thing.

"The shadow?" I venture.

George's eyes meet mine.

"George, I saw the same thing last night. In that window, too. A shadow figure." I stand up, taking the towel and the shards up with me. I throw them in the trash can next to the fridge behind me. "I thought it was my reflection but..." I trailed off, not quite sure how to finish that sentence. I turn to go to the guest room closet where we keep the broom but see that the door is firmly closed. I know I left the light off. And I know I left the door open – Shadow was sleeping in there. "George, why did you shut the door and turn the guest room light on?"

"I didn't."

My chest tightens as I hear a long, deep, rising meow come from behind the door.

CHAPTER FIVE

"Shadow!" I swing open the door, and a cold breeze sweeps past me. Shadow meanders out, stretching her paws far in front of her. She doesn't seem bothered. I go into the room, seeing the box of DVDs where I had left it, the bed made, showing an indent where Shadow had been. Going over to my altar table, I take inventory. Chalice, athame, statues, crystals, all accounted for. My cloth is a bit ruffled, like a cat's paw or a small hand had gone across it, but nothing is missing.

"Wait," I say aloud, putting my hands on my hips. "My pendulum. I thought I put it here last night when we got home. It's where I usually keep it." I check the floor, thinking maybe Shadow walked across it and knocked it down. It's not under the table nor the bed; it couldn't have slid far on carpet.

I go into our bedroom, open the hamper, and find my jeans from yesterday. I check the pockets.

George has followed me around the apartment silently. "My pendulum is missing," I say in disbelief.

"Do you think that Shadow took it?"

I shake my head. "No. I swear, George, I've never heard of

something like that happening. A haunting following someone out of their space. Maybe it just followed the pendulum."

"Are you sure it's a haunting? Is that even how energies work?" George asks, shaking his head.

"I don't know. That shadow we saw reminded me of what I saw in the kitchen at the house." I pause, still clutching yesterday's jeans. "Are you still interested in this place?"

George hesitates. "One more look won't hurt. It won't be easy to find a house that size in our budget again."

WE'RE PULLING up to 117 North Front Street. I don't have my pendulum, though part of me hopes it'll be here today under the table or out in the driveway. Maybe it fell out of these abysmally tiny pockets. They always make women's pockets imperceptibly small, when they think to give us pockets at all. Lynn left the door unlocked, so we head right in.

"Lynn?" I call. Her car is empty out front. I don't see her in the front yard anywhere.

There's no answer, so we come in a bit further. I peep into the study before crossing into the main foyer – it's my favorite part of the house so far.

George walks in ahead of me to the kitchen, taking his time it seems. I'm glad he likes the house as much as I do.

The study is as charming as it was yesterday. I want to open my laptop and get right to writing at that delightful desk. It's the first time I've felt like writing in at least a week. Remembering the desk, the top drawer, and the papers I found, I head in. Without Lynn for a minute, maybe I can see what's in there. Sitting at the desk again, I begin to gingerly open the drawer so I don't crush anything.

It opens too easily. It's been emptied, I realize.

Lifting the drawer out, I check the back. There's nothing there. Did they disappear along with my pendulum?

I hear what must be the back door close. I stand up from the desk and go to the foyer. "Hi, Lynn! Everything okay?"

"Yes, just finishing up a call!" Smiling as ever, she straightens her skirt and stands in the kitchen doorway. "How was the drive?" She beckons me in to sit.

"Pleasant as always," answers George, seated at the kitchen table. He's at the head of the table again, in front of the back door. The door and the window above the sink are letting in the afternoon light, illuminating the table. I sit at the other head of the table across from him, my back to the gas stove – something else I love about the house.

Lynn goes around me and takes her place in front of the kitchen sink as if we're continuing yesterday's conversation. She puts her illusive folder down and opens it. "This is what we know. You'll be happy to see there've only been two families, really, that have owned the house."

I'm reaching for it as soon as she opens the folder. Photocopies of typewritten pages, I scan the top – *F. Harr, 1919*.

"The original build date is definitely 1865. Here's a copy you can have." She flashes the paper at me. "And full disclosure, the home was likely damaged in the 1889 flood as all of the homes here were. It has undergone many renovations since then including the basement – we can head down there next since we didn't have time yesterday." There's something different about Lynn, a collectedness she didn't have last time.

"That would be great," I smile, leaning in to scan the deed she holds. Fancy 1800s script like a diploma. It looks legit enough to me. The title is in the name of John Baker. No mention of a wife, but women couldn't even vote then, so I'm not surprised. "So the Baker family owned it until they passed it on to the Harrs in..." I pause, looking back at the first paper I had pulled out. "1919?"

Lynn nods. "Pretty unique, right? I thought you'd like that." She grins at me. Today she isn't tense, and she hasn't reached for her vape once. George isn't looking at the title closely; he's watching Lynn and me. His arms cross his chest, and he leans over the table. I think he sees it, too. She's confident today, yet she seems to be holding something back. Who did she talk to? And where are those papers from the desk?

I flip to the next page, dated 1955. Thirty-six years after they bought it, the Harr's son Lionel inherited it.

"Are there any renovation documents? Is that something that would be shown at the time of sale or...?" I ask Lynn, looking at the next pages of hard-to-read photocopied photocopies.

"Well, as it was an inheritance before the recent sale, that isn't usually something documented upon deed transfer. The house was sold in almost this exact condition to the family who recently vacated. They prefer to remain anonymous." She clears her throat uncomfortably and then goes on. "I believe they repainted but didn't need to do much else. You'll see the most recent inspection there." She reaches over and pulls out the paper from the bottom of the stack. "It's all in order."

So, realistically, only three owners since 1865. John Baker, two generations of Harrs, then the mystery couple. That's interesting: a haunted house with no real problems until the last owners, unless the Harr families were indifferent, were in control, or are the ghosts themselves.

"Is the Harr family still living?" I ask.

Lynn looks to the side, reaching her hand towards the vape in her pocket for the first time today. "I don't know – if they are, I haven't met them."

"And they had the house during the 1972 flood?" I meet her eyes as I ask this question.

Lynn's blue-black irises don't waver. "I suppose so."

I leaf through the pages one more time then pass them to George. "Can we keep them?"

"Sure, they're photocopies and public records," Lynn's lips thin into a tight smile.

"Thank you for this research, Lynn," I smile in return. "I appreciate this. George, are you ready to check out the basement? I want to see the upstairs rooms again, too."

George nods, looking at the papers, and we stand to follow Lynn. The basement door is under the stairs, nearly imperceptible – the banister takes the attention from the shadowy alcove. She opens the door, and I notice its handle as I move to follow her down. It's the face of a gardenia in full bloom.

Lynn turns on the switch at the top of the stairs, and we descend. I like that the wooden stairs feel solid, although the railing stops as we clear the ground floor. Whether it's the concrete darkness or the energy of the space, I feel a chill rise up my neck. Like Persephone entering Hades, I feel a sense of foreboding as I touch ground onto an unseen floor in complete darkness.

At the bottom, Lynn pulls an old-fashioned chain, and a single bulb reveals the gray cement of the floor and a small perimeter around us. It looks like the basement goes on for the full length of the house.

The smell here is of dust, must, and old. Like the home of someone who only used a room or two for the past several decades. It's not mold, though. That's promising.

Lynn continues to the wall a few feet from the bottom of the stairs and flips a heavy industrial switch. A line of lights flash on. The ceiling is low, but it hasn't stopped previous owners from making the most of the space. Like a massive storage unit, it's filled with covered furniture. I lift the corner of a cloth, revealing a side table. Heavy, by the looks of it. I wonder if this is Victorian. This might be more to my taste than the pieces we'll be bringing.

"Does the furniture come with the house?" I ask as Lynn stands against the wall. She left the folder upstairs and doesn't seem to know what to do with her hands.

"Yes," she says, swinging her arms slightly. "It was here when the last couple moved in. I don't think they took anything, actually."

"This is original furniture?" I try to mask the excitement in my voice.

"Or from the Harr's, but yeah." Lynn is clearly done with my haunted house questions. I see her reach for that pocket again. The smoke break will come, Lynn.

George is walking around the basement, lifting a few covers here and there, then replacing them. The light reaches every corner, and I appreciate that. "It's well lit, isn't it, hon?" I call to him. He's a few hundred feet away leaning over a pile, looking behind something.

"Yeah. I still wish I had a flashlight for these nooks and crannies," he says. It'll be so fun to excavate down here.

I don't know why, but I'm hesitant to explore right now. I take a quiet, deep breath and look at Lynn, pretending to be looking at the lights behind her. She is too quiet today. I miss her usual energy on house tours when she's buzzing with fun facts and cool perks. Today she's just present, her face unreadable.

"I'm ready when you are," I say as George comes back around the stairs. The reinforcements after the floods must be holding, it's been a bit wet outside as fall sets in. George starts up the stairs, and Lynn follows, leaving me at the back of the line. I don't want to make a scene and complain, but I don't like being last. There's an uneasiness that sets in, being the last at the bottom of the stairs to a basement, especially an unfamiliar one.

"Can you get the lights, Kendra?" Lynn asks. I feel like she's testing me.

"Sure thing," I say, glad that I sound more confident than I feel.

I sigh, and to avoid being left down here longer, I reach up and pull the cord.

Darkness plunges around me.

In the split second it takes to turn off the light at the wall, I swear I see a lightning strike. Like ghosts, the outlines of cloth over the furniture seem to glow in the remaining hollow of light from that single, ancient bulb. It's the trick of sudden darkness, I know that, but then I hear something.

Footsteps. No, crawling.

No.

It's a sheet rustling.

I hurry up the stairs, no longer heeding how this looks.

CHAPTER SIX

I get to the top, and Lynn is standing in the doorway.

"Basements, always creepy, right?" She tries to lighten the mood. Thanks, Lynn.

I hack a short laugh, at a bit of a loss for words. Behind me, I hear another laugh, higher-pitched, longer than my own. Lynn and I look at each other, and I feel a shiver run down my spine. I swallow and step past her into the foyer, standing closer to George than I normally would in the presence of company. He puts his arm around me.

"Did you see this doorknob? It's beautiful," he smiles as he gestures toward the door, but his face changes as he looks at mine. "Kendra, what's wrong?"

Ignoring him for a second, I look at Lynn. "Lynn, did you hear that?"

Her face is stricken. Then she shifts, and something behind her eyes changes. "Hear what?" She asks the question almost rhetorically. The inflection is unnatural.

I don't answer, but I keep my eyes on hers. "You heard it too, then."

I look at George, and he is glancing from me to Lynn. Still standing by the door to the basement, I gently shake his arm from my shoulders and move out to the foyer. "Shall we see the bedrooms?"

As we head upstairs to the bedrooms, I turn to George. "As I came up from the basement, we heard a child's laugh, or maybe a young woman's. I also heard a sheet rustle when I turned off the bottom light. It's like they were playing with me."

"Maybe that's a good thing," he says as we step onto the landing of the first half of the stairs. The light from the window there is strong today without the haze of twilight closing in. I almost didn't notice it before.

"You might be right," I give him a wan smile. I notice Lynn is waiting at the bottom of the stairs again.

"Lynn," I lean over the railing. "Why don't you go outside for a smoke break?"

She smiles, warmly and with teeth. I'm floored. "If you're sure you're okay in here! I'll just be on the porch off the kitchen. There's a couple of rockers out there."

She turns on her heel and heads to the kitchen. "There's a great view of the woods by the river from that side of the house," she calls over her shoulder as she exits. That's the Lynn we know and love – always the salesperson.

Facing the wide hallway from the top of the stairs, there are two bedrooms on either side. I instantly fall in love with a room with big windows overlooking the street: I can see myself using it as a sewing and craft room. My altar should be up here too for easier morning and bedtime rituals.

Almost on cue, George says, "I want this windowless room. It's great for developing film."

He sounds excited, but for the life of me, I can't remember the last time he had to do that. Always the photographer and ever the purist, I can see George wanting to settle into a quiet life in the house – taking his time, watching film develop, perfecting his craft.

George is behind me, taking longer in the master bath to check the taps. I head out into the open space, taking it in. This floor alone is bigger than our apartment. I hear the tap switch off, and in a minute or so, George comes out. Placing his hand on my shoulders, he says, "Are we ready to go?"

"Almost," I say, putting my hand on his. "Let's go up and try the lights in the attic rooms again, see if it was a fluke. That should be fixed before we move in," I add that last part for the practical effect. I know I'd move in today, regardless. But at least it's sunny, and I can see this time.

The rooms are as we left them, but the wallpaper – yes, more wallpaper – is now visible in the midday sunlight. The sun is directly overhead so both rooms are fairly well-lit, the slanted ceilings casting shadows across the floor in each room. The walls are lined with paper of an ill-fitting pattern. It's white with pink stripes, with pink flowers and bows between the stripes. This cheery, feminine decor doesn't line up with the furniture or atmosphere. Maybe this was a sewing room for a mistress of the home or a baby's room in the Victorian days where children were seen and not heard. It makes me a bit sad to contemplate.

In this light, I can see the chair in the left-hand room better. It's a medical chair, reclined as it was yesterday. I don't know why they'd put that in this room – maybe to keep it out of the way. There is a thin table to its left against the window.

The right-hand room is empty except for a metal-framed twin bed.

The windows are curtainless, and standing within the room on the left of the stairs, we can see that the paper is yellowed along the door frame where the morning sun must shine.

"I'm not sure what, if anything, we'll do up here, but it's not a deal breaker." George is standing in the room with the bed, flicking the light switch to no avail.

"It's a better place for storing decorations or towels than the basement," he replies. "And it's less creepy." He jabs me playfully.

Going downstairs and meeting Lynn, she locks up, and we shake hands and walk to our cars. George and I get into his sedan.

Sitting in the car, watching Lynn pull out, George slaps his hands on the wheel. "Well. Lunch?"

"Yes, I'm starving," I say dramatically, laying my head back on the seat. "Let's stay local. I think there's something further down on Front where the old hotel used to be; we don't need to GPS it. Let's just see what we can find."

"Let's see what the local color is like. And how they feel about getting some more," George raises his eyebrows, as if to say, 'laugh at my joke, please.'

I can't help obliging him. "This will make or break this decision." I keep my tone light but can't resist squeezing his hand in a show of empathy. I can't imagine that extra layer of consideration for others' reactions that he has to endure.

Heading up North Front Street along the river, the road runs parallel to the elevated railway track to our left. We pass spaced-out homes and trailers before arriving in the center of town a minute or so later and parking in the square by the pharmacy.

"Right here is where I saw some photos from 1918 at the end of the first World War," I tell George, pointing to the town hall. "Bunting up there, you know, thick red-white-and-blue ribbon and banners. And this pharmacy," I say, jumping onto the curb in front of it, "was there too, but cuter with a wooden awning."

"I bet it was cuter," George says, with a laugh in his voice.

He comes up on the curb next to me and takes my hand. Walking to the corner, across from the town hall, he jabs a thumb behind him, "I guess we're eating at Bitting's?"

I can't help myself. "Yes, and did you know, it was an old hotel?"

George shakes his head, smiling. "I bet you already know more than some of the locals."

"I'll be asking for any and all trivia," I grin.

"I pity the waitstaff."

As we approach, George heads to the door and opens it for me. It's a classic diner, right down to the bell ringing as we enter. I look around, noticing it's empty except for one man at the far corner, seated with his arms crossed on the table in front of him. He looks up as we come in but then returns to his food. That's a good sign.

We wait for a few minutes before a woman comes out of the kitchen.

"Hey, folks, will it be the two of you?" She says with a voice louder than the library-like silence around us seems able to handle. She skates down the edge of the counter, picking up menus and smiling at me and then George. Personable, warm, but also curious in a friendly way.

"Just passing through?" She sharply nods her chin to the counter, looking at the seats we stand behind. "Have a seat, then. I'm Wanda." She scurries about the counter, then walking out from behind it, she heads over to check on the other customer.

She moves with life in her hips, bringing a sense of joy to the place.

I like her already.

George and I look at our menus, large and oversized, with hundreds of items and combination platters to pour through.

"I'm thinking breakfast for lunch, what about you?" George

43

says, turning on his stool to face me, exaggerating how difficult it is to see me over the menu.

I playfully nudge him with my elbow, placing my menu down. "I'm getting the chicken salad. No, a Reuben. I'll ask Wanda what's better," I decide.

As if summoned by the universal signal, Wanda makes her way back over to us when George puts his menu down. "What'll you have then?"

"Two pancakes, two sausages, two eggs sunny side up, and two pieces of rye toast, please," orders George. He was ready before we even got in here – he loves diner breakfasts.

"You got it," Wanda looks to me without writing down his order, a true professional.

"Reuben or chicken salad?" I ask, tenting my fingers.

"Chicken's old, go for the Reuben. He butters both sides of the rye – it's delicious," Wanda answers quickly. She's a woman of confidence. I like her more. "Anything to drink?"

"Sweet tea," says George.

"Water's fine."

Wanda prepares our drinks, grabbing two cups from the rack under the counter and then going to the pitchers at the back. When she returns to put them on the table, grabbing two straws from her apron, I dare a question. "Wanda, have you lived here in Newport long?" I hope that's not too forward. "We're about to put an offer in on a house here," I add to make her feel more comfortable. Funny, she's the first person we've told. There's something about a seasoned waitress in a diner that invites you to bring them into your confidence.

"Well, it's a bit boring if you like excitement," she starts, "but I've lived here all my life."

"We're homebodies; I write and work part-time. He is a photographer," I explain. "I'm Kendra," I smile warmly.

"I'm George," George chimes in as he takes a drink of his

sweet tea, squirting a modicum of lemon from the slice on the rim. "I grew up in a small town in New York, actually. I'm looking forward to less excitement."

"We're moving from the city," I add.

"It'll be nice to get some new folks in town, especially young folks like you all. Apart from the weather, nothing new comes here. Lots of floods; though we haven't had a good one in almost 40 years," Wanda says, "I remember '72 a bit. I was only eight, but it swept away Front to Main. Well, actually, the whole town out to 6th Street. But 'swept away, Front to 6th' doesn't rhyme," she gives a little wink.

I laugh with George on that one. He's the giggler of the two of us, but Wanda brings it out in me. "We haven't met a lot of folks here," he breaks in, "but we really like the atmosphere of the town."

Nodding, I say, "It's great writing stimulation."

Wanda pauses. "Depending on the genre, I couldn't agree more," she says, turning away back to the kitchen.

I turn to George. "I bet she means horror," I raise my eyebrows.

"Or she means small-town Americana. You know, Harper Lee, Jeanette Walls," he shakes his head at me, "It's got that Appalachia or southern vibe a bit," then he hastily qualifies, "in the good ways. Dare I say it, I can walk around safely here." He laughs.

I smile wanly. "I sure hope so."

Wanda brings our food with a smile but not a word. She takes the pitcher of sweet tea and refills George's glass. She heads around the corner to top off the other gentleman. He nods without looking up from the table.

I'm picking at a few of my chips when I look at him. He looks familiar somehow. He has deep-set blue eyes in a scruffy face, deeply tanned from a lack of wearing sunscreen over the years. He's wearing a trucker's flat-brimmed cap, with the plastic meshing showing a head of graying dark hair. His button-down is open over his white shirt, a construction vest over it all. His large hands rest on the counter. "Thank you, Wanda," he mumbles his voice scratchy.

"No problem, Charlie," she says with a smile. I eat a potato chip, chewing slowly. George didn't seem to look at him at all; instead, he pops a whole sausage in his mouth.

Taking a bite of my sandwich, I'm glad I took Wanda's advice. She comes back over to us, and I say, "This is excellent. Thank you for the recommendation." Taking another bite with relish, I notice she's absently leaning on the back counter.

"Everything okay?" I ask, interrupting her reverie.

"Hmm? Oh, yeah," she nods. I notice she's looking toward Charlie. Then looking at me, she asks, "Which house are you all looking to buy?"

"117 North Front," George answers with a smile. The address rings around the diner, and George blushes.

I notice Charlie's shoulders rise to his ears, tensing, but he doesn't look our way.

"Well, I hope you like it. It's a great house with lots of character." She looks as if she would say more, her hand on her hip, looking at a fixed point in the counter before her.

"Did you know the owners before?" I ask.

She shakes her head and lowers her voice. "Not the latest, they didn't stay long. But I knew the Harrs well. They always gave out full-size candy bars at Halloween. They enjoyed the crowds and costumes." She chuckles, a gentle sound of memory. "I remember one year Mr. Lionel was a scarecrow, and we didn't know until we came up the walk, and he sat up. I never screamed so loud," she laughs again.

"Why did they sell? It sounds like they really loved the place." I need to paint a picture.

"When Ms. Eileen died, I think Mr. Lionel just wanted something smaller. Moved away." Wanda toys with her apron strings, looking at the knot. "I don't know if he's still with us, actually." "Did Ms. Eileen die in the home?" I realize as I ask that I shouldn't have; Wanda's face snaps up to mine.

"I'm not sure," she says curtly. "I think she was sick, that's all."

I wince internally, forcing myself to pick up the second half of my sandwich, silently willing George to save this new friendship.

"Sorry about Kendra." George puts down his fork. "Her morbid curiosity for local history gets the better of her," he smiles, making eye contact with Wanda before she can turn back to the kitchen.

Wanda hesitates and then heads around the counter toward Charlie. He hasn't moved, but he hasn't drunk any of his sweet tea, either. Wanda says something quietly to him, but he doesn't seem to answer. He pulls a worn wallet out of the back pocket of his stained jeans and leaves a twenty-dollar bill on the table, not waiting for change.

Wanda watches him leave before clearing Charlie's plates. When she comes back around, placing the plates in the sink at the back counter, she is contemplative again. "This town has nothing but history," she finally replies. Then meeting my eyes again, she says, "But it's not all good. You might find yourself wanting to pray a bit longer at night."

I nod in agreement. I don't believe we pray the same way, but I appreciate the sentiment.

As we finish our meals, Wanda asks after us and brings us refills but doesn't break from small talk. We leave a good tip, and as we leave, she calls after us, "See you again soon, then," and smiles, wiping her hands on a towel.

· · ·

Driving out of town, I'm starting to get used to how small it is. Two grocery stores, one on either end; the pharmacy and restaurant in the middle square; and the river on the east side. That's it, as far as I can tell, except for more houses and a fire company.

"Let's cross the river," I say, leaning back, resting my foot on the seat, pulling my knee towards me.

"Sure," George stops at the stop sign and turns left to cross the Paul Reider Bridge.

Looking over the edge of the metal bridge, I see the dark green of the Juniata rushing past beneath us, the mud of the last rain gone but the river maintaining its depth. I can't help but think of the two devastating floods. 1972 was one thing, but for 1889, without warning systems or the rescue protocols of today? It would have been devastating.

On the other side, there are a few homes, a bit newer, and a gas station.

"Not much but neighborhoods here," George notes, "should we turn back?"

"No," I shake my head. "Let's just see."

George is right. It's just homes. And at the end of the homes, a bend through the woods. Scenic. The leaves have all changed and fallen here, the skeletal branches reaching out in every direction. When we come out on the other side, and it's only more homes once again, I relent. "Okay, let's turn back."

"Right," George makes a mock salute and turns left. "Let's go down here to the end and see if we can find a way back."

"Lead on."

We follow the road for a couple of minutes to the end of a neighborhood with small, one-story '70s-style homes. We realize we can see the river again, though it's not close enough to hear. "We must have doubled back on the river with that bend," George asserts.

Pulling my hands into my sleeves, I sit up a bit from my slouched position. "What's that over there?"

At the end of the cul-de-sac, there's a flat plain of land. "Maybe it's a protected land or bureaucracy won out here," George posits. "It's a bit creepy at the end like this, unfinished."

"They probably ran out of money or people didn't want to build in the end," I think out loud. "Or maybe this area was damaged by the '72 flood. These homes seem pretty '70s, don't you think?"

"Oh, I bet you're right. Property values surely plummeted with flood insurances skyrocketing."

Slowly going to the end of the cul-de-sac, we pass homes no one seems to live in. The green shutters, matching on all six homes we've passed, are chipping, the once-white siding flaked and gray.

As George pulls up to the end, about to swing the loop to turn around, I look out my passenger-side window.

"Hold on," I intone in a low voice. Thinking. "I'll be right back."

Taking my phone, I get out and head to the flat tract of land. It's slightly bumpier up close like a building site prepared a long, long time ago. The grass is also much longer than I thought, and I raise a silent ward against tick bites, tracing a circle with an 'X' through it on my thigh as I walk to shield against them.

In a few more paces, I hit my foot on something. A flat stone. I kick aside some brush and high grass and see carved letters.

It's a headstone.

CHAPTER SEVEN

I can't make out much, "Sm-" and "189-", maybe *Smith, 1893?*

Swiping my foot along the grass around it, I find a chipped bit of stone sticking up. Walking further, another stone. This one is black on top, the name and year almost completely obscured as well. An eighteen is visible, and it also looks like a nine or another eight.

After about ten minutes of grid-walking, dragging my feet low to detect what I can, I find seven different stones. Two have potential to show the date with the right cleaning. Four are really damaged, chips of stones more than finished pieces. I shudder, realizing that many are destroyed by the construction process. How long did they dig? Were there stones around the other houses' land? Why wasn't this preserved?

The last stone I find is the most promising. It has a clear date: 1889. The year of the flood. The name is a bit harder to read, but it starts with an E; it might be 'Edwards'. I know I will be researching this in the county records when I can find where they're saved. I took pictures with my phone of the stones I found, just in case. I look back towards the river. I can see the roof of our house through the winter trees. I feel that now-familiar chill at my neck again, like when I touched down in the basement for the first time.

Going back to the car, I tell George what I found. "I think I should come back with a toothbrush and some dish soap or something, get in there, clean them up, and figure this out," I explain. "It's disrespectful, and what if the people of the town don't know?"

"I'm sure they know," George says. "It's probably a sore enough subject." He reaches over and grabs my hand. "I'm glad you care so much, but let's not make waves, okay? Do your research if you want. I know you can't help it. But let's wait before we ask any questions."

I nod reluctantly, still looking out the window at the grave-yard. "I don't know how people can do things like this. Haven't they seen *Poltergeist*? It doesn't end well to build on a cemetery."

George chuckles. "I guess they're uncultured swine."

George turns on the car and, within a few minutes, we're back on the main road, going over the bridge. Crossing through town, we pass the fire department, grocery store, and Dollar General.

"Not much to do in town, is there?" I remark.

"No, not really," George taps the steering wheel in a rhythm as we drive the slow speed limit. Twenty-five miles per hour feels very slow after years of highway driving. "I guess we could take a day trip to Philly or Harrisburg, or maybe some of the other small towns around here to do fun stuff. Danville seems interesting," he says.

Propping my elbow on the window, I put my hand to my cheek. "At least we can't hear the highway from here. And the train will be sort of romantic, I always liked the sound of train whistles."

"You say that now; I'm sure it runs all night."

"Actually, I don't think I've heard it since we got here. I wonder about that. We are pretty close to the tracks." I take out my phone and search *trains to Newport, PA*. "Huh, the train stopped running in the 1940s," I say wistfully.

George laughs. "Only you would be sad we're not going to have to hear a train going by throughout the day."

I smirk at him and pull my hand into my sleeve before turning back to the window, sinking comfortably into my seat as I watch the cornfields flicker by, interrupted occasionally with thickets of forest.

We're heading back toward the highway to Harrisburg when I have an idea. "Let's go home without taking the highway. It'll be good to get a feel for the land around here." I open Google Maps and turn on 'avoid highways.' Our ETA goes up by 20 minutes, but we're in no rush. "Maybe we'll see a cute place to stop for coffee."

"An adventure it is, then." George turns on the radio. The cadence of an '80s rock song I can never remember the name of swells around us. "Road trip jams, my favorite." The song gives character to the atmosphere as we drive. The next song is similar; we must be picking up a throwback station. It's apt for the surroundings.

"So, let's talk about the practical side of this house," I start. "I know we've talked about it, but are we sure, completely sure, it's worth it? You said, 'within our budget' earlier when we left the house, but it's only within our budget if we sink the rainy-day money too."

George doesn't answer right away. He keeps his eyes fixed on the road as he responds, "You know how I said I didn't feel it? The energy, or whatever?" I nod as he continues. "I think I did. It's been on my mind in a different way. It's like it's a homecoming. I really like that house, Kendra. When I saw that room that could be my office, it was all I could do to *not* put the offer in right then and there."

"You're giving me goosebumps," I giggle. "Are we really doing this?"

George nods and takes a hand off the wheel to grasp mine. "Plus, I think we can sell the furniture in the basement. It's gotta be worth a lot – some of it is over 100 years old." He grins, squeezing my hand. "And it's time we got our own home. We're not getting any younger."

I watch him out of the corner of my eye, surprised by his conviction.

"I really want this, Ken," he says softly.

"So do I," I agree, nodding my head. He glances over and gives me a reassuring smile, and I can't help it. I feel myself returning his grin, butterflies filling my stomach as the realization sets in. We're going to be new homeowners.

We pass a Wal-Mart with its original all-caps logo and star in the middle. Several tractors slow down our progress, taking in the last of the hay. Little creeks flow in the fields, serpentine paths edged with thick, graying plant life. The first frost must have come and gone; it's hard to notice those things in the city.

"Living out in a small town, we'll be so much more aware of the weather, of the seasons coming and going," I muse romantically. "I'm excited about that. It'll really be good to feel the wheel of the year. Go to some corn mazes."

Almost on cue, we see a flag on a wooden tower in the middle of a cornfield, in the post-harvest field of beige. Rounding a corner, the sign comes into view: *Jack's Pumpkins and Corn Maze*.

"Want to go?" George asks, eyebrows up, chin down as he meets my eyes, already slowing down to turn.

"Uh, yeah!" I say ecstatically. I love fall activities.

We turn into the corn maze and park. It's a Wednesday at four o'clock, not very crowded, but they seem to be open.

"We should get pumpkins on the way out," I say as I get out of the car.

"Naturally," George agrees.

Tickets are only five dollars per person, and there's hot apple cider for a dollar per cup. We each get one and head to the maze.

On the way to the entrance, we pass hay displayed and arranged as adventures for children, in any way imagination can conjure: conventional hayrides, a small train pulling hay bales around a track; pits of hay like a ball pit rimmed with hay bales, of course; a fortress of hay bales for climbing and jumping off of; a hay maze, tarped over so you have to crawl on all fours; and even a hay sitting area. There's a small petting zoo with an ironic sign stating: "DO NOT FEED HAY TO ANIMALS." I chuckle a bit at that. There's even a new activity, well, new to me: pumpkin chucking with a slingshot, two dollars per pumpkin. I suddenly wish I was ten years old again.

The entrance to the maze is right next to its exit. We can see the flag tower maybe a quarter mile away. This maze doesn't give you an outline like some do, so we're going in blind, but we'll have the maze to ourselves with more than two hours before dark to figure out how to make it out again.

Heading into the corn maze, I take George's hand. There's something romantic about a corn maze. We make a left turn and then a right. Then, sticking with a straightaway, we find ourselves in a half circle, making our way back to the main path.

"This is a bit more of a challenge than usual," I remark.

"They must be using fancy rotating corn plows or something," George jokes.

Back on the straightaway, we come to a T. "Did we make a turn somewhere?" I rub my chin. I don't remember seeing this when we were just here.

"I didn't think so. I guess we should go right – if we made a right coming from the other direction, that's a left now, so maybe we just didn't see this other option." George is a good strategist. I do love that about him.

Making the right, we continue for a few minutes without any turns visible. It feels like the corn is narrowing toward us, the smell of the damp earth and the musty, drying corn suddenly oppressive. "George, how long have we been in here?"

George doesn't answer right away. "At least 20 minutes, maybe more. I didn't think it could be this big, but I guess it's always hard to tell."

We find ourselves at what looks like a dead end until we approach it and see a narrow path to the right.

I stop at the end of the lane.

"This isn't a haunted corn maze, right?" I ask, half serious. "And where's that flag tower? We should have seen it by now."

"I'm pretty sure a place like this doesn't have a haunted corn maze. Besides, we'd see or hear something by now. I guess we make this right – all these rights should lead us back to where we came in at least."

George leads the way down the narrow path. It's getting chilly, the tall corn shading us now as the sun sinks toward the west.

We come upon a left turn. "What do you think?" I ask George. I notice I'm talking quietly, though I don't know why. I feel a chill up my back.

"Let's keep going," he responds, just as quietly. "We should be closer to the end by now."

We continue and find another T juncture – a left or a right.

"Hold on a minute," I say, almost to myself. I kneel on the ground, guided by my tingling intuition, and place my hand on the soil. If only I had my pendulum, I think. It's well-trodden ground, and it's only slightly damp in the way everything is outdoors in the cool of autumn. I look to my left, then to my right.

Suddenly, I feel a cool curtain descend over me like an ice bath. My flesh rises in goosebumps, and yet a drop of sweat pours down my temple, running into my eye. I'm keenly aware of how quiet it has been since we arrived. We haven't seen a soul since the ticket counter. It's a school day, but we got here at four o'clock, and it must be at least five o'clock by now.

I turn to George to ask the time – he's carrying both of our phones – and I see he's not behind me.

Standing up, I look around. "George?" I say, my voice cracking a bit. No answer.

"George?" I raise my voice. Wait. Still, I don't hear him. I walk back the way we came, the sun getting closer to the horizon with each passing minute. I force myself to stay calm. He wouldn't leave me in a corn maze without a phone.

"George!" I'm feeling frantic now, I can't hold back the panic setting in.

I turn around, ready to head back and try the next turn, and I see him.

That is not George.

A person of nondescript height, with the shoulder set and short hair of a man, or boy nearing manhood, is standing at the end of the straightaway.

In the growing shadows, I can't make out his features, but I can tell from the square of his body that he is looking toward me. "Hello?" I call. "Did you see my husband? Glasses, Black, dad bod?"

The man doesn't move. It's as if he doesn't hear me.

I approach him, slowly. I feel unsettled, scared even. I'm alone in a corn maze with this man. As I get closer, less than ten feet now, I can see he's definitely a teenager at the youngest, at least my height. Overalls, or maybe a button-down? He's difficult to see. But sunset isn't for another hour, right?

"Excuse me," I start, looking down at the path for a second, an unconscious reaction to fear. I look back up, prepared to meet his eyes, and I gasp, quickly closing my mouth. His gray, cold eyes stare intensely back at me, not six inches from my face. I stumble backward and fall, my arms breaking my fall as I land. I scurry backward away from him, as fast as I can. He doesn't move, continuing to stare at me, expressionless. He has a shaggy mop of dark black hair that covers his ears. Now, I can see that he's wearing dark pants and suspenders over a light-colored shirt, buttoned to the very top button. His mouth and arms are unmoving. He blinks and turns his head toward me, slowly, a curious onlooker to a spectacle.

I freeze like a scared child and close my eyes as his fingers reach toward me. Unable to move, I scream as his hand clamps down on my shoulder.

CHAPTER EIGHT

"Kendra? Kendra, baby, are you okay?" George is leaning over me. He's kneeling on the ground, his hands on my shoulders. His eyes are wide and worried, his brow furrowed. As he comes into focus, I see relief pass across his face.

I'm lying on my back in the middle of a corn maze. The sun is overhead, only slightly casting shade acrossthe path.

"What time is it?" I ask hoarsely. Clearing my throat, I try again. "Did I pass out?"

"It's five-fifteen, honey. You squatted down and put your hand to the ground. Then you stayed there for like, five minutes. You wouldn't answer me. And then," He takes his hands off my shoulders, helping me to sit up. We both sit down right there in the mud. "I don't know what happened, you just fell over. I knelt by you, and then thirty seconds later, here we are. It felt like an eternity, but it couldn't have been long."

"There was a boy, did you see him?" I ask, already knowing the answer.

"No one has passed us in this maze, Kendra." George draws his brows together. "What did he look like?"

"Black hair, gray eyes, white skin. Emotionless. Maybe late teens, early twenties. The way he looked at me," I stop, mouth suddenly dry as I remember the boy's cruel eyes. "He didn't say anything. I was looking for you, and he was all of a sudden just there, where we had been standing. Here at this crossroads."

Crossroads. "I know I'm always finding the spiritual in everything," I begin, after mulling on the thought a second, "but that's a common place for these things."

"What do you mean?" George asks, pulling his knee up and resting his chin on it.

"Crossroads are the meeting place where we can connect with spirits." When George doesn't respond I clarify further. "A ghost," I say. "Maybe it was a ghost."

"It's not always a ghost, Kendra."

"But sometimes, it is. He had on a weird outfit. Black overalls, a white button down, buttoned up to the neck, with dark pants?"

George sighs. I hear the relief in that sigh but also the exhaustion. "Mormons? Amish?"

I shake my head. "Not with overalls. Not with that haircut. He felt... old. Wrong."

George stands, slowly, then extends a hand to me. "I guess it's more research for you, then."

"I guess. I don't know, why would a corn maze –"

A wind picks up. "I think we should just focus on getting out of this damn maze," George says, pulling his brown suede jacket tighter about him. He never zips it up.

I pull my hands into my sleeves and nod. "Yes and get another apple cider."

I look to George, and he points to the right. We turn right. In a couple of meters, we turn right again and find ourselves at the center. Two lefts, a right, then another left, and we find ourselves out.

"Well, that was a lot easier than I thought it would be," George says. "I'm not sure what that was about back there."

We're passing through the gates, both too tired to get another drink, and I stop.

Going back to the ticket counter I ask, "How long is that supposed to take? The maze, I mean?"

The girl behind the counter puts down her phone. "Um, I don't know, I think twenty to forty-five minutes or so. You guys took a while," she says in the tone only teenagers have mastered.

"I was wondering, are there any spirals or circles within the maze? Like, that would send you back onto the path you came from?" Any stupid questions she'll chalk up to dumb city folk confusion, I hope. By the looks of the hand still on her phone, there won't be much thinking of this conversation, anyway.

"No, this is the pattern," she puts her phone down reluctantly, and shows me a basic, box maze pattern on the paper to her right.

"Can I keep this?" I pick up the paper.

"Sure," she says, already picking up the phone and swiping it open.

Back in the car, I show George the map. "It's like we were transported by that spiral. Even the darkness felt deeper, at least when I was looking at that boy. I don't know, it's weirding me out." I put my face in my hands then lean my head back on the seat of the car.

"Let's get back to the apartment," George says. "I'm sure we just went through a fake path some kids carved out by breaking the line."

"I hope so. It was awfully narrow." George guides the car back onto the road, and the bumps slowly wear down the tension in my shoulders. Closing my eyes, I don't reopen them until I feel the car rock back and hear the engine switch off.

"We're back at the house, sleepyhead," George says. He sounds as tired as I feel.

Heating up the last of the Chinese leftovers, I write a bit before bed. George is in the makeshift office he's set up in the corner behind the couch where we would have a dining table if we weren't couch potatoes.

We don't talk about the day until we're lying there next to each other in bed.

Pulling me onto his shoulder, George kisses my head. "Tell me, honestly, baby. Is this related to the house?"

"I don't know," I start, but I can feel George's knowing eyes on me. "Well, I can't *know*, but I think so. I do know that the character in the corn maze was not the kid I talked to. He was much older, and more –" I don't want to say the word that first came to mind, but I'm too tired to go euphemism hunting. "This boy was sinister."

George swallows. "I don't know if we should take the house," he says. "I know you love it. I do, too, but maybe this is why it's nearly in our price range."

"'Nearly' is the key word; what if I can't find a teller job there? What if the winter slump for photography lasts longer than expected? What if we can't sell that furniture?" I pull my hands into my sleeves. "What if I can't handle what we find in there, George?"

George leans his head on my shoulder. "Not that I'm not worried about it." He points those brown eyes up at me. I can't help smiling. "I don't know how witchcraft works, and I don't feel ghosts or anything. But I know you. I feel *you*. You've got this, Kendra." When I don't respond right away, he tries again. "And anyway, if that man isn't who you talked to, whoever you did will need your help."

I lean my head on his. "You know I can't resist helping a ghost cross over." I sit up straighter against the back of the bed.

"You're right. It's in our price range because we're moving to a sleepy town that peaked two World Wars ago. It has nothing to do with ghosts. The house is great. It's in good condition, and the research shows there's no one to be afraid of. A family lived there for at least two generations. I can handle it. Let's do it." What I don't say out loud is that I know I'll write my book there. I don't want to jinx it.

George doesn't speak again. It already feels like ours. We outgrew this apartment years ago, and the cats deserve a bigger place. Okay, we deserve a bigger place. Our own offices. Two floors. A balustrade.

"Okay," he finally says. "Let's officially do this."

THE NEXT MORNING, I'm laying out the cat dishes while George sits down with our coffees. "Are we still feeling settled?" I ask.

"Absolutely. You know, I slept really well. I'll take that as a sign. No ghost nightmares or anything. Or worse, finance-related panic." He takes a sip of his coffee while I take out my phone, giving him a mischievous look.

"Give me a minute," I say with a smile, turning to George as I leave the room.

I go to the guest room and bring a stick of nag champa incense on a flat, wooden incense holder from my altar. "Do you mind if I try something?" I ask George, a bit sheepishly as I re-enter the room.

He looks at the incense in my hand and smiles. "You don't need my blood right?"

I smirk. "No." My smile fades as I continue, "I just want to protect our space."

George gestures permissively. "Then by all means," he smiles.

I place it on the table in front of us as I prepare for Lynn's call, asking for protection. "Element of Air, blow away negative energies. Element of fire," I light the stick, "may your flames blaze up around us in protection from spirits who seek to harm us." As the incense ignites, I see a spark grow and then fall to a normal steady burn. A good sign.

"Element of Water," I gesture my hands around our kitchen table, creating a sacred circle with us and our cell phone in the center. "Cleanse this space and keep it clean and pure, may no negativity or harmful spirits enter here." I feel a cool calm descending in the kitchen. I look down at the cats eating in their bowls; they seem content, always a good sign.

"Element of Earth, ground and center our intentions. Allow us a clear, safe, seamless path to purchasing 117 North Front Street, Newport, Pennsylvania." I waft the smoke of the incense up and around me, and gently toward George. I smile to see him not reject it. It dawns on me then that he hasn't been as privy to my rituals as I assumed. He's doing great.

I take a deep breath and sit at the table. "So mote it be," I whisper to myself.

"What does that mean?" George asks.

He never asks this much about my Craft. This house is a good idea. I smile when I answer, "It's like 'amen,' it finalizes the..." I pause, unwilling to say the word 'spell.' "...the protective circle." It's not *not* true. I'll get there. "Let's call Lynn."

Lynn answers on the second ring. "Hi, Kendra."

"Hi, Lynn! George and I would love to put an offer in," I burst with excitement.

I can hear her returning the smile in my voice as she replies, "Great! Oh, you guys will love it, Kendra! I'm so excited for you both! I just have a few questions, and then I can send your offer to the buyer today!"

As George talks through the legalese with Lynn, it starts to feel final. An acceptance of the end of a phase of life, and the embrace of a new one.

Come what may.

CHAPTER NINE

Closing is a breeze. Lynn is more than happy to have our first offer accepted, and the loss of the nest egg aside, I am too excited for words. We boxed up our entire apartment and stayed with Alicia, George's sister, for Christmas. She and her wife had us over for the week between our lease's ending and the house moving. As an only child, the sibling dynamic fascinates me.

We secure the keys by Christmas, and by January 4th, we are finally moving in. The furniture is already in place, the last of the boxes are in the car, and my stomach is in knots with excitement about finally spending our first night in the house.

I haven't quite figured out my transfer to working at the new bank, but I'm glad for the break to unpack and make our house our home. Bringing in the last box, I place it on the living room floor. Turning around and walking into the foyer, I step back and look up. Hands on my hips, I heave a deep breath. I take in the 'balustrade,' the lamp, the gardenia details every-where. The atmosphere is warm and buzzing, but maybe it's just me. I look around for any hint of a spirit, but I don't see anyone yet. Luckily, I also don't see any shadowy figures either.

We've already decided which rooms are for what purposes, and I start sorting items from the boxes. Putting on my favorite playlist and some headphones, I get to work.

Luckily, the heat is working throughout the house; another piece of the second inspection that pushed back the move-in date a couple of weeks.

The home is heated by an old-fashioned wood stove circulating system. It's almost as old as the house. You fill the stove – accessible by a door in the kitchen – with wood, and it circulates throughout the home. It's oddly economical, considering how old it must be. Only once every seven or eight hours does the fire need more wood, and there's a slotted ramp of sorts on a timer to dispense it. We add more wood once a day, and we're set for another fifteen hours on a winter's night, even longer as the days warm.

The pile of boxes at the stairs – for the bedroom, my altar, our offices (okay, George's office, my craft room) – will be for George to lift when he gets back from his shoot later tonight.

I start with my books, bringing them to the study. There's not a lot of room on the already-bulging shelves. I'm still floored that the books come with the house. I would never be able to leave my babies behind; unless I were dead, I guess.

I wonder how old some of the books are. I fight the temptation to go to the shelves and start fiddling around. I might have to reorganize or redistribute to blend my books with the bursting collection. There will be plenty of time later to read and sort. Even as I think it, though, I feel a strong reluctance toward the thought. I won't get rid of a single one, I decide.

Going over to the bay window, I slowly start to pile the books. The first book I pick up is George Eliot's *Silas Marner,* a classic of feminist literature. Great taste, mystery reader.

Several National Geographic magazines from the early 2000s. And, shockingly, journals. There are several with yellowing pages and scrawling cursive. I open one, and then another. In each, the pencil has faded to an illegible script. I sigh and place them in a pile, carefully, when my phone rings.

I don't recognize the number. "Hello?" I answer, hoping it isn't spam.

"Hi, is this Kendra Hill?"

"Speaking. May I ask who's calling?"

"This is Fran, I'm an agent with the Solare group." My heart is in my throat, beating through my skin as I try to focus on her next words. "I read your excerpt in The New Yorker, and I'd like to request the full manuscript for *Bleeding Glory*. I think it's got great potential."

Suddenly my throat is the Sahara Desert. I swallow, hoping she can't hear it. "Hi, Fran! Wow, thank you! Thank you for this opportunity," I try to finish on a professional note, but the excitement is killing me. "Yes! I am in the process of moving now and still unpacking everything," I start, the panic that I haven't actually finished the manuscript yet finally starting to sink in, "but if I could have some time to get it to you?"

The pause before Fran answers is interminable. "No problem, I completely understand. How does six weeks from now sound?"

I instantly begin doing the math. Six weeks. I've got at least a hundred pages left, not to mention the tone shifts and the consistencies to double check and the character arcs to solidify... I shake my head like a dog stepping out of a river. "No problem at all, that should be plenty of time. Thank you, Fran!"

"Okay, Kendra, sounds great. I'll send you an email, and I'll be looking forward to reading the full book!"

"Thank you, Fran! Have a great day."

"You as well!"

I don't know how long I stand there over the open box of dishes in the center of my new kitchen before I return to reality. I can't believe it. A manuscript request.

I've read up and done my research. This makes or breaks it. Editors aside, I need her to like this book and believe in it, but how can she believe in it if I don't? I make a mental pact with myself to write today. To write, and to set up the study. Forget the rest of this house, that unpacking can wait.

I close up the box of dishes and keep looking. What was I looking for? Oh right. Cleaning products. When I find them, I open the cupboard under the sink to put them away and feel a cool breeze coming out. Sitting in front of the sink, I turn on my phone flashlight and peer inside.

There's a strong smell of must, and I hope it's not mold... the inspection should've caught that. Looking around, it's extremely dark in the left corner where the cupboard continues beneath the counter.

The draft seems to be coming from there.

Even with my flashlight on, I can't see well; I'll need a real one to see all the way to the end. Turning off my phone flashlight and putting my phone in my pocket, I stand up to grab the box of cleaner. The draft, strong as a breeze, is chilling my ankles. I feel goosebumps growing on my skin as I lower the box to the floor.

The draft slows again as I sit down, probably the rules of convection or something. I start taking the cleaning products out one by one, leaving aside a roll of paper towels, all-purpose cleaner, and window cleaner. I empty the box and begin placing the dish soap, floor polish, extra mop heads, and all the additional cleaning supplies on the cupboard's floor. Suddenly the draft picks up. It pushes over the roll of paper towels behind me and blows dust in my eyes. Squinting, I use the neck of my shirt to wipe my eyes.

When I open them, I'm staring at a cloud of sparkles. I rub them again, and the sparkles clear, my eyes gaining focus.

Eyes.

Glittering blue eyes stare back at me from a pale face I can barely make out in the darkness. Wide, round, and watery, I know at once these are the pleading eyes of a girl. A young woman.

Unafraid but too stunned to move, I blink, mouth gaping. "Hello?" I whisper, looking between the two eyes, close enough that I can't focus on the pair.

I blink again, and they're gone.

Air moves past my face in a gust and then stops. I slowly reach my hand under the sink, just slightly.

No draft, no coolness.

I sniff the air there. It smells of dust, but not as damp nor aged as it did before.

Maybe I got used to it, sitting here for a while.

Or maybe whatever was in there left with that last, swift draft.

As soon as I say it, I freeze, chilled and unnerved. I inhale a deep breath slowly, and then in a quick motion I turn around.

Behind me, under the table, I don't see anything. But I remember that first day in this house when I tried to communicate. Is it a child? Are they hiding from that shadow man?

I hear a click from outside the kitchen.

"Kendra?" George's voice is unnaturally loud to my heightened senses. I flinch and then clear my throat.

"In the kitchen!" I stand, taking the cleaners and paper towels I need and putting them on the table. Breaking down the now-empty first box, it feels like a challenge to whatever was there. We are staying; this is our house now, too.

"Making some progress?" George asks, looking at the broken-down box stacked by the back door.

"Yes, some. It is overwhelming, honestly. But we've got this." I decide not to tell him about what I saw. Not because it doesn't matter, but because I have a feeling in my bones, in my spirit, that this is the beginning, not the end, of activity here. I'm not scared; I'm just unraveling the puzzle, piece by piece.

"I moved in the last of the boxes from my car, but you'll need to take them upstairs, Muscles," I jibe him.

"You got it," he says. "I brought home pizza, want to eat in here?"

I'm not scared, but I'm not relaxed either. "Let's eat in the living room like the millennial trash we are," I attempt a joking tone.

He reads the discomfort but misplaces it. "You're exhausted. Let's take a break and watch some TV."

"Okay, here, take these," I reach into the first box of plates and forks, passing him two of each. "I'll be right there."

I grab the cleaning products and follow him out.

Dropping off the bottles and towels in the study so I won't forget to grab them later, I put them on the desk. Doing a double take, I look at the desk.

A drawer is ajar. I reach over the desk to shut it, and then hesitate. My hand wavers. Instead, I pull the drawer all the way out.

Sitting in the top middle of the drawer where I had found the papers that mysteriously disappeared after the first day, is my pendulum.

CHAPTER TEN

L ying in bed, the sheets put on and boxes all arranged at its foot, I'm fingering the pendulum, wrapping and unwrapping the chain across my hand.

"Isn't it strange, George?" I ask for the tenth time.

"It is, Ken."

"George, I wonder. Did that man take it? Why would he give it back?" I can't make sense of it all, but I know I shouldn't attempt to talk with them again yet. When George doesn't answer, my mind goes over the events of the day, and it suddenly hits me. My phone call with Fran. "George! I completely forgot. My book! An agent called today, and she wants the full manuscript in six weeks!" I can hear my tone shifting from excited to terrified.

George gives me a side hug, the best we can do lying in bed. "I am so proud of you, baby! I knew it! But is the book finished?"

I chuckle at that, maybe a bit manically. "Nope!"

. . .

I DREAM that I'm sitting in the middle of a massive bed of gardenias.

Within the vibrant yellow of their petals, brighter than the sun against the verdant green of their leaves, I'm wearing a cream-colored sundress, admiring a bloom in my hand.

The sun is high overhead, but it isn't too hot: a beautiful spring day just beginning. Looking up from my bloom, I gaze out across a field of green grass dotted with trees in various stages of May.

From behind one, I spot a face. A girl, I think.

I can't make them out, and as I shield my eyes from the sun to get a better look, they pull themselves behind the trunk. I smile and raise my flower to them in greeting.

But they won't reappear. Are they hiding? Or were they just a figment of my imagination?

I WAKE, refreshed. Unexpectedly, I am less shaken by what happened yesterday; instead, I'm curious. Like I'm getting closer to the answers to this mystery. Like the answers want to be found.

"How did you sleep?" George asks me, sitting up in bed. He runs his tongue under his top row of teeth.

"Good, actually. Excellent. Ready to tackle the unpacking." I sit up beside him, leaning on his shoulder. "How about you?"

"I dreamed I was spitting up teeth. They just kept falling out of my mouth." He rolls his neck, then turns, kissing me on the head. "Otherwise, not bad. It's been a while since I've had a visceral dream like that." He gets up, going to the wardrobe. "I'll be back late, most likely. The shoot is a couple of hours away."

"I'll wait for dinner until you're home," I smile, rising. I kiss him on the cheek. "You know, witches believe that dreams of teeth falling out are a sign of new changes. So moving into a new house, it wouldn't surprise me that you'd have one of those."

"Doesn't make it any less creepy," he replies, heading into the bathroom.

I take my pendulum off the nightstand and place it in my pocket; after slipping on my favorite housedress that actually has some pockets. Sliding into my fuzzy socks, I feel ready to unpack a bit more today. I shake off that feeling of neglecting my writing. First things first: my altar.

After washing up and saying goodbye to George, I cross the hall to my craft room. I pause in front of the fireplace, taking in the solidness of the brick and stark-straight wooden mantle. I can't wait to decorate this.

Sherry and Shadow are adjusting well. For having never had such a massive area to explore, they've surprised me with their excitement. Though they haven't ventured beyond this floor, they seem content here.

Looking around the room, I notice wide windowsills. I'll be able to use this front-facing window as an altar shelf or at least for cleansing my tarot cards and crystals under the full moon. I'm excited for that.

Dragging my altar table over to the window I begin unpacking. Within a half hour I have an empty box – my magic books are on a shelf under the altar table, and I am ready to consecrate the space.

Taking up my athame, I call the quarters and draw a sacred circle. I light a stick of incense – nag champa – to cleanse the area with smoke.

Lighting a white candle, I say a quick consecration: "Elements of Air, Fire, Water, and Earth. Bless this space as magic's hearth."

I close my eyes, envisioning a shield of protection around

myself and my altar, two bubbles of white light enveloping and connecting us both. I draw an invoking pentagram, a five-pointed star drawn from top to bottom, over the surface of my altar table to invoke the positive energies of the elements in the space, focusing on strengthening this bubble of protection.

On an impulse, I draw a second invoking pentagram in the air in front of my heart. Focusing on the lit candle in front of me, I set the intention for the space: envisioning it as a space of grounded celebration, a place for joy, peace, and growth. I focus on the energy of a full moon, and the feeling of the eight individual Sabbat holidays – Samhain on Halloween, to Beltane on May Day. I close my eyes again, blow out the candle, and release the elements from their quarters, the space still humming with the energies of protection.

Placing my athame down and lowering myself to my knees, I sit with the space. It feels so good to have a whole, massive room to dedicate to witchcraft. We'll put a desk at the far end for me to sew at and a futon against one wall in case of extra visitors – and for reading. That will require some shopping, to find a comfortable futon. Maybe there's something in the basement that can work in the meantime.

Taking a deep breath, I turn my thoughts to the blue-gray eyes.

I try to remember if there was anything else there to see. They appeared in the kitchen, the same room as the first incident when I saw the shadow under the table.

Under the table, under the sink. It's like they're hiding. From what? Other ghosts? Me? I will need to ask to find out.

As I scurry around our bedroom, putting away clothes and sorting the knick knacks on our side tables and windowsills, I notice there doesn't seem to be any activity up here. It's calm, it's warm, it's dry.

I start to wonder if the dampness from the river affects the activity downstairs. The height of the ceilings, the wires, the pipes running in the basement and underneath the sink – they all increase the electromagnetic currents. It can give anyone a sense of disease.

My intuition tells me I'm not just seeing things. I know better. The missing papers and the pendulum appearing in the desk drawer is no accident. This house is full of mysteries. I want to go downstairs and write, but my procrastination is holding me back from going into the study.

After I finish the bedroom – George will be chuffed to see his clothes all out of boxes – I hear scraping and digging in the litter, and Shadow whooshes past me. I'm glad they're using their bathroom but less enthused that I'm going in right after her.

I walk to the bathroom where Shadow had just been, and I put the box labeled "Guest Bath" on the sink, crossing to the window by the toilet. I open it a crack to let the cold January air take some of the smell out.

The window is old, thick glass with two worn metal handles to pull down or push up the window from the bottom. Getting my grip, the heels of my hand under the handles, I push. It doesn't budge. Squaring my legs I try again. I feel it move but not enough to release any air. With a grunt, I push one last time, and it budges about two inches. The window's jam shows splintering white paint, the same color as the frame. Turning back to the sink, I go to the box, taking the guest shampoos and bar soaps and pull aside the old curtain on the shower.

A dead mouse, dried and curled with age, is staring up at me.

I shriek and drop a bar of soap into the tub with the mouse, my heart thumping in my chest. Stepping back, I try to breathe deeply and put the shampoos on the sink. My stomach turns as I think of the mouse's twisted body. George will have to take care of this tonight.

Breaking down the empty bathroom box as I walk to the kitchen, I take quick stock of how many boxes are left in the living room and foyer. It'll get done; I repeat to myself.

TWO HOURS LATER, I am exhausted. The backdoor is inaccessible due to all the broken-down boxes in the way. I should take them down to the basement, but I still feel uneasy about it, so I take them to the door of the basement, at least.

Doing my best to gracefully lean a dozen worn-out boxes against the wall across from the basement door, I wipe my hands together, thinking about lunch.

The doorknob catches my eye again. It's intricate, brass I think, a full gardenia in bloom. My dream comes back to me. I didn't remember it until now, but I was in a field of gardenias. Who was behind that tree?

My stomach grumbles, and I run upstairs to change for the grocery store.

LEGGINGS UNDER MY HOUSE DRESS, my black woolen peacoat hiding my bralessness, I grab a cart and head for the lunch meat aisle. Seeing corned beef, I think back to that day in the diner, where we met Wendy... no, Wanda. I never told her we decided to move here. Maybe George and I should go back to Bitting's and check in. I grab some turkey, Swiss cheese, and pickles. On the way to the bread aisle, I snag some mayonnaise from an endcap. It's nice to be in such a large grocery store with stocked shelves and ample room for shopping carts, after Harrisburg's crowded corner shops and 7-11s.

I grab some potato chips and iced tea, and I'm heading to check out when I see someone familiar ahead of me.

The man from the diner. Charlie. He's in line at a cashier. I get in line to check out beside him. Pretending to look down the aisles as if I forgot something, I'm able to study him. He's wearing a similar outfit with the addition of a worn leather jacket and boots. It hasn't snowed in a while, so maybe he's a farmer. He turns his head and meets my gaze. I smile, trying to look friendly. He doesn't smile back. I drop my eyes and look ahead at the checkout counter, mindlessly placing my items down. I watch as he pays and walks over to the tobacco counter.

"$12.36, ma'am," the girl behind the counter repeats herself.

"Oh, sorry, yeah," I take out my phone and grab the card from the back. I had been engrossed in listening for Charlie's gruff voice.

As we're waiting for the machine to run my card, I hear him order chewing tobacco. Disgusting, not riveting. I feel a little silly for caring so much, but it's a small town. This might be the most entertainment I get.

"Thanks," he says to the tobacco cashier as he heads for the door.

The bell of the door jingles closed as the card reader finishes. I sign and take my receipt, smiling at the cashier.

I'm heading to the car when I see Charlie again, walking to what I assume is his truck at the back of the parking lot, an old rusted Chevy with its empty truck bed haphazardly tarped. He unlocks his truck, stepping up inside. I take my cart back then turn toward my car.

Getting in and turning my engine, I realize Charlie isn't moving. I wait a minute, adjust my seat belt, and check my mirrors. No change. He's just sitting there. I turn toward the back seat of my own car then turn to face the wheel again. I feel too silly and hungry to wait much longer, so I shift into drive and head out of the parking lot.

As I pass his car, I realize I don't hear it running. Pulling through the spot to his right, slowly, I peer at him inside, concerned. His body is slumped forward with his head leaning over the wheel. I stop my car and get out onto his passenger side.

Tap, tap, tap. I lean over and gently hit the glass of his passenger-side window. He whirls his head to meet my eyes. His expression goes from shocked to lost to angry in a nanosecond. I back up with a grimace that I hope says "I'm sorry," mouthing the words to him as I put my hands over my heart apologetically. It feels like a slow-motion pantomime as I back into my own car, fumble at the door handle, get in, and drive away.

Mortifying, absolutely mortifying. Why would I do that?

BACK AT HOME, I try to focus as I eat my sandwich, not even thinking of the ghosts here in the kitchen. It's a good sandwich, a nice day – more sun than expected in January.

After I wash my dish, I know I should be writing, but I decide that I'll feel more settled if I finish unpacking first. I move on to the kitchen and find the cupboards wiped clean. If only the previous owners had taken the same care with cleaning the study before they left.

As I'm unpacking, I find an old flashlight, the kind we kept for power outages back in the '90s. Big, heavy, black metal. I put away the plates, utensils, and bakeware, but I can't stop thinking of Charlie. How small was this town? Did he recognize me? Do I need to make friends so I can stop being so nosy? All questions I don't have answers to. Except the last one: 'yes.'

"What do you guys think?" I say. The ghosts aren't quite the new friends I should be making. There's no answer, though part of me really expected one.

In another hour, I have four more boxes broken down. I take them to the pile by the basement stairs.

The door is open a crack.

"George?" It's only four, and the sun hasn't even set yet. There's no way he's home already and didn't come say hi. And anyway, I would have heard the front door if he had come home.

I open the basement door more, daring to reach in and turn on the stair lights. Nothing but dust greets me. They didn't clean in here, then. The basement, the study, the attic – the only places so far that feel old, abandoned. I turn off the light and close the door.

Surveying my finished work in the kitchen, I take the bag of potato chips upstairs.

George will be impressed that I did all of this today. Little does he know, I'm procrastinating tackling that study.

The bedroom, my 'crafts and Craft' room, the bathrooms – finished. The kitchen – finished. George's office will be for him to complete.

I amble into the guest room, munching chips. It was the easiest room to complete. George and I did it last night when we made up our bed: sheets down for the first guests, extra towels in the drawer of that plain white wardrobe. Maybe I'll paint flowers on it or something. This room needs a reading chair, and we might be in luck finding one in that basement. Despite all the work, I feel too restless to read or write just yet.

Moving from a two-bedroom apartment to a massive house, I realized we don't have as much junk as I thought.

Going down to the living room, still avoiding the office, I

unpack and sort through the decor there, as sparse as it seems now with so many shelves to fill. It's fun to work with the design, to look at all the empty spaces and imagine the possibilities.

Finishing there and breaking down the remaining boxes, I move to add them to the growing pile by the basement. The door is still securely closed. I push it in to be extra sure. With the sun setting, I'm feeling uneasy again, thinking of the ghosts.

I do one more sweep through the kitchen. It's clean. My lunch dishes are clean, too, so I put them away. Standing at the kitchen sink, peering out into the twilight, I watch as the streetlights come on. The sun is completely down, the warm purple glow receding into black night, silhouetting the other houses in the neighborhood.

It's past five-thirty, and I've finished every room as best I can. The broken-down boxes are stacked in the hall, and I am not going into the basement without George. There's no escaping it. I need to write. I have at least two hours before George is home.

Going back upstairs, I grab my laptop bag and charger from my Craft room. I'll make dinner while I write in the kitchen, I decide. The energy is so scattered in the study; close, oppressive. Like there's no room for me. Halfway down the first set of stairs, I remember the bag of chips, so I go back up, into the guest room.

The bag is on the floor. I pick it up, and it feels less full than before.

Shadow comes out from under the guest bed, chirping at me. I shake my head. First drinking out of our water glasses, now eating my salted snacks. This cat will be ordering takeout next.

I walk slowly out of the room, gesturing for Shadow to follow me. She's oddly reluctant. I don't mind them eating up here. We're keeping the food in the bathroom by their litter, so, if anything, *they* should mind. But I want them to feel comfortable here. I roll up the bag of chips and hoist the laptop bag properly onto my shoulder. With my free hand, I scoop up Shadow. A check in our bedroom shows a sleeping Sherry. Alright, she's off the hook for now. Shadow starts mewling as I step onto the top step.

"I know you hate being held, Shadow," I soothe. "We're just going downstairs." I pull her in against my body, using the back of my chip-holding hand to cradle her tail so she feels supported. When we get to the landing, in front of the window, she starts to squirm. I teeter, holding her against me. I can't make it down the steps, and I don't want to hurt her. I bend my knees and let her down. She jumps like I placed her in lava and darts past me back up the stairs.

"Cats," I mumble to myself, shaking my head.

Putting the chips in a cupboard, I plug in my laptop next to the sink. I'll have to be careful not to clothesline myself on this when walking back and forth to the sink.

The flashlight is still on the corner where I left it, a comforting sight. I sit with my back to the entryway, facing the sink and counter next to the back door. From this angle, it appears to be pitch black outside. The streetlights further down aren't glittering as I thought they would. It's not quite six. I haven't heard from George, and my snacks are holding me over, so I'll write a while before I start the pasta.

I open my laptop, and the document that is my debut novel stares me blankly in the face. I'm about 160 pages into a book with no heart. I know it, my intuition knows it. I haven't even let George read it yet because it's just not happening.

I clear my throat and read out the start of chapter eighteen: "Catherine isn't sure, but she doesn't like her job. Working in fashion was supposed to be fun, but nothing is fulfilling in measuring tapes and sweat stains." I pull my hands in my sleeves and lean back in my chair. "Too sterile," I murmur. I delete and retype, delete and retype, trying to describe Catherine's emotions with some reality. "Ugh!" I groan, smacking the backspace key several times. Again.

I pause and hear a scraping sound. It sounds like a chair being pulled out. I look around for the cats, but I don't see or hear them. Pushing my chair back, I lower my head under the table to my left where I had seen the pale eyes before.

No one is there, but the sink cupboard door is open. I pause a minute, wondering if this is my brain looking for distractions from writing again. The scraping sound begins again.

I shouldn't be relieved by paranormal activity.

I grab the flashlight, swing both sides of the sink wide open, and don't hesitate. "Goddess give me strength," I whisper to myself, and then louder, "who's in there? It's okay, I just want to get to know you."

I shine the flashlight slowly across the dark, left corner. In the far back, once again I see a shimmering cloud of – I don't know what. Moving along the cupboard, there's a wide cobweb, rusted washers under the u-bend, and an old cut wire. I realize the cabinet extends into a corner space, wider than I would have guessed. Where I saw those blue eyes shining at me.

I reach in, tapping my knuckles on the cupboard floor as if knocking on a door. I turn on my flashlight – It's not working.

I shake it and tap its head on the palm of my hand. I try it again. No dice.

And then: there it is again. The breeze.

"Are you playing hide and seek?"

I don't know what makes me say it, but I'm feeling more annoyed than scared at this point. Maybe they didn't scare away the last owners but simply annoyed them away. I pretend to look around me under the table and in the right-hand cupboard. Then, turning back to the sink, I say in a sing-songy voice, "I found you!" I turn on the flashlight. It works for a second, then sputters out. I peer into the dark of the cupboard, searching for those blue eyes and whatever else I might find waiting for me.

CHAPTER ELEVEN

I t's pitch black. No eyes staring back at me, no faces. The breeze picks up and moves off again. Listening intently, I hear nothing, but I decide to get up and follow the air. Standing in the entryway, I wait. Then it comes again, passing my face. The chill starts across my cheeks and ripples down my back. I turn and look, and in the glow of the yellow foyer, I can almost see a shimmer. I step forward between the front door and the basement. Out of the corner of my left eye flickers a silver sparkle, like a glittery dust mote, drifting down in front of the mirror. The presence I felt the very first time I entered the house. It drifts toward the study.

"Are we playing tag or hide and seek?" I chuckle, slowly following them into the study. I peek around the corner and can't see anything. The room is dark, the bay window only letting in a sliver of light from the streetlights.

"Hello..." I musically call into the room, walking slowly around and looking in the bookshelves. I creep around to the back of the desk, gently pulling out the chair.

"Gotcha!" I squat in a quick movement, hands on my knees, looking in the recess of the desk.

I didn't turn any lights on when I came in, but a glassy ray of fluorescent streetlight is shining between my shoulder and the far corner of the desk. I don't see anything at first, and then I hear movement, like a small person adjusting their position. The ray of streetlight, only an inch or two in width, is coming through the window, and it suddenly illuminates the left side of a child's face. Nearly transparent, I look at the girl. She isn't smiling, but she doesn't look scared.

I'm talking to a ghost, but I'm worried she's scared?

"It's okay, honey, I'm Kendra," I say. I don't want to scare her off, so I don't move a muscle. I simply smile, keeping my hands on my knees. "We just moved here. Do you live here too?"

The girl nods, her head passing through the light. Her hair glitters a bright blonde.

"Do you live here alone?" I turn my head to the side slightly.

She shakes her head.

"Are there other children?"

I swear she huffs in answer.

"I'm sorry, I thought – how old are you?"

She hesitates, looking to her right, the white of her eye oddly bright in the dull light. She turns her gaze back to mine, not answering me.

"Can I sit with you here?" I ask. My legs are cramping.

She nods, and I rock back onto my butt, landing on the ground a bit faster than I expected.

She laughs. A gentle, tinkling laugh like small bells being rung in a large, open field.

I laugh too, and then cover my mouth, the sound is so loud

in the quiet. We meet eyes, mine and hers both wide. I'm conscious that she's hiding for more than the sake of a game. I pull my hand away from my mouth and smile at her. She returns the smile coyly, not showing any teeth.

Sitting down, my body no longer blocks the light from the window, and the streetlight almost fully illuminates her. She is entirely opaque, her dress high-necked and ruffled, a color only describable as a blue haze. In a different colored light, I feel instinctively it would look different, as well. Bangs cover her forehead, and wide waves of hair fall past her shoulders. She could be thirteen, fourteen, maybe fifteen years old. Young, but not a child; not then, anyway.

"Are there others in the house?" I ask again. She nods and holds up a finger. One. "Just the two of you?" She smiles sheepishly, and then, she screws up her mouth and looks up. She doesn't know how to say it, but she has something else to say.

"You're the only two kids – uh, young people... but there's others?"

She nods vigorously.

"Are they nice to you?"

She freezes. She starts to fade like she's backing through the desk. "Wait! I'm sorry, let's just –" I try, but she's already gone. I look at the space for another few seconds, and then stand, hoping I'll see her by a bookcase.

In the mirror across from the door, I see the silhouette of a man. He's looking into the room from the doorframe, but I can't see him here, only his reflection. He glides out of frame and moves toward the stairs – or basement. I sit in the desk chair. I'm not playing hide and seek with *him*.

After a few minutes, I go back to the kitchen to cook the pasta and think on this, fiddling with the pendulum in my pocket. Who had taken it, and why had that girl been so scared? What does she know of that man?

. . .

WHEN GEORGE GETS HOME, I tell him about our roommate over dinner.

"Didn't Lynn say the last couple tried to engage, and it made it worse?" He runs his hand through his hair. "We just moved in, here, Kendra."

"I know, I know, but maybe they didn't differentiate. It's not just kids here, George. I saw a man in the mirror. He scared the girl away just by showing up." I move food around on my plate. The pasta is good, but I'm buzzing with thoughts now that George is here to talk this over with. "I think she was hiding from him, and she might not even be as young as she seems. Her dress, her demeanor, made her seem younger but maybe in her time... I don't know, but I know there's nothing to fear with her."

George heaves a sigh, pushing away his dinner plate. "Anything else I need to be prepared for?"

I give him a questioning look.

"I'm working from home for a while. No shoots for another week," he smiles half-heartedly. "Maybe this'll be good. They might be intimidated by both of us being home."

"Or the girl might be too scared."

AFTER DINNER, I go back to the study and pause at the desk. I know I should write, but this nervous energy, the mental fatigue...

I look down at the dusty window and sigh. Reaching for some cleaner by the door, I focus on cleaning the window.

Working my way top to bottom, I pull aside the curtain to get a better angle at some of this dust. I get to the bottom, and in the bottom left-hand pane is scratched: *Clara 89*.

"Clara," I say out loud, leaning in to read it more clearly. My breath fogs over the name, and I wipe it off. In the reflection are those gray eyes. I whip around, and there's no one there. In the foyer mirror across the room, a shadow passes.

CHAPTER TWELVE

I'm kneading dough on the new table, the flour coaxing the scent of pine still fragrant from its surface. Sunlight pours in, illuminating my work. No need for candles now that spring is here. I brush a lock of brown hair out of my face, then use the corner of my dress sleeve to clean the flour from my forehead. Finishing up, I place the dough on the counter to rise. Wiping my hands on my apron, I go out to the hall to check the clock in the foyer. Half past eight already. Clara should be down for breakfast by now. "Clara?" I call up the stairs, softly. I don't want to wake the others.

No answer.

Disappointed, I go back into the kitchen. These mornings are our time together, before the rest of the house is up and we have to be on our best behavior. I open the backdoor and look out. I see a footprint in the mud. She must have snuck past me when I was stocking the woodstove this morning. I start to follow it, then walk back inside and deposit my apron before leaving again, closing the door behind me.

The footprints continue here and there where she pressed her *shoe into the mud. I follow her tracks past the treeline, lifting the hem of my dress to keep it clear of mud. "Clara?" I call again. No answer, save for the whispering wind. I look around, and as I step through the tree line into the woods and head toward the railroad tracks, I feel that I am alone. Checking for trains, I cross the tracks when I don't hear a whistle. Before I can get to the river, I hear the rustle of a dress in the fallen leaves still coating the forest floor. I turn toward the sound, heading south along the tracks. "Clara? Clara!"*

I WAKE, lifting myself back on my elbows. I look around and see George's silhouette in the bathroom, startled for a minute as I come back to reality. I remember the dream; I feel like part of me is still in it. Subconsciously I dust my hands together, half expecting flour to be on them. The table in the kitchen was new – I remember its piney smell. The backdoor – I was looking for Clara.

I need to stop talking to ghosts before bed.

I shake my head and roll out, joining George in the bathroom.

George is in awe of my unpacking prowess the day before. "You even plugged in my razor. Thank you, baby," he says, kissing me on the head as I brush my teeth.

Shadow brushes across our legs. Drying my face, I remark, "A master bathroom isn't half bad, room for the whole family in here," I laugh, hanging the towel and squatting down to pet Shadow. She trots out to the bedroom, and I pick out my outfit for the day: a dress with a lovely wheat pattern over a solid navy.

"Want to make breakfast with me?" George asks, "I have some editing to do, but eggs are calling me first."

"Absolutely," I say, sliding into my slippers. These hardwood floors are lovely but a nuisance in January. Which reminds me: "Did you top off the wood last night?"

"Yes, actually, it was strange. There were two more logs in the furnace than I remembered putting in the other day. It's not as cold as we think, I guess," he shrugs, pulling on his tried-and-true hoodie over a t-shirt. He's wearing pajama bottoms, a staple of at-home productivity.

In the kitchen, I rearrange some pots and pans while George monitors the eggs. "I think I want to hang a ladder or a bar here for the pans to hang, I've always loved the look of that."

"And we should get new curtains. These are drab and dusty," he tugs at the one closest to the stove, shaking it out a bit.

"Speaking of, did I tell you what I saw in the corner of the mirror when I cleaned the bay window in my study? *Clara 89*, carved in the corner. I've read that in old houses, diamonds could be used to carve into glass to leave your signature. She must have lived here, maybe the daughter of the first owner." I wrack my brain for their name. "Baker," I snap my fingers.

"Must've been doing well to get his wife or daughter a diamond," George posits. "I wonder how this town was doing back then."

As he says it, something clicks. "1889 was the year of the flood."

I lean back against the counter, chewing my thumbnail.

"I know that look," he says, flipping the eggs. "Research is coming," he says in a mockingly-ominous voice.

I roll my eyes and turn around to get two plates down.

Sitting at the kitchen table, I look around again at the space, so cheerful in the morning light. It's not even nine a.m. yet, so the sun is warm and bright as it streams through the kitchen window. "I'm surprised the cats haven't followed us downstairs yet. They'd love these sun patches."

George swallows and nods. "I'm sure they're just over-whelmed with how many stories there are here. The middle level alone is bigger than our last place. All they've ever known is a two-bedroom apartment."

"Yeah, but I tried to carry Shadow down yesterday, and she practically clawed her way back to the bedroom from the stairs."

"She does hate being held," he tries, but I interrupt him.

"It felt like more than that. You know cats see spirits and are more in tune to them. Have you experienced any activity upstairs at all?"

"No, actually. Maybe that's it," he's looking at the remains of his egg with an unfocused stare. "Clara. Huh."

"Yes, maybe. Could always be unrelated, though. It's an old house with probably a dozen or more people living in it over the years. Our girl could be anyone." I finish my egg and sit back. Standing up, I go over to the back door and remove the curtain. "I think I'll do the laundry today while you're home. You're right about these curtains." I move to the kitchen window and remove them as well. Rounding them up around the living room and then going to the study, I pause at the glass inscription. Running my finger over it, it's easier to read in this light than last night's darkness. It's a decent cursive for a decidedly difficult writing medium such as diamond-on-glass. She wasn't a kid, or maybe she had great penmanship. The family must have been doing well.

I sit on the bay window and try something.

"Clara Baker?" I say into the ether of the room. Looking under the desk, I see no one. The mirror in the hallway is empty as well.

"Clara?" I try again. Nothing. I've left my pendulum upstairs on my altar, or I'd be tempted to try it again.

As I stand up to leave, I turn around and look in the corner, between the desk and the end of the bookshelves. It's dark, and I feel a presence there, swaying like they're uncertain. "Clara, is that you?" The presence steps closer, and I see the outline of a man.

"George!" I call before I can stop myself. The man steps closer, and the gray eyes look at me from beneath a dark black mop of hair. I've seen those eyes before. That button-up shirt. Those overalls. He steps back as suddenly as he stepped forward, and I feel him recede as George comes running into the room, panic in his eyes.

"Kendra?" He comes around the desk and puts his arm around me, turning me to face him.

I whip back around. "That man – that man from the corn maze," I stutter. I don't know why I'm whispering. I clear my throat and make myself talk at a normal volume. "He was in that corner," I point. "He was looking at me last night after Clara left; after I read her name from the glass."

With his arm around me, George takes me out of the room. I peek in the mirror as we pass – empty again. Sitting in the living room, we look at each other in silence for a couple of minutes. "I think we need to talk to them again," I venture. "But I need to do some research first."

The curtains forgotten, I go upstairs to pull on leggings and warmer socks. I'm going to the library.

THE LIBRARY IS an easy building to miss if you don't know it's there. It's small, sided with faded alabaster vinyl. Entering the building, there are a few tables and a couple of aging armchairs in the middle with shelves at the back and along the walls. I'm the only one inside when I clear my throat at the reception desk. No one is around, no bell to ring either.

After a few minutes of waiting, a heavyset woman comes out from the back office, curls piled on top of her head in a loose '60s style, thin bangs over her forehead.

She inclines her head, looking at me, direct and serious. Okay, this is one of *those* libraries then.

"Hello, I'm Kendra Hill. My husband and I just moved here." Best to start on a personal note, I think. Small towns and all.

"Welcome to Newport," she says bureaucratically.

I wait for a follow-up, but none comes. "I'd like to open a library card, please."

She pulls an ancient ledger out from under the desk. It's then I notice there's no computer on the desk. It's 2019, and there's no computer. As I wait for her to pace the pages forward, I look around. No computers in this library at all. The shelves go straight back with more books lining the far wall.

"I like the peace here," I try. "It's a dead silence, just books and more books."

"It's a library," she says. I look for a nametag, but she isn't wearing one.

She turns the book toward me, and I fill in a line with my name, address, and today's date. She turns it back to herself and closes it, then reaches into a drawer and passes me a paper card. I write my name on it, and she takes it, giving it a stamp. She turns to leave.

"Excuse me, Ms. ...?"

"Shenk." She turns her head, not her body, to meet my eyes.

"Ms. Shenk, I had some questions about records or old newspapers. Can I view those here?"

Ms. Shenk turns fully and approaches the counter again. "From which year?"

"I was curious about the flood of 1889," I start. "The papers from around town, obituaries, and any pictures would be really helpful."

She pauses, looking down in thought. "Local history. That flood is well documented, it affected most of Pennsylvania. It rained for days. A dam burst in Johnstown. A lot of people died. Some people's bodies weren't found for years. Some washed up states away."

She looks up. "There's a book you might try." She comes out from behind the desk, heading to the non-fiction section. "No relation," she says, passing me a book by one William H. Shank. "Common name in this area. Mine's spelled with an 'E,' though."

I smile at her. "Fun coincidence." When she doesn't return the smile, I add, "Are there any newspapers or articles in local papers about the flood?"

"Oh yes, very many. Most are on microfilm. If you have the time, I can show you how to use the machine. It's in the back." She's already walking, and I follow.

The microfilm machine is almost like a big microscope or an eye-test machine – there's room for both eyes to look down the dark corridor to the past.

"This is the catalog." She gestures to the latter half of the 1880s section. "You're going to want May 31st onward." With a stern look, she adds, "Take notes, only. None of these materials are to leave the library."

"Of course." I nod. "Do you have a notepad?"

She looks at me for a minute, and I feel like I'm being read under a microfilm projector, myself. Then, she nods, and crossing the small room to what looks like her personal desk, she opens a drawer and hands me a yellow-lined notepad, the kind with thin papers and wide lines printed in red ink.

"Thank you, Ms. Shenk." I smile again. I don't need to have it returned. I did my daily shielding meditation; her energy is not going to sap mine.

She turns to go back to the front desk, I guess to leave me to my privacy. Giddy, I start to pull down the microfilm copies of newspaper after newspaper. There are three different publications all covering the flood: *The Newport Ledger, The Liverpool Sun*, and one simply titled *The News*. Page after page until my eyes are dry as bone, I read scrawling notes without looking up. No missing persons lists, no Bakers, but lots of damage reports.

After an interminable amount of time, I pull back, widening and blinking my eyes. Yawning, I look at my notes.

Yeesh.

This'll take some pacing.

I raise my hands above my head and then suddenly remember Ms. Shenk. Calmly lowering my arms to my sides again, I look around. She's seated at her desk with a book in her hand. She's engrossed, her pointer fingernail between her front teeth. I pull out my phone. It's almost one o'clock. Then I look at the lock screen – four missed calls from George and a text that reads, "I think Clara's here." I unlock my phone to call him back and see another text. "Upstairs with the girls. Call me back."

Hastily but carefully, putting away the microfilm, I smile and thank Ms. Shenk, pulling my arms through my coat sleeves as I sprint to the car.

Something doesn't feel right.

CHAPTER THIRTEEN

I pull into the spot diagonally and get right out of the car. The door is fighting me as I try to unlock it, and when I finally get the key to turn, I open the door in a rush. Running up the stairs to the bedroom, I'm out of breath. No one is in here, except Shadow sleeping on the bed.

"Kendra, I'm in here," George calls, his office door is open. I dash inside.

"What happened? I'm so sorry I had my phone on silent, I was at the library, and there's this librarian who's pretty uptight and –"

"It's okay. We're okay. I just panicked at first, but I came up here to seek refuge with the girls."

I heave a huge sigh and sit on the stool he keeps by his desk chair for his feet. "Thank goodness," I force a laugh. "I'm relieved. I thought the ghosts were bothering you."

"Oh, they were," he chuckles, but I hear the nerves in his voice. "I was trying to work in the downstairs study. Figured since you weren't home, I'd try out the energy. There was a draft coming in, so I fiddled with the window but couldn't find a source. I got up to move to another room, and I saw someone run past me, behind me, in the mirror's reflection."

"Were they shorter than you?"

He nods. "I swear I could see long hair or a dress behind her, in a split second as she passed. Like I said, she was behind me so I couldn't get a great look."

"Did you talk to her?"

"Nooo," he says in a long, descending tone. "Nope. I ran like a living little girl up the stairs to cower with the cats."

I pull my hands into the sleeves of my coat – in the rush, I didn't take it off when I got home – and put my elbows on my knees, resting my head between my hands. "Alright, I'm going to try something," I say decisively. George raises an eyebrow. "Something witchy," I add sheepishly. When he smiles, I straighten up a bit.

I stand in front of my altar table, centering myself, grounding in the moment. "Goddess, guide my hand in aiding this lost soul. The winds of change, help me to usher her on to where she needs to be. Goddess, protect me from the man. Fires of creation and destruction, protect us," I pause, smiling at George, blushing, and then adding, "and protect Clara, too."

I take a bundle of sage and a clay dish I use to catch the ash when clearing or cleansing. I had picked the sage on a hike in California years ago and made enough bundles to last me a lifetime. "I should've done this the night we moved in," I mumble, grabbing a lighter from the altar table.

Lighting the sage, I continue. "Flowing waters, grant me your gift of patience as I work with and find answers to these mysteries here in our new home. Mother Earth, help me to ground and be grounded here, to feel welcome here, and to be a part of this land I'm now on."

I start in the bedrooms and work my way throughout the house. I draw banishing pentagrams, five-pointed stars drawn from bottom to top in each corner, over each window, in front of the fireplace, and in the direction of the cats as I pass through the bedrooms and large hallway. George comes out of his office, smelling the burning sage.

"Sorry about the smell," I say, blushing redder.

George shakes his head and smiles. "I'll come with you," he says.

I feel relieved. I hope this works – it's been less than a week and I'm tired of feeling unsafe in my own home, and Clara is not the culprit of that.

Heading down the stairs, I cleanse and clear the air, the large window, and the stairs themselves, paying particular attention to the landing where Shadow freaked and jumped out of my arms. I waft the smoke over the balustrade and balusters and once at the bottom of the stairs before I head into the kitchen. Usually, during the clearing of a home, the sage needs to be relit. This bundle is burning brightly – a good sign that the smoke is clearing away the negative energy but also a sign that there's a lot that needs to be cleared.

Repeating my incantation, invoking the healing powers of air, fire, water, and earth, and asking the Goddess' blessings in our home, I do the same in the kitchen, drawing banishing pentagrams in each corner, opening each cabinet to let the smoke fill and clean any negative, stale energies away: evil or benign.

As I approach the back door, I see my reflection in the now-curtainless window. Behind me, I can see George's as well. Drawing a large banishing pentagram from floor to ceiling, I envision the smoke banishing the negative energy as it curls away from my sage bundle. I trace the outline of the door, and as I move across the bottom of the door, sealing the rectangle, I see a third figure's reflection enter the room behind me.

Making eye contact, I say, "Any negative energies that seek

to harm us or the good spirits of this house, be banished here today, by the powers of air, fire, water, and earth."

The figure dissipates in smoke as I complete the rectangle.

I ask George, "Did you see that?"

"What?" He looks around and behind us.

"In the reflection, in the door. The man was behind us but dissipated as the smoke rose and sealed the rectangle. I don't want to jinx it, but maybe it's that easy." I smile.

Moving to the window over the sink, I do the same. The figure does not reappear. I open the cabinet under the sink as well, wafting in a large amount of smoke, squatting down, and using my breath to blow it into the space. We move to the door of the wood stove and do the same then head out into the foyer.

Going into the living room next, I repeat my invocation and blessing to clear the energy, sealing the banishment of negative energy at each window. I do the same at the front door, then looking at the mirror, I banish and seal it as well.

"Let's do the outside of the door." I pull open the front door and draw a banishing pentagram on the front mat and send smoke up the door, sealing a second banishing pentagram on the front of the door. "Nothing can come in, at least," I say as I close the door and lock it. I take note that it's still sunny, not even five o'clock yet.

Heading into the study, I take my time. I repeat the invocation and blessing again and clean every bookshelf, seal the window, even open the hidden cupboard under the seat of the bay window and send smoke over its contents. I draw a large banishing pentagram in the corner by the window in which I had seen the man last night, sealing the wall like a door. It's possible in an old house that it could've been one, and the ghosts might not notice a change like that.

Looking around the study, I peer into the mirror. I listen and breathe, inhaling the fragrant smoke of the sage. This is a massive house compared to my usual needs, and the sage bundle is almost halfway used. "Ok, we have two floors left," I say.

Then I realize something.

Neither of us has been in the basement or the attic since we moved in.

"George," I ask, "did you take the boxes down to the basement for storage?"

"No, I recycled them. I haven't gone down there." He says it like he's realizing it too.

"I haven't gone down either. Isn't that strange?" I sit in the study chair, letting the sage smolder. There's a decent collection of ash in the dish, I notice, holding it in my right hand while my dominant left keeps the bundle aloft.

George rubs his chin. "That is a little odd, but I guess we don't have any reason to. It's only been a couple of days."

"The attic is a finished third story," I start. "We should want to be up there, right?"

"I mean, there's no lighting yet," George states, always practical-minded. "But we should clear the whole house while you've got the sage going." He's not a believer, but I smile at his enthusiasm. "It can't hurt," he adds, reading my smile.

We stand, walking to the basement door. I clear the outside of the door, drawing and sealing another banishing pentagram. Opening the door, I do the same on the other side. "I'm not letting any of that," I gesture down into the basement with the sage bundle, smoke curling to the ceiling, "come up here."

I flick on the lights. "Shall we?"

George nods. "Wait," he lifts one finger then heads to the kitchen.

Looking down the basement stairs, I can't look away. Part of me wants something to appear, validating this feeling of impending doom. It's just the electromagnetic field, I remind myself. Electromagnetism makes people jumpy, that's all.

"Okay, let's go." He's holding the flashlight. "I put in fresh batteries after what happened to you last time."

I lean my head onto his shoulder, unable to use my hands to touch him. I suddenly feel an urge for human contact to ground me.

"Okay, let's go." I nod.

I spin the sage bundle in my hand, letting the smoldering embers catch fresh leaves. The smoke grows, and I repeat once again, invoking the elements, asking them for blessings upon me and George against any harmful energy that lingers here.

At the bottom, George turns on the flashlight, and, walking to the bulb, he pulls the string. Going further, he flips the switch. He sighs with relief as the lights flicker on.

"I don't like it down here, Ken. Let's move around and get back upstairs." He makes his way to me, going around a piece of tarped furniture.

"We can't be afraid of our own basement," I say. "We should get a few friends or family together to clear it out down here."

As I finish that sentence, a draft starts again.

"Clara, is that you?" I ask into the basement's muffled depth. Turning, I watch the smoke follow the breeze, blowing with it. I follow the smoke with my eyes and then with my feet.

George behind me, the smoke leads us to a corner with what looks like a table or a stack of boxes, maybe a wardrobe. I look at George, and he looks at me. We don't speak for several heartbeats, watching the smoke bounce off the furniture. I start to draw a banishing pentagram when the breeze picks up.

The sage goes out.

Turning on the flashlight again, George shines it at the

collection before us. It's angular, like a box on top of a table. We meet eyes, and I nod. He grabs a corner of the tarp and pulls.

It's a doll's house.

A large, Victorian doll's house with an open face and several rooms. Next to it is another tarped section, a corner of the once-white cloth resting in the frame of the house. He pulls it off too, gently. Boxes. Somehow, I know those boxes contain dolls, furniture, and maybe even little rugs or animals for the house.

"Don't worry, Clara." I smile. "We wouldn't get rid of your house."

Taking the lighter from my pocket, I relight the sage. Washing the smoke over the house, I say a blessing.

"Are you sure that's a good idea?" George asks. "Aren't you making a few assumptions here?"

I shake my head. "Clara is not the problem nor the one to fear."

We're standing in the far right of the basement, probably under the kitchen. I turn to the right end of the basement and draw a banishing pentagram in the corner then smooth some smoke around the area. The draft of air has not returned, and we walk around the area deosil, or clockwise, clearing and banishing as I walk. We must have passed over a dozen tarped belongings of families past.

"Who knows what we might find down here?" I ask George, feeling overwhelmed.

"We'll get my parents out here, for sure. They'll be a great help." George's parents are always antiquing throughout upstate New York and Massachusetts.

"We could auction some of this toward the mortgage." I quickly add, "But not the doll's house. We'll check with Clara on anything we don't want." I feel a sense of relief from somewhere behind us, but it might have just been me, happy not to have any incidents again.

George switches off the lights, then pulls the cord and turns, gesturing me first up the steps. "Such a gentleman," I smirk. He pats my butt in a hurrying way. He hasn't turned off the flashlight.

Back upstairs, he turns off the flashlight. "I'll save the battery power for the attic," he says. "Almost done."

It's nearing sunset, which is when I want to start writing. I do my best work from twilight to midnight. I nod. "Let's keep moving."

As we arrive at the top step of the attic, I find myself exhausted. "This house is huge," I sigh.

George yawns and sags his shoulders. "Almost done," he says again.

In the attic's small hallway, George switches on the flashlight as I repeat the invocation of blessing one last time. We turn and clear the room on the right first, banishing and sealing the window, and again at each corner. I pause in the center of the room.

"It feels stale in here," I remark. "Not bad, just stuffy."

"I bet no owners have used it since it was first built, if even then," George posits. "It's probably for maids – why else would it have finished floors and separate rooms? Built in the 1860s... I'm just glad it wasn't the South."

"I second that," I nod in agreement. "The energies could certainly be worse," I say as I knock on the wooden doorframe.

Crossing the hall, George goes first to shine the flashlight ahead of me. The window here is much darker, south-facing. We amble past the reclined chair. I draw a banishing pentagram over each corner, watching the smoke flow up to the ceiling and across the walls in the small room. I brush over the reclined chair as well, but the smoke goes up and away from it. I try again, but it won't hit the chair.

It's an old leather chair, cracked and worn. It reminds me of something barbers would use in the old days.

If we move it to its upright position, I suspect it would break, so I don't want to touch it. Leaving the room and coming to the stairs, George follows me down to the bedrooms. Going over to my altar, I say a blessing of thanks. The bundle is a tiny nub, burnt down to the stubs of stems. I decide to let it burn down and clear my body with the smoke, front and back, crown to feet. I pause and look at George. "Do you want to cleanse yourself, or is that too weird?"

George shrugs. "Better safe than sorry." He puts his hands out on either side of himself and spins slowly as I waft the smoke up and around him.

When we're facing each other again, I smile at him. "Thank you for being so cool with this."

"Thank you for taking care of us on this. Spirits are your domain, not mine." He's keeping his tone light, but my intuition says there's more on his mind. I give him a suspicious look as the bundle fizzles and fades.

"Really, I trust you. I don't fully understand it all, but I want to. It's not for me, but I am glad you know what you're doing."

I lay the bundle in the ashes of the dish. "I hope I do. I've never had to use magic like this, not in my own home." I place the dish on my altar. "Not with my own family at stake."

I decide to keep the ashes. I'll mix it with sea salt to make protective black salt. It'll be a great extra precaution outside around the perimeter of the house like a shield.

Placing a finger on the blackened stumps of sage leaves, I verify that the fire is done. I yawn and stretch, taking a second in mountain pose: straightening my back, my hands palms together in front of me.

"Ready for dinner?" George asks.

I nod. "And baby, thank you so much for keeping me company through this. I hate to admit how uncomfortable I've been feeling here." I go over to him and take his hands then wrap my arms around his waist. "We did the right thing, right?"

George rests his chin on my head. "Yes," he says. "I really love my office, and the girls are happy here. The cats, I mean," he jokes, but I know he's relieved too. Believer or not, it feels good to do something against the uneasiness.

"You're not worried?" I stretch my arms around him. "I haven't found anything, no banks are hiring, and my book is by no means bringing in any money anytime soon, even if this agent meeting goes well next month." My heart leaps. Next month will come too fast.

I feel George shake his head back and forth, his chin still resting on top of my head. "My intuition might not be as developed as yours, but this is our house. We're meant to be here."

We stay in each other's arms, and I wonder if he's thinking the same thing I am: this has to work out. All of our money is sunk into this house.

As we head downstairs to make dinner, the cats follow us. Shadow stops on the landing, looking down at us. Sherry chitters and chirps a bit then skips down to us. She follows us to the kitchen and starts sniffing around. A few minutes later, Shadow comes in and brushes against George's leg before hopping into a chair then up on the table. I don't have the heart to make her get down.

"I think it worked, babe," George smiles at me.

CHAPTER FOURTEEN

Clara has been quiet but ever-present so far. Somehow on a Saturday, George doesn't have a shoot, I'm ahead on my writing, and my dad is off work, so I call him, and he agrees to help us move some things and look through the basement.

I run through the things we need to get done. First things first, we'll move the dollhouse upstairs. I'm thinking we'll put it in the living room. It's a fun piece, and we have room for it there. Next will be some untarping and figuring out what to do with everything else.

I'm at the kitchen table with my laptop, reading over my writing so far and sipping coffee while George finishes washing the breakfast dishes. There's still something missing. I close my eyes and clear my mind, entering a slightly meditative state. I repeat in my head, three times, an affirmation for my book. *Bleeding Glory is an authentic story of Catherine finding her way to accomplish her dreams. Readers will love her as much as I do.* On the third repetition, I realize I don't know her that well. I start a random scene, disregarding the progression of each chapter, writing about Catherine's favorite outfit. I lean over my laptop, tying in a story of her childhood love of fashion. The mantra changes as I type: *this is relatable, this is real!* I knew this house would help me get this story together.

"Pleased with yourself?" George asks, wiping his hands on the dish towel.

I look up at him and realize I'm smiling. "Yes, actually. I'm thriving as a full-time writer," I take a sip of coffee, leaning back in my chair luxuriously. "I could get used to this."

"You know, we've committed ourselves to this house. Put all our money in," George begins, "and yet, the wood stove is more efficient than we expected. Groceries are cheaper out here. There's less temptation to go out to eat since there's only one restaurant."

"Yes, and?" I think I like where he's going with this.

"Well, in the spirit of commitment, why don't you embrace this full-time writing? Enjoy your time with your book for now." He comes over to me and takes my hand. "I have shoots booked all April and May for engagement photos and next comes the wedding season. I'll have graduations as well. There's plenty in savings from holiday photos, and I'll be enjoying my downtime too until spring. It'll be good for us to have the time to get the house in order for ourselves, together." He lilts on 'together,' an excited schoolboy playing house. "Besides, we haven't had real time to ourselves since..." he pauses, remembering, "since the summer after senior year when we were apartment and job hunting. And this time, we won't have the financial stress of unemployment weighing on us."

"Just the student loans, now," I laugh. I tilt my head back, beckoning him down to me for a kiss. He obeys willingly.

"So much uncertainty, so much possibility. We've really made it, George. Can you believe we really have our dream house?" I sigh romantically, standing and pulling him into a hug.

He puts his arms around me, kissing my head the way he loves to; the way he knows I love. "We're living the dream," he murmurs into my hair.

After a pace, we separate, and I close my laptop. "Alright, are we ready to tackle this basement today?"

He nods energetically. "Very much. I think it'll feel much less claustrophobic once we get those old pieces out. Do you think there are some valuable things there?"

"I'm sure of it if the dollhouse is any indication. Not that we would sell that, ever," I add loudly, for Clara's benefit, "but the tables or any clocks or what have you can definitely move. We could even host an auction here. I hope my dad knows what to do."

"I'll video chat my parents as well. They're always available," he chuckles. "I'll text them now and let them know."

I take out my phone and see a text from my dad. "Dad'll be here around one, he says."

"Awesome, plenty of time for a walk to the river," George says spontaneously.

"I love the way you think!" I say, pulling my hands into my sleeves and taking his hand as we walk outside.

There hasn't been much snow since before Yule, and though brisk, the sun is shining, and there's no wind blowing – great walking weather.

Living at an intersection, I love the privacy of abutting the old rail track and a small alleyway. Alleyways have very different meanings in a small town as opposed to a city like Harrisburg – here, they mean peace and quiet, not risky when you're just trying to take out the trash. We go out the back door, lock it, take our house key, and head for the tracks.

"Our first walk around the neighborhood!" I skip a little,

reigning it in, just in case any neighbors are watching. I'll save my crazy for a little later, once they have a chance to get to know us. I'm excited to explore on foot. The world is different at this pace: more tactile than driving. I can see the weeds clearly for the varied plants they are; the trees are individual oaks and ash instead of a rush of brown slotted with sun.

Scaling the dry, dead grass on the ridge of the railroad track, raised nearly six feet above the road, we come to the edge of the tracks. George takes my hand, and we dash across the tracks, finding ourselves in a wider-than-expected section of the woods.

"To the river, or do you want to explore along here a bit?" George asks, crunching leaves underfoot.

I look down the stretch of woods on either side, the river before us. "Let's head a bit further north, away from the bridge," I point to the left.

George salutes with his free hand, guiding me ahead with his other hand still in mine.

The trees are open but dense enough that the ground is thickly coated with dead leaves in varying states of decay. Some still retain an auburn crispness, others are dull, gray, and withered beyond recognition. The smell is heavenly.

I stop in front of an old, thick-trunked oak. "I wonder when this one was planted? Maybe even before the railroad tracks." I drop George's hand to hug the tree to my side.

George lays a hand on it. "It's still healthy," he says as he pats the trunk.

We continue another few minutes, enjoying the cool air and rays of sunlight dashing down through the naked branches.

"Shall we head to the river?" George asks.

"Absolutely," I nod, taking his hand, and this time, taking the lead.

The river is further than expected, about a five-minute

walk. We hear it before we see it, rolling along at a decent but leisurely pace. "Imagine tubing down this!" I exclaim, standing at the edge. At this rise, we're looking down into the river, a deep green, less muddy than when we drove over it in the fall.

"No rain for a while," George remarks, remembering the last time we were here. "Did you find anything out about that cemetery by the way?"

I had completely forgotten about my research over the past couple of days. I had taken the notepad – I hope Ms. Shenk didn't mind – but I haven't looked through it since. "I didn't, but I only made it through about half of the newspapers, and I focused on 1889 and the flood first."

"I guess we have things under control now anyway," George remarks. "No trouble with Clara, and that man is gone."

I pause before answering. "I'm not sure it'll be as easy as regular sage clearings, but I think our presence is accepted by the house, and Clara is in better... spirits." I raise my eyebrows at George.

He chuckles right on cue. "I'm glad she's not as afraid."

"I'm glad you care." I kiss him on the cheek. "You used to be a doubter," I add.

He puts his hands up in resignation. "Not since Gettysburg. You talked to people you couldn't have known were there, and research verified every last bit of information. A troop of twenty-six men from Georgia nearly all under the age of twenty-one, dying in exactly the spot you said they did? I'm a believer in empirical evidence." He doesn't sound scared, but I like the hint of respectful confusion in his voice. "Whatever or however, that activity was real in our home just as it was in Devil's Den. You're the expert on this, I'll always follow your lead." George takes up my hand again and kisses it.

I grin back, blushing. "I don't know, there's a big difference

ELYSE WELLES

between feeling a few ghosts on a battlefield and helping a young woman in my own home. It feels more dangerous, more serious."

"You're taking it seriously, though, and I think that's what matters," says George, squeezing my hand.

We both turn and watch the river for a while, taking in the smells of clean, moving water paired with the cold of the January air and the decay of the leaves. I kiss him and then pull him into a big hug, enjoying the warmth of his body against mine in the winter air. "Let's start heading back." I pull back from him, pecking him on the lips one more time.

As we near the tracks, the sound of the river starts to fade. "I wish we could hear it from our house," I sigh, "but it's lovely to be so close to running water and a forest, no matter how small it is."

"Let's walk back south from here, then we can cross the tracks. We came further north, remember?" George suggests.

"Great idea, baby," I swing our arms as we walk, hand in hand, enjoying the crackle of leaves beneath our feet.

"We should be at the house now," I say, and just as I turn to head closer to the tracks, I notice a spiky collection of twigs: a bush or shrub. It seems out of place amongst the trees and their leaves. Getting closer, I realize it's a gardenia bush. Leaning down to check the stalks, I see it's not beyond saving.

"I'll be back for you in a few months," I whisper to it.

When I stand and turn around to leave, I feel a peculiar sense of deja vu. I look back toward the tracks then begin heading in that direction. George follows, his hands in his pockets, looking inquiringly. I get to the tracks and then turn, looking toward the bush. "This is where I was," I say. "In my dream. I was in a bed of gardenias," I point to the gardenia bush. "Someone was behind that tree. I thought it was a young girl."

George shrugs. "How do you know this is the spot?"

I shrug in response. "I just do. It was early spring, I think. Warmer." I pace a bit toward the bush. "And in another dream, I was heading over here. I was calling for Clara... I'd followed her steps in the mud." I kneel down, fingering the dead leaves of the bush. One comes off in my hand. "I could hear her dress in the leaves." I stand, looking at the dead leaf. "I was calling for her."

George takes his hand out of his pocket, holding my hand. "That's it? Nothing scary happened?"

I laugh shortly. "Ghosts aren't scary. In my dream, I wasn't looking for a ghost. It felt like I was looking for Clara. I was wearing an apron, baking bread, and then I took it off to go outside." I pause, closing my eyes to think. "I might have been wearing a long dress. Like a different time period. It felt like I was looking for her because she's family. I don't know how to explain it."

George rubs his thumb on top of the hand he's holding. "You've been investigating this almost non-stop. Don't worry about it."

I smile back. "It was the night I found her name carved in glass. You're probably right, she's just on my mind." I drop it with George, but I know there's more to it.

BACK AT THE HOUSE, I'm taking my shoes off as my phone rings.

"Hi, Dad!"

"Hi, Bug. I'll be there in about thirty minutes." I hear the whooshing sound of the highway on the other side of the line. "Not too much traffic for a Saturday."

"Thank you again, Dad. We're looking forward to showing

you the place." I smile into the phone. "You'll be the first family to visit."

"I'm honored," he says dramatically. "See you soon."

"Drive safe. See you soon Dad," I say, ending the call.

"I'll tidy up my office – he'll want the grand tour," George says, hanging his coat and heading to the stairs.

"I'll do a sweep down here first, then tidy up our room and my altar," I say, his retreating form already on the landing.

The house hasn't had time to get dirty yet. I haven't even considered how much more cleaning this will require, but I can only hope the robot vacuum can handle it down here. We haven't set it up on its charger yet, but after hauling some furniture out of that basement, I think we'll need to.

The kitchen is clean, and the dishes are still drying, so I leave them be. Looking at the kitchen sink, I think of Clara.

Checking to make sure George is upstairs, I clear my throat. "Clara?" I call, kindly. "My dad is coming to visit today. We'll move your dollhouse up here. What do you think of putting it in the living room?"

I wait for a temperature change, a draft, a sound. "Clara, are you around?"

There's no response. I shrug and head to the study. To *my* study – I need to start saying it that way.

Putting my hands on my hips, I inhale deeply as I take in the organized chaos. It's a space that had claimed itself decades before I was born. I haven't been able to write in here yet. The kitchen, my altar room, even the living room, but for all my good intentions, this space just feels like someone else's, and I don't know how to start on it without disrupting it. The study feels like a living thing in that way: like I want to keep it happy. Like I need to.

From the desk, I clear the few books I had unpacked and put them back on top of their boxes in the corner by the bay window where I'm keeping all my other things for now. I haven't seen that man in a while and hopefully keeping my things there will remind him it's not his space anymore. It seems Clara hasn't felt scared or threatened. In fact, it feels like even she is fading away. I can only hope that's a good thing.

Heading upstairs, I tidy our bedroom next, making the bed despite Shadow's protestations – she stays under the covers at the foot, a persistent lump. Sherry is in George's office with him where he's made great progress settling in. I don't know how he made it so cluttered in so few days, but at least the mess is contained.

I look at my altar. The room is tidy, my altar too – although I still need to make that black salt. But Dad is coming over. I sigh, opening the drawer in the front of my altar table and gently placing my statues, athame, sage bundle, pendulum, and jars of salt and water inside. I offer a murmured apology to deity and leave only my candle on the tabletopand temporarily, the ashes from the house clearing .

In the back of the drawer are empty jars. I reach to the back and find one, empty the ashes into it, then seal and place it in the drawer. I take the dish with me to the guest bathroom sink, giving it a wash with hand soap, then dry it on the hand towel. Putting it down for a minute, I sniff and am reminded of the litter boxes. Best to empty those before Dad comes. He'll notice that, alright. I open the sink cupboard to look for a plastic bag. Reaching to the back, I knock over a bottle of glass cleaner, and I hear it roll against the backside of the sink. I take out my phone, turning on the flashlight. I grasp for the bottle towards the back of the sink.

My hand goes straight through.

The sink is backed with loose fabric.

I lay down and empty the cupboard of extra cotton swabs, cotton rounds, and cleaning supplies, and shine my phone's light to the back. The floor is solid wood, but behind the u-bend it is a simple, solid-colored cloth, beige or gray, it's impossible to tell in this light.

"Kendra?"

I jump, smacking the top of my head against the sink.

"Oh baby, I'm sorry! What are you doing down there?" George kneels down next to me, gently placing a hand on my head where I hit it.

"Jesus, George! Just look for yourself," I say, mad and in pain. He kisses the top of my head, taking my anger with his lips as his hand takes my phone from me.

"An empty sink?" He's shining the light into the cupboard.

"The back, dingus," I say, crossing my arms even though I'm feeling better.

He pushes his hand to it, realizing as I did that it's just cloth. He pulls it aside. "It's a curtain," he says in a tone of great discovery. "And look," he reaches further and then pulls his hand back. "Here, hold the light," he passes me the phone.

Extending his arms further into the space, I shine the light over his shoulder. A few seconds later he starts withdrawing, a box in his hands.

Sitting back on his heels, the box on his lap, he looks up at me in wonder.

"I don't think it's treasure," I say ominously. I don't feel anyone with us, not even Clara; not even the cats.

There's a knock downstairs.

"Shoot, that's Dad," I say, jumping up.

George puts the box, unopened, on top of the sink. "I'll clean up in here, you go greet your Dad. And don't worry: I won't open this without you," he adds with a wink.

Opening the door, Dad is standing there in a familiar stance. Hands in his pockets, looking up at something. This time, it's the trim around the door.

"Ladybug!" He stretches his arms out to me, and my love for him washes over me.

"I'm so glad you're here, Dad," I don't hide the genuine gratitude in my voice. "Being a homeowner is more ambitious than I realized," I chuckle.

"It's definitely a trip," he says. "You're doing great so far, though, by the looks of it." He walks past me, looking up at the foyer lamp. "Tiffany? Excellent. And that railing!"

"It's a balustrade," I say in my best British accent. "The realtor made a point to say so," I chuckle again. I have really missed my dad.

"Well, it is masterfully crafted," he says in an equally-terrible British accent. "And what's this?"

He ducks his head, entering the study. "It's like a history museum! Where are you going to fit your massive book collection in all this?" He picks up the astrolabe, turning it gingerly. "I'm surprised you've unpacked a single thing with this massive distraction right here." He moves down the shelves, turning and poking at different decor and book spines. "Speaking of, are you doing much writing?"

I nod vigorously. "Yes. As a matter of fact, I am doing some of my best work... as of this morning. Not in here, though. I don't know. It just feels heavy, hard to focus."

"It's a bit dark and dismal, but I thought you might like that atmosphere. The dust might keep you sneezing though." He pantomimes a sneeze, holding a finger under his nose to stop it, like one of the Three Stooges.

I find myself laughing again. "And there's more news! I had an agent request a full manuscript! I have a little over five weeks to get it to her."

"That's fantastic, Bug! Really great! I hope she'll like it."

"What are we smiling about in here?" George enters, smiling.

"Kendra's good news. She's practically published," Dad says, shaking hands with George and exchanging a casual man-hug.

"And are we surprised?" George smiles at me, then turns back to our guest. "What do you think of the house so far?"

"Well, I'm taken with this room and the foyer. Not a bad front door either, very sturdy," he nods with approval.

"Well, the kitchen is this way," George says, leading us on, the house tour beginning.

After my dad passes him, George puts his hand on my back and leaning close to my ear whispers, "Shadow and Sherry won't go in the bathroom, I think it's that box. I moved it to our bedroom."

I give him a confused grimace, my brow knitting. On the top of my thigh, I use my finger to trace a protection sigil: three interlocking circles. Then, standing next to George in the kitchen entryway, I do the same on his back. It can't hurt.

"This is the kitchen!" I gesture, Vana White-style. "The back door and, you'll love this, the heating element is an old wood stove. And it auto-refills," I say enthusiastically. I decide I'm just going to enjoy today. No reason to worry about a stupid box right now.

After too much time spent exploring the wood stove and a brief tour of the living room, we head upstairs. George shows him around while I go in and check on the girls. Bless his heart, George cleaned the litter boxes as well, though I'm not sure where he stuffed the trash – probably a bag under the sink; but that's tonight's problem. The girls are both in my craft and Craft room, enjoying the meager patches of sun still coming through the west window. "I'll put my sewing machine there," I say, pointing to where Sherry is in repose.

"Well, kids, you've picked a good one," my dad intones, nodding his head.

"There's one more floor!" I say in mock exasperation, "And then it's down to business in that basement."

Stepping up onto the landing and peering around the attic rooms doesn't take long. "No wiring up here," Dad remarks. "You'll need floor lamps, I think." He absently flips the switch in the right-hand room.

"Right, good point. That's some hope then," I say. "I was bummed about the overhead lighting. And who knows how we'll get that chair down."

"What chair?" Dad says.

"In the room there, on the right," I say, pointing. I'm standing on the top of the stairs, no room in the tiny hallway for more than Dad and George.

"There's no chair in there," he says, opening the door wide and checking again.

"Right by the door," I brush past George, who backs up into the other room. He peers around me himself to see.

"George, you saw it too, right?" I turn to look at him.

There's no chair in the room.

"There's a big leather recliner from a barber's or a dentist's, right?" I ask again, feeling like I've gone clinical.

Dad backs up to let George pass. George blinks. "Yeah, I could've sworn..."

We all stand in silence for a minute.

Then I get out my phone flashlight just to be sure. Peering around the room, there's no sign of any chair.

But getting down on the floor, I see scratches and divots like a heavy object sat here. A chest, a box, a wardrobe – or a large chair.

CHAPTER FIFTEEN

Coffee brewing, I place sugar and a carton of milk on the table. I sit with my back to the sink, feeling like Lynn all those months ago when she first told us of the ghosts. I don't even vape, but I could use a hit. I clear my throat as the coffee pot starts dripping.

"Well, I guess we can tell you it's a haunted house. There have been two ghosts so far, but after –" George breaks off.

"After we cleaned the space, we have only seen one," I finish for him. I don't want to explain sage's benefits for cleaning and clearing energy right now. "Clara. She's a young girl, I've seen her a couple of times at night. I really don't feel threatened by her, but that chair really freaked me out. We haven't spent much time up there yet: we've been here less than a week and there's just been too much to do. But Dad, I swear, we didn't think that was something spooky or haunted or anything. It was just an old chair every time we went up there." I shake my head slowly. I've only ever heard about the residual haunting of a piece of furniture like that.

"We sleep fine, and the cats were wary of the downstairs at first, but they've warmed up," George explains.

Dad echoes my motion, shaking his head. He rubs his hand down his mouth, then holds his chin in his hand, elbow on the table. George and I look at him, not sure what else to say.

"Well, it was a great buy, a great location, a beautiful home. It's bound to have some bugs," he says. "Does it have bugs?" His eyes widen.

"No, nothing structural." I laugh. He always says I'm the dramatic one. "The basement isn't even damp. They did serious renovations to the foundation after a big flood in the '70s," George says. "Energy is affordable, the taxes are fair. It's a great house, we're willing to work with it, but sorry we had to scare you back there."

Dad chuckles, a sign of his usual mirth returning. "I haven't even seen the basement yet. Anything in store for me down there?"

George and I look at each other. I speak first. "There's a Victorian-style dollhouse and some boxes we think are related to it," I explain. I smile, then giggle a little. The whole situation is a little ridiculous, really. "We think it'll look excellent in the living room."

"There are a lot of great finds down there," George continues. "I think we'll find some decent auction pieces. My parents said we can video chat with them about anything we think looks valuable. Especially if there's anything from the Civil War era," he says, turning to me. "You know my mom and her collecting historical 'souvenirs' related to the Southern defeat or the Northern victory." He and I share a laugh, then he turns to Dad, saying, "They're antique connoisseurs like all retired New Englanders. And, of course, they have their favorite collectibles they're always looking for." George stands to get the coffee pot. Pouring three mugs, he sits back down, and we sit quietly as we pass around the sugar and milk to make our coffee.

"Your mom would have liked this whole mystery," Dad breathes a short laugh. "She liked ghost stories."

I raise my eyebrows at him. "I didn't know that," I say in surprise. Mom died when I was seven – there's so much I didn't get to know about her. "Did she ever see one?"

Dad nods as he lets his steaming cup warm his hands. "A couple of times. Actually, before you were born, she took me to a bed and breakfast *because* it was haunted. She woke to see someone at the end of her bed, and she woke me up, not because she was scared but because she was afraid I wouldn't believe her. Of course, it was gone when I came to, but I believed her. She was so excited." He looks wistful like he always does when he talks about Mom. But I'm glad he talks about her – and I think he's happy to talk about her, too. I wish he'd talk about her more; I wish I could get to know her as she really was. As a woman, not just a mom. I'll never know her woman to woman, adult to adult.

"She saw ghosts more than once?" I ask after a quiet beat, shaking off the introspective gloom coming on. I wonder how Mom would have reacted to Clara under the desk the other night.

"Her friend, Audrey or Aubrey or something, back in high school. She lived in a haunted house. It had a wall that was added after it was built, but it used to just be a hallway or throughway so, sometimes, she said, she would see a man-shaped-shadow-thing walking through it like they were passing down the hall. She saw him once at a sleepover. She told that story all the time." He takes a sip of his coffee. "I bet she'd have some thoughts on this." He takes another sip. "She'd want to spend the night to find out more. And to check on you guys, make sure it's safe here." Another sip. I think I get what he's driving at.

"Would you like to spend the night here tonight, Dad? We'd love to have you. The guest room is open, already made up, and the guest bathroom has shampoo, soap, and even extra toothbrushes," I smile excitedly.

Dad doesn't hesitate to agree, smiling back at me. "That would be great, Bug."

I suddenly feel much calmer knowing Dad will be here: another opinion, another witness to anything unnatural. I make eye contact with George, and I see he's feeling the same way. He pushes his glasses up the bridge of his nose and lets out a deep breath.

We drink our coffee, and I ask about his work, "Slow as ever," and George updates him on some of his recent photography shoots. When the mugs are drained, I clear the sugar and milk, then run some water in the mugs. "I'll wash these when I cook dinner later," I say. "Or when we order pizza," I say, looking sneakily at George and Dad like we're kids at a sleepover. I feel giddy, safe, warm, like pulling into your parking spot and running up to the house when the sky darkens with rain, locking the door behind you just as the thunder starts and the first drops hit the window.

Dad goes out to the car for gloves. Carpentry has its benefits in this regard, and he might be a good help when we look at this old furniture for stability and sturdiness. Waiting for Dad, I turn to George. "What do you make of all this?"

He shakes his head before I even have the question out. "I can't even understand how a chair can just disappear. Did we ever sit on it or touch it? I've been racking my brain, and I don't think I did."

"No, we didn't. I didn't want to." I shiver, a bit for effect, but also authentically. George doesn't answer as he runs a hand through his hair, still shaking his head.

Dad comes back in and hands us gloves which we slip on to protect our hands from splinters and dusty old things. "Oh, hold on," George puts up a gloved finger and goes back to the kitchen. He comes back with the '90s flashlight. "I'm ready now," he says, smacking it against his hand like a nightstick.

George goes on ahead, turning on the light at the top of the stairs and heading for the single bulb before the switch. "The breakers are back here, too," he says, proud he remembered that – he knew that Dad would ask.

Dad doesn't go down right away. "This door handle," he says. "Gorgeous flower. Geranium? No, gardenia."

I start. "I'm impressed, Dad. Yeah, it's a bit of a theme. They're on the balustrade too," I say 'balustrade' in a British accent again. He chuckles and follows me down the stairs.

"You know, gardenias were a bit of a fad for a while at the turn of the last century. In the Victorian language of flowers, gardenias meant innocence, purity, gentleness. And secret love." I don't have to turn to know he's wiggling his eyebrows up and down.

"Wow, Dad, I didn't know you were such a romantic," I say, as we arrive at the bottom of the stairs. I feel safer than the last time I was in this basement. "Secret love, huh?" I ask rhetorically. A chuckle dies in my throat as I hear a quiet laughter: the tinkling giggle of girls in another room. It couldn't have lasted more than a second. I look at Dad, but he doesn't seem to have heard. I look around and see a silver sparkle float around behind the stairs and then disappear. I don't feel any change to the energy; still safe, still comfortable. Come what may, I know it's good to have Dad here.

"Oh yeah, Ladybug, all those fine details of wood crafts-manship were part of my training. Can't get that at the Home

Depot." I sense a tone of resentment, but it's gone almost as soon as it came.

George flips the switch and Dad whistles, long and descending. "You weren't kidding, what a space."

"Yeah, not like the house needs it, but we could finish this space, and it would be a four-story home," George replies.

"Dad, is there any harm in untarping it all?" I ask, starting in toward a large piece of furniture.

Dad shakes his head. "Don't see why not. We'll move it all out soon enough, anyway."

Armed with our gloves, we start. First is a table: long, and lower than a dining table, yet higher than a coffee table. "Weird, but maybe people were shorter back then," I shrug. I have two colors of sticky notes – red for "sell", and green for "keep." I mark this one red. "Right, George? Sell?"

George and Dad both nod. "Gives me the heebie-jeebies," Dad says. "Not sure why."

As I attach the sticky note I feel it too, feeling unsettled, but I shake it off and go to the next one to pull off the tarp.

Boxes. I lift the lid – they look like old printer paper boxes, now dusty and a bit soft but not too damaged. Inside are what seem to be gas lamps, and, blessedly, they seem empty, wrapped in papers. "I'll look through this for a minute. You guys carry on with the rest."

George scoffs, "Nice try, just put the boxes you want to investigate on the stairs, we'll look through them together." He looks at my face, my impatience evident. He chuckles. "I know you're curious, but we'll be curious together in the coziness of the living room."

I sigh and agree, taking the box to the steps. It's heavier than expected for lamps. The next two boxes are assorted glassware, also wrapped in thin paper. Some bowls, some sconces, and I have to cut off my searching as Dad shakes his head at me.

I move the next boxes one at a time, and when I return to Dad and George, they've taken the covers off several more pieces. We're almost a quarter of the way around already. There's an old piano, stool, and a few wicker pieces. I mark them each as "sell." As tantalizing as an old piano sounds – pun intended – the repairs and space required in a home where neither of us play is rather unappealing.

We move swiftly around the basement for another fifteen minutes, then we find ourselves at the dollhouse. "We are definitely keeping this," I remind Dad, "we'll put it in the living room."

"Are you sure you don't want to switch it out for the piano?"

I'm already shaking my head before he finishes. "This is much more stylish, don't you think?" I'm embarrassed to explain it's the ghost's dollhouse, and I don't want to offend her.

Dad laughs a short laugh. "Yes, that is true. These boxes seem to all have accessories for it." He lifts the lid of the first one and then picks it up, taking it to the stairs.

I'm alone for a minute, then George comes by. "Have you heard or seen Clara today?"

I shake my head. "No, not really. I know it's silly, but I don't want her to hide from us. And I don't feel she's left us, either. I don't know what's going on." I lean down to get the second box, and, either from weight or age, its bottom starts to fall out.

George rushes to help me, his hands under the box. Through the bottom falls a bone-white doll, naked, no hair, its face either smudged or scratched off. "This is chilling," he says good-naturedly. Then, he puts it in on top of the box, which he shuffles over to the stairs, resting on both of his forearms. I lean down to get the third box when something behind it catches my eye. Something blue, appearing powdery in the strained light and dry with dust. I pull the box toward me, getting a good grip, then drag it out.

It's a ribbon. I reach over to grab it, but it's stuck on something. "George?" I call.

"Yeah?" he says. He sounds far away.

"I could use that flashlight when you can."

In the thirty seconds I'm waiting for George, something flashes behind the ribbon. Shiny or moving, I can't tell. I silently weigh the options, and I'm not sure if I should hope for rats or ghosts here.

George appears, the light shining past me. The ribbon is hanging from the top corner of a short shelf, and it's stuck under a box resting on top. George, holding the flashlight, stands behind me as I lift onto my toes, bringing the box down to the ground. The ribbon is freed, and I grab it once the box is securely on the ground, coiling it around my hand. It's in good shape, all in all. I put it in my pocket.

The box we retrieved is oddly light, and I open it to find yellowed quilts. I'm reluctant to touch what is likely excellent bedding material for rats, and close the box, dragging it out with the third dollhouse box. "This must be the women's section of the basement," I note. "Quilts in here, dolls and accessories there." I turn and look at the shelf. It's a changing table with shelves underneath for baby accouterments. I take out the sticky notes, tearing a red one free.

"Don't be so hasty," Dad is suddenly here, butting a word in. "You never know, you kids aren't even thirty yet."

"I know, Dad," I say as kindly as I can, but I don't hide the frustration in my voice. We've had this conversation before. George, grabs my hand, but doesn't say anything in my defense.

I use my other to place the red note on the changing table when George stops me. "Just give it a couple of years, maybe. We won't renovate or use this space for a while. We can keep it in storage down here, use it for a storage table, and if we ever need it for something else, we'll have it."

I give him a look, then sigh. "I'm not putting a green one on either, though. It's a maybe, that's all."

George doesn't reply but leans down to pick up a box to take to the stairs.

Dad clears his throat, embarrassment shifting him into action. He takes one of the boxes to the steps. As George lifts his second box, I catch a glimmer of light. Turning toward it, I catch sight of a low window in the corner of the basement. I wipe cobwebs and dust from the surface, murmuring a short apology to the spiders. I jump, trying to see through the window, but I can only make out some grass. I can't tell what part of the house we're under, but I think it's the back porch.

Trying again, I jump – and feel pressure on my right side, like a hand. I lose my balance. I put my hand on the baby table to catch myself, and it slides to the left – into the dollhouse.

"No!" I shout, watching the scene in slow motion. The changing table smashes into it, leaving a huge gash in the side. "Oh no, Clara I'm so sorry," I say, then cover my mouth. Dad, having come running at my shout, looks at me with a confused expression on his face. I feel my face redden, suddenly grateful for the poor lighting.

Dad doesn't say anything, just looks at me, confused, a dozen thoughts crossing his face. If we hadn't just had an exchange about kids, I'm sure his first question would have been, *Who's Clara?*

Before Dad could open his mouth, George shifts his feet, then says, "Clara is the nice ghost who... stays here in the house. It was her dollhouse, we think. She's made it clear she wants to keep it."

"How do you know her name?" He shakes his head. I instantly feel guilty for trying to keep it from him. "I don't – I don't..." his anger, his confusion, his fear even. It's palpable. I feel horrible.

"Dad, I'm sorry. I didn't want to worry you. She's nice, really. I can show you how we know her name: she carved it into the window in the study, *Clara 89*. There was a big flood here that year." He nods slowly in slight recognition. "We think she might have died then. This whole area was wiped clean in seconds, the water traveled at tsunami speed." I shake my head, refocusing.

"That sounds awful," Dad says. "I know you think Clara's nice but shouldn't she..." he lowers his voice, "move on?" I smile at his thoughtful tact.

"I agree, and I hope I can help her. But you never know. Maybe that's not what's next for us, or maybe she's just happy here." Thinking of death, I suddenly feel very aware we're in the basement. Dad and George, the focus of the task of organization, and the daylight creeping through the small window was a comfort, but the crushing feeling of the low ceilings comes back to me. "Let's go upstairs. We reached the first wall: that's huge. Let's finish this tomorrow."

George claps his hands. "I agree." Then rubbing them together, he adds, "I know a great restaurant."

As I follow George up the stairs, I touch my hand to my side, to where I'd felt the push. I don't want to mention it; it sounds crazy already, and the sage worked.

I think.

BITTING's is nearly empty once again, but this might be considered busy. There are at least five other groups eating here. I see Wanda with a tray on her arm flurrying to the back table where we'd seen Charlie months before. I hope she doesn't remember our conversation, or if she does, that she remembers it fondly. I like her, and since she's lived her whole life here, I think she's a good person to know.

The hostess, a cheery teenager, seats us and gets our drink orders. The atmosphere is different now at dinner. Families, elderly couples, a couple of middle-aged men at the counter. Chatter permeates the air.

"Cute place," Dad remarks, knitting his fingers on the table and looking around.

"We haven't been here since before moving in," I tell him. "I love the vibe. It's timeless."

"It reminds me of Pittsburgh in the '8os before it sort of modernized. I bet the plates are massive," he says, dramatically opening the menu.

George laughs, "I get a kick out of these huge menus, too. Kendra was laughing at me last time," he opens his menu and repeats the same joke he tried back in the fall.

I roll my eyes. "You are two of a kind," I grin.

The hostess comes back with our drink orders: two waters, a cola for Dad. "Wanda will be with you in a minute," she says before going back to the entrance.

I decide on the Reuben: it was great last time. Wanda comes over. "Well, if it isn't the investigators." She puts her hands on her hips. "Did you take the Harr house, then?"

I laugh, hoping she doesn't hear the nerves beneath it. "Yes ma'am, and we love it so far," I smile broadly.

George nods, "It's got great bones, that house. Great style, too."

"Well, I'm glad to hear it," Wanda smiles. I'm relieved. "What'll we be having?"

She looks to me first. "On your recommendation, I'll have the Reuben again, Wanda."

"A burger and fries, all the fixings, please," George orders.

Dad squints at the menu. "I'll do the same, actually,

George. A burger please, ma'am. All the fixings, but no ketchup," he gives her a warm smile.

"You got it, handsome," Wanda winks.

"Just the charm this town needs," Dad says as Wanda leaves. "I might have to move here, too," he says as he returns her wink.

"How is it back in the city these days?" I ask. I'm not sure what, but something's kept me from asking until now.

Dad exhales through tight lips. "Well, truth be told, Ladybug, business isn't what it used to be. Philly is expensive, and people are going to big brand home improvement places for cabinets or have become victims of the DIY craze, refinishing old ones themselves. People aren't building homes and putting in custom built-in cabinets; they're using minimalist storage techniques or just have less furniture in general. They're renting more than buying. Or maybe I'm just not in touch anymore." He takes a sip of cola, pulling his glass in between his hands, looking at the table. My heart aches. Then he pushes the cola back from himself again and looks up, smiling like a ringmaster. "So, now is as good a time as ever I suppose to formally announce," he does a pattering drum roll with his hands on the table, "I'm retiring!" He looks at us expectantly.

"Dad, that's great news! I'm sorry you feel like business isn't good, but I think you're right: it's time to enjoy your golden years." I smile as warmly as I can, the sadness of his talents fading spinning in the back of my mind. "You can redo our cabinets if you feel bored or fix our dollhouse," I add, remembering how much he loves to be helpful. "And you can stay with us anytime. We have more house than we know what to do with as it is."

"I won't be staying in that attic anytime soon, but I'd love to stick around and keep an eye on things with you all," he grins.

"My parents are all the way in Massachusetts, and my

sister is in Pittsburgh now with her wife. It would be great to have family close by, whenever you want to stay. Stay this weekend and see if you can stomach the ghosts," George wiggles his eyebrows.

Dad grimaces. I wince, wishing George hadn't said that. "I want to know more, too. Your mother would've been at the library all week figuring this out," he opines.

"That's what I did a few days ago. It's a small library, but they had microfilm records from three newspapers, all dated from the 1800s. I have notes, I'll show you tomorrow." Then I remember. "And maybe tonight we can bring up the boxes and dollhouse. I'm excited to clean and fiddle with it. It'll really look great in the living room, right?"

"If you say so. Sometimes they're creepy," Dad says. "So, I guess it will fit."

George laughs. "Knock on wood, we really do sleep fine. Oh, but we did find an old toolbox. I'm sure you can help us figure out what that could be about."

Wanda comes by, a wide tray on her shoulder. "Order up!"

"Divine. Thank you, Wanda," Dad says. The old flirt.

We eat joyfully, the excitement of the future palpable. I smile widely at George between halves of Reuben. He warmly returns it. I'm so grateful for the way he bonds with my dad. It's been nearly a decade we've been together, and they have had such an easy relationship. All we've ever had was each other, Dad and I, so it must have been hard when George entered the picture. Looking at them now though, I feel at ease.

I look over at the booth just across the narrow aisle. It's a family, also eating mostly burgers. I notice the way the dad is laughing with the older kid while the mom wipes the younger one's mouth. I'll give it to George; parenting doesn't look *all* bad. She makes eye contact with me, and I blush, then smile.

She smiles back. She's not much older than me, probably my mom's age when she died.

Wanda appears, shaking me out of my momentary sadness. "How is everything?"

Dad wipes a bit of mayonnaise from his chin with his napkin. "Excellent," he grins.

"When you're ready," Wanda says, depositing our check at the edge of the table. "Pay at the front. And be back soon, hmm?"

"Absolutely," George answers.

In a while, we finish up, and Dad picks up the bill. Squinting, he holds it away from himself. "I'll take this one," he says.

"No, Dad, let this be our treat for all your help today," I try, but he's already taking his wallet out of his jacket.

"I can still treat my girl. I'm not on social security yet," he jokes.

At the counter waiting to pay, I notice Charlie is one of the men on the stools. As I look his way down the length of the counter, he looks up, feeling my eyes on him. He makes eye contact with me, and I smile at him. I swear I see a flush on his bushy cheeks. He picks up his coffee mug and takes a sip, holding it close to his face. I can't tell if he's returning the smile or not.

"Do you know him?" Dad asks, looking Charlie's way. Charlie seems to notice, shifting uncomfortably in his chair, putting his mug down, then picking it up again.

"Not per se, but small town means I've seen him a few times. He seems lonely," I add in a lower voice.

"Don't worry about him. Every town has a few like that," Dad replies shortly.

It's my turn to blush now, hoping Charlie couldn't hear him from his place several stools down. I look at George. He gives me a sympathetic smile and rubs my back. Then he does something I don't expect. He looks over at Charlie, who is watching us out of the corner of his eye. He gives a small wave. And to my amazement, Charlie returns it. With a smile.

Dad pays, and we thank him; I look back at Charlie as George holds the door for me, wishing I'd had the courage to go over and say hello.

BACK AT HOME, we hang our coats. "I know it's dark, but let's bring up those boxes at least, start looking through the doll's things."

"I think Clara will understand if we wait until the morning, Ken," George says, stretching. It's not even eight, but we're all tired.

"I thought it could be fun to go through those boxes tonight." Then I remind him, "You didn't let me look through anything yet."

He rolls his eyes, only half-mockingly. "Okay. Let's do it," he says and goes to the living room, taking his gloves. Dad and I do the same, just in case. I might have pissed off some spiders today.

Opening the basement door, I realize we left the lights on. "Shoot, we have to be careful with that," I say to George.

"I turned them off," he replies. "I swear I did."

"I don't remember," Dad says, "but ghosts who turn lights *on* are new to me."

I shrug and go down first to get a box. As I get to the bottom, I see a rush of movement to the right of the stairs, back by the dollhouse. I shiver, standing in place, unable to look away from the spot where I saw the movement.

"Clara?" I whisper. No answer, no breeze. I feel goosebumps rise on my flesh.

George is there behind me. "What are you looking at?"

I roll my shoulders. "I thought I saw something."

As I say it, I see another movement shuffle by the dollhouse. Right by where I was pushed.

Dad is holding the top box. "Let's go kids, what are we –" He stops, seeing it. "Rats, right?" His voice quavers.

I take out my cell phone slowly, pointing it to the spot and then turning on the flashlight. A shimmer floats past, a reflection on glass; or one of those flitters I saw passing before?

"Clara?" I try again. No answer. I step forward, not feeling afraid, only feeling uncertain. I inhale slowly in measured frustration as I realize: when I burned the sage, I didn't clear the basement's energy. "Who's there?" I ask, hesitant to receive an answer.

Air lifts the curtains of the dollhouse, like someone rushing behind it. Not caring what Dad thinks, I try again. "Would you like the dollhouse upstairs?" No answer, no draft of wind comes in reply. But the dollhouse shifts forward, creaking. As it settles, it's moved nearly an inch forward like it was pushed from behind. I turn and look at Dad and George. Dad is gaping at the house, not noticing me looking at him. George meets my eye. I go to the house, slowly, peeking behind it.

The shelf behind the house starts to move, rocking backward and forward. A box starts to fall. As we stare, it slows, suspended at the edge of the shelf. We wait. It doesn't resume. I lift a hand to the box, sliding it back on the shelf. I hear Dad and George exhale behind me, and realize I'd been holding my breath too.

"We're bringing it upstairs today," I say, getting a grip underneath one side. George comes to me, and we lift it.

Dad, shaking his head, moves some of the boxes on the steps aside, and takes the steps two at a time ahead of us.

CHAPTER SIXTEEN

W ith the dollhouse upstairs, I see now that it's smaller than it seemed in the low basement. Now we can see it was painted green with a roof of beautiful German-style eaves. The individual shingles seem to be attached by hand and are varnished in dark brown. The rooms inside have wallpaper, similar to that of our own house, with varied colors and textures. The attic is one wide flat room, three rooms on the upper level, and a large living room, dining area, and kitchen on the bottom floor.

Looking at the empty rooms feels like a strange sort of omniscience – this house, too, was empty and unlived-in just a week ago. I'm impressed that the dollhouse is in such great condition. There's no sun damage and no bubbling of the wallpaper. Sitting down in front of it, I gingerly run a few fingers over the wallpaper in a few rooms. It wasn't wallpaper. It was hand painted directly onto the dollhouse walls.

I hold my breath as I peer around the miniature rooms, taking in the moldings around the doors, at the middle of the living room. A small, empty fireplace is on the left wall of the living room, the limit of the house. I look around the side, and the chimney goes up through the roof. Gently angling the house, I see the gash I put there and wince.

"I'm so sorry, Clara," I murmur to myself, if not to her. I breathe in and feel for her with my intuition, my third eye. I don't have any sense of her right now, but by now, I know she's a great hider.

"It's a shame, but I can fix it," Dad says. He's standing behind me, a cup of tea in his hand. "I'm glad you guys had some chamomile. I love a cup in the evenings."

"I know, Dad." I smile, rising. "Me too."

"I thought as much." He jerks his head toward the coffee table where a steaming mug is sitting on a coaster. George is seated at the couch with his laptop, editing photos I imagine. I join him, Dad following and sitting in the chair to our right.

"This room feels fuller with the dollhouse here, right?" I smile. "Maybe we should bring up a table from downstairs for it to sit on. I'm sure there's one there." Suddenly I feel Clara. I look and see a glimmer to my right by the house. I didn't unpack any dolls yet. Maybe she's looking for them.

"We'll move quicker tomorrow. We're nearly halfway, and once we get everything sorted, I'll video chat my parents," George says. "I texted them that we'll be calling tomorrow, instead."

"It'll be nice to talk to Isaiah and Margaret," Dad says. "Are they doing well?"

George closes his laptop. "They are doing well, enjoying retirement. Mom found a Southern Baptist church last year not too far from their home. She's dragging Dad along," he chuckles. "You can share your news with them and get some tips on the easy life," he grins.

"I'll bet. I hope they're keeping warm up there," Dad replies, taking another sip of tea.

"We'll have to ask them in the morning," I say, feeling antsy to get back to the dollhouse. I sip my tea quickly, glancing over at the house. I see Clara sparkling there, and still looking, I swear a second presence is dancing beside her. I watch as the two glimmers intertwine, floating into the rooms of the house.

"Kendra?" Dad says. I snap to, jostling my tea and then gripping it tighter, both hands in my sleeves. "I was asking if you found anything at the banks around here."

I shake my head. "Not yet. Truth be told," I take another sip, "I'm enjoying the break to work on the house and write. I have written a lot," I finish my tea in a long draught. "In fact, I should be writing right now, but there are more important things to do," I smile at him, and he smiles back. "I've missed you Dad," I say.

I remember spending the whole week of Christmas there last year. I feel like it hurt him that we went to Alicia's this year, but we hadn't seen her in a while either. Buying this house feels like a shift into a new phase. A phase for family. I lean toward Dad before continuing. "We're going to do better, now. It's time to settle down and make a life in one place instead of feeling like we're in survival mode in the city."

"I concur, doctor," George butts in. "This house means it's time to accept middle age," he leans forward, a hand on his back.

Dad laughs. "You kids enjoy your twenties. You'll know middle age when it hits you, don't you worry. Until then, be young and have fun." He finishes his tea, putting the mug on the coffee table.

I get up, taking our mugs to the kitchen. As I pass the doll-house, I hear a drifting giggle from the ground. I turn and look at Dad and George: they don't seem to have heard it.

There's no sound nor activity in the kitchen, but as I turn to leave, I look to where the cleaning supplies are beneath the kitchen sink. The dollhouse probably hasn't been cleaned for a hundred years or so. I grab the white vinegar – I won't be using anything harsher – and a rag for a light dusting. On the way back, I use my foot to push the two boxes of dolls and furniture from the top of the basement stairs to the side of the dollhouse.

"Are you doing that tonight, Ken?" George asks. I hear sleep in his voice.

"What did Dad just say? Enjoy our youth," I put down the cleaning products and turn the house, lifting it slightly to avoid scratching the floor.

"Playing with dolls is regressing a bit," Dad jokes, but his voice sounds hard, like gravel. "Don't scuff the floor. We'll bring up a table tomorrow."

I pause, hearing double for a second, and turn to him. "Say that again, Dad?"

"Don't scuff-"

"No, about the dolls."

"It's regressing a bit," he smiles, and his voice sounds like his own again. "I'm just joking, Bug."

I hesitate and return his smile weakly. "Oh, ok. I thought you said something else."

I know I heard it though. His voice was different. Deep. Menacing. And so did Clara; the sparkles – both of them – are gone. A gruff, menacing male voice had scolded me for playing dolls. I try to shake off the cold chill rising up my neck as I look around for a source, but there's nothing. All traces of Clara are gone.

Taking the dry cloth, I hesitate in front of the house. "George, do you have any canned air?"

"Of course." He gets up and heads to the stairs. "In my office," he adds, ruffling my hair on his way past. Then he turns to Dad, "Mr. Hill, I'll show you the guest room and shower if you want to get cleaned up or settle in. It's nearly ten."

"I'm not so old that ten is bedtime," Dad replies as he follows him to the stairs. "But a shower sounds nice."

"There are extra toothbrushes and everything in the guest bathroom cupboard!" I call after them. "And move the litter boxes to my Craft room!" I get a secret thrill calling it that openly, a fun double entendre only for me. Dad doesn't know I'm a witch, and I think I need to keep it that way.

It's then that I realize the cats haven't been downstairs at all today. "George!" I shout. He doesn't answer. When he comes back down, I'll remind him to check for them. Their food is still up there, so I'm sure they're sleeping in the bedrooms somewhere.

In the quiet, I face the dollhouse to begin cleaning. I lightly dampen the cloth and begin wiping the edges of the rooms. A dark brown comes away on the cloth, and I check the varnish. It's intact: only the dust is coming away. I may have been right on the mark in saying it's been in storage for a hundred years. The Harrs must have moved it when they redid the basement. Why would they keep all of that down there after a renovation?

As I move on to the floors of the house, glitter flickers at the corner of my eye. "Clara, what do you think?" The giggle comes in answer, echoing and low. I smile, turning my head to face her. I jerk back involuntarily. A girl is sitting there. Her golden hair frizzy with the activity of a long day, her bangs needing cut, hanging over her eyes.

"Sorry, Clara. You scared me." I stare.

She's so real. I'll never get used to this. Her dress is white, pinned up to her neck, a short ruffle on either side of the buttons, bordering a ridged pleat that ends in an elegant u-shape at the bottom of the row of buttons. Her legs are tucked under her long skirt, her hands loosely folded on top of her lap.

"Clara," she says, pointing to herself. Then she points at me.

"Kendra," I answer, pointing at myself. "George," I say, pointing behind me, not taking my eyes off of her, afraid she'll disappear. "He's the younger one in glasses. Darker skin, curly, dark hair."

She nods and then cocks her head like she has another question. "My dad, the old man," I try. She smiles again, softly, not showing any teeth. I realize she's not as opaque as I thought, but translucent, like a hologram.

"We're all happy to have you here," I say.

I hear steps behind me and look over my shoulder, expecting George or my Dad, but the person darts away, hiding behind the wall. A dark head of hair peeks around the corner.

"Is that your dad?" I nod my head back towards the wall, not turning my head.

Clara shakes her head but doesn't say anything.

"Your mom?" I try again.

"Found it!" George's voice, calling from upstairs, jars me. I shut my eyes in a wince, jumping a bit in my seat. Clara's gone.

I look at where she had been and slowly lift my hand, drifting into the space where she had been seconds before. I feel a slight chill. I withdraw my hand quickly and smile sheepishly at the space.

"Sorry," I whisper. And then louder, to George: "Thank you, honey!" I'll tell him about this in bed tonight. "Is Dad settling in?"

"Yep, he's in the shower. I hope it's all in working order. And I'm glad I saw the decaying mouse before he did," he says with a shiver.

I pale. I forgot to tell him. I'm glad the cats didn't get it first. Speaking of which, "Did you see the cats up there?"

"Shadow was sleeping on the guest bed. I think your dad

will enjoy her company tonight," he chuckles. "Sherry was in your altar room when I moved the litter boxes in."

I sigh with relief. "Don't call it that," I whisper. "Not around Dad."

George narrows his eyes at me. "Do you think he'd care?"

I shrug. "I'm not ready to find out." I stand up from in front of the dollhouse and change the subject. "I notice the cats aren't coming downstairs anymore."

"I'm not sure why, but I wouldn't worry about it. They're cats, they're lazy, and their food is up there," George lists, logical as ever.

"Good points," I say, too tired to say more. "I want to open this box and go through everything, but I feel we need to clean this first. Especially if Dad wants to fix it."

"I'll start on the outside of the house. I'll go to town on these windows and little eaves." He holds the can of air to his eye like a scope.

"I'll be right back. I'm going to try to find a duster," I reply. I watch as George settles in to clean the wall at the front of the dollhouse. No sign of Clara or whoever that other person was.

I walk to the kitchen slowly, looking around the corner by the door where I had seen the dark head appear. No sign, no glimmering trace of anyone or anything.

I flip the light, checking under the table. I hesitate, then open the cabinet under the sink, slowly, just in case. I sigh, and using my phone flashlight, peer around for a duster. I can't remember if we brought one but I'm trusting we did. Sure enough, there's a box of duster heads in the right-hand corner. No handle, but this will do. I close the cabinet and stand, catching my own reflection in the window above the kitchen sink.

A few paces behind me stands a girl – a woman.

Dark hair frames her face, only her eyes clear in the reflection. I don't know if she sees that I can see her. Resisting the urge to turn around, I focus on the reflection. I blink, and in that split second, she seems to be closer.

I blink again. She's standing right behind me, staring down the back of my head.

I whirl around, unthinking, heart racing. She's gone.

CHAPTER SEVENTEEN

I 'm laughing with someone. The ceiling is low, but sitting here on the floor, the room feels less cramped. There are no windows, and a small bed fits just between the two walls at the back. I look over at it, perfectly made, and smile. I turn and see Clara, her cheeks rosy, her mouth in a lippy grin. She has her doll in her hand, and she reaches into her apron pocket and retrieves a second one.

It's dark in here. I can't see much except that this doll has dark hair and an apron on, like me. I smile back, and she offers it to me again. "It's you, silly," she says. I blush and take it from her, holding the doll's delicate body in my hand. She stands to go, but I take her hand. "Stay," I say, blushing. She blushes back.

I WAKE up thinking about the dolls. Was that Clara's mom? It certainly felt motherly, with the apron and everything. George and I did well with the dollhouse last night, but I left the dolls in the box. They'll need to be dusted as well, but I hope they'll be in good condition.

After washing up, George and I open our door. Dad's is open too, and the guest bath is unoccupied. Coming downstairs, I see Dad in the kitchen brewing coffee and frying eggs.

"Good morning, sleepyheads! Another sign of aging is waking up early." He flips a pair of eggs in the pan, "But you learn to make the most of that."

I go over to him, giving him a kiss on the cheek and reaching into the cabinet to his right for mugs and plates. "Thank you for breakfast, Dad. This looks delicious," I smile.

"It'll be okay, at best – you kids don't have any bacon," he jibes good-naturedly.

"I'm glad we had eggs. We haven't done any real meal prepping yet," George explains, getting the milk out of the fridge and pulling the sugar jar in from the corner of the counter.

I start making my cup alongside George, filling in Dad about our cleaning the dollhouse last night. "I'm even dreaming of dolls now," I say with a chuckle. "Speaking of dreaming, how did you sleep last night?"

"Well. Quite well." Dad nods, bringing the pan to the table and laying eggs on each plate. "You're right. It's a comfortable house at night."

"Ready for more excavation?" George asks, sitting with his cup of coffee and pulling his plate of eggs to him.

I bring forks to the table and sit down at the end by the fridge. "I am. I hope we find a good table for the dollhouse and maybe some nice side tables and a chair for the guest room and my Craft room."

"I'm sure we will. We've got a ways to go. Are Isaiah and Margaret free to chat later?" Dad asks.

George nods between mouthfuls. "They're as excited as Kendra to know what's down there. I'm surprised they're not visiting, but the recent snow has made a mess of the roads up there."

After breakfast, we suit up with gloves and head back to the basement. Passing the dollhouse to grab the gloves, I notice the dollhouse accessories are scattered on the floor. I shake my head. Clara must have been playing last night.

Back in the basement, I'm starting to get used to the feeling of its low ceilings and dim light. We jump to organizing much quicker, with a purpose. The grime of the window cleared, the southern wall of the basement is brighter. We can see that the wall is made of cinder blocks, the grout still a dusty cream color.

From the corner of the southern wall, we find two matching side tables with fine craftsmanship, according to Dad; a wide, flat table, not far from where we found the dollhouse, that will be perfect for it to rest on; and several small tables and book-shelves. I mark all but the side tables and the wide table with red sticky notes.

Under the stairs is a collection of boxes. "This will take a while," George sighs. We start with the top, pulling each one out and placing them in a circle around us. I open the first.

"Blankets," I shudder. "I'm not looking through this." I imagine rats or snakes and nudge the box a bit with my foot. Nothing comes out, but I don't feel much comfort.

"We'll take it up and shake it out onto the yard," Dad suggests. A pragmatic man.

George opens the next. "Dishes," he says excitedly. "These could be worth something if they're a full set." He moves to the next box before Dad can. "More dishes, a tea set or large pitcher, it looks like." He glances between the boxes. "The same pattern too, a big yellow flower."

I step over to him, looking at the dishes to confirm my suspicion. Yes. Gardenias.

Dad opens his box and finds something only he would be

excited about: old lightbulbs and mechanical doodads. Wires, plugs, springs. "I wonder if any of this stuff could work," he ponders, running a gloved hand under his chin before catching himself. He shakes out his hand and rubs his chin on the shoulder of his shirt sleeve. "I'll fuss around with this while you play dolls tonight, Bug," he grins at me.

The stairs now clear, I step over to investigate. Shining the flashlight – George won't come down here without it – I see that the stairs are as solid as they feel when you walk down on them. "Dad, is this normal? To make such good stairs in a basement?"

He shrugs. "They must've been thorough folks," he says. "I've seen it done and would've done it myself in any house of mine that has a basement. You don't want the stairs breaking on you." He comes over to me under the stairs and inspects them for himself. "These are new," he determines. "Well, newer than the home. I'd say '70s or early '80s."

"The Harrs redid the basement in '72 after the flood," I tell him.

"Ah, yes, well this basement's appearance makes some sense now. The cinder blocks, the cement floor, it's all very modern. Secure. Great work, great work indeed. You could easily finish this space and use it as a billiards room or whatever recreation your generation enjoys," he muses.

Interrupting his reverie, I pick up a box of the gardenia-printed china. I'm not going near those blankets even if they're lighter. "Let's move these upstairs, get a glass of water, and we'll continue," I propose.

George nods, picking up the other box of porcelain, and Dad takes his doohickies and the blankets in one go. "Don't hurt your back. I can grab that," George tries, but Dad is already passing him, stepping onto the stairs.

"I got this, it's – not – heavy," he says, straining his voice in a joking way.

Back upstairs, I open the box of china in the kitchen. It's beautiful. Yellow gardenias on striking green leaves against an elegant, simple white background. The plates are rimmed in gold. I lift them out, taking the stack of large plates and placing them on the table. There's a newspaper separating them, and I balk at the date. 1891. Ads for furniture, rentals, and gardening tips are still visible on the yellowed page. I gingerly remove it, knowing it could crumble easily, and place it aside the plates. Underneath are smaller plates of the same design, a set of six. In the corner of the box are gardenia teacups, which I take out first, one at a time. Removing the stack of plates, I find saucers. A complete set. I stack them all together and place them next to the sink, then return to the living room to retrieve the next box. There's balled-up newspaper in the bottom of the box, sadly unreadable. I try to unfurl it, and it pieces away in my hands.

The next box yields three more pieces of newspaper, the classified ads – a dressmaker took out a half page, showing off the latest design. I'll flatten this under a mattress and try to frame it for the front hall. I place it delicately on top of the other preserved newspapers and remove the pitcher, tea kettle, milk, and sugar dishes from the box. There are also six small bowls, and I marvel at the serving sizes people must have been accustomed to. Mentally, I compare that to a plate at Bitting's today and laugh a bit internally.

Dad and George come in to get some water, after fooling around with the mechanical bits I imagine. "Anything good in there, Dad?" I ask, waving a hand at the dish set.

He whistles a descending tune, impressed. "Well, that is something," he says.

George sighs. "Let me guess, we're keeping them."

I nod enthusiastically. "Gardenias are the lifeblood of this house. It would be wrong to get rid of them." As I say it, I feel a presence at my right side near the kitchen sink. I don't turn to look, but I feel a sense of approval.

"These are great finds," Dad says, picking up the newspaper printed with the dressmaker's ad.

I go over to him, worrying my fingers at the newspaper in his hands. "Hold them at the edges gently! I'm going to press them and have them framed for the entryway," I say.

"Good idea. Your mother would've done the same," he adds, smiling. I smile back, a shared smile of loss, both of us feeling warmed by remembrance.

Back in the basement, we realize we've made more progress today than we thought. "We'll call my parents soon. They'll be begging for those dishes, for sure," George says, and I shoot him a look that says I'm not compromising. "But I'm sure some of this furniture is more valuable than it looks, too," he says, meeting my eyes with an accepting nod and a smile.

The far wall to the north of the house is all that's left to be uncovered. We find four big bookshelves, two on their sides against the wall. We mark them all with red sticky notes; as sad as I am, we have no room for them, and the shelves in the study are more than sufficient. There are two more boxes filled with more blankets or tarps of some kind. And a bench for the piano. I lift the piano seat and nearly drop it – there's a drop lid. I open it and find sheet music, weathered but still readable. John Philip Sousa – very patriotic. If Dad wasn't here, I'd ask Clara, but I don't want to freak him out. Leaving the music where we found it, I go over to the piano. Someone's opened the lid. "Did you guys do this?" I ask.

"What?" they ask in a chorus.

"Open the piano?" I ask again as they come over with a box in each hand. They both shake their heads no, Dad looking at me and then to George. George sighs. I shrug my shoulders. Maybe Clara wanted to play it one last time.

Following them up the stairs, they place the last of the boxes with the rest. "While we're gloved, let's see what we're dealing with." I open the first box and find, unsurprisingly, a gardenia-printed tablecloth. And underneath, spiderless, snake-less, and without rats, a set of six dinner napkins, once white, and embroidered with gardenias. "Wow," I intone under my breath.

"Wow is right," George says. He has opened the other box we'd just brought up, and the blankets inside turned out to be lovely, handmade quilts. Two, queen-sized. Both featuring gardenias. "It's a bit of an obsession, no?"

I laugh. "I think it's charming," and then I add, "the Victorians had a whole language of flowers, you know. But even then, gardenias weren't common, not that I know of. They must have commissioned all of these things or made them them-selves," I point to the quilts and the napkins. "I wonder why they were down there."

"Why wouldn't they have taken them when they moved? Or if they died, why didn't their kids? And in a hundred years, the Harrs redoing the basement and everything, no one used them, but no one sold them? That's unsettling to me," George says, sliding the boxes to the wall distractedly. It's not like him to be uneasy, but he's right.

"I'm not sure. Maybe my notes can give us some clues about the 1889 flood and any connection here, but the Harrs, moving it all back into the basement?" I pace in frustration. "I don't understand it."

Dad flops onto the couch. "Well, all I know is, I'm glad we didn't see any ghosts down there today." He laces his fingers over his stomach and leans his head back, closing his eyes.

"Are you okay, Dad?" I ask.

He cocks an eye toward me. "Hmm? Oh, yeah, just tired. What d'you say to lunch before calling the Levys for an appraisal?"

It's then I realize my stomach is grumbling. "I say that's a great idea, Dad."

George nods. "How about that pizza we never ordered?"

After about ten minutes of Googling and checking every food delivery app, we realize that, for all of our research before moving here, we forgot to check for pizza. "The nearest place is a fifteen-minute drive," George says, "but I'm up for it."

"I'll go too. Keep you company," Dad says, rising from the couch with a grunt.

"I'll stay here with the ghosts," I grin.

They leave with an order of two pizzas – one cheese, one pepperoni – having been decided. Remembering Dad's suggestion from earlier, I take the boxes of quilts and blankets out to the yard, dumping the contents on the grass. Breaking down the boxes, I take them over to recycling bins at the end of the driveway. Remembering the cats, I rush back in, closing the door. I go upstairs to find them both, making sure neither ran while I left the door open. I exhale in relief. Shadow is in the guest room, and Sherry is kicking sand in the litter box – hopefully *only* in the litter box.

Going back downstairs, I quiet my steps and slow my pace at the landing. Peering around the corner to the living room, I peek at the dollhouse. No activity. I go over to it, passing the two boxes of glassware which I had forgotten – my next task – and see a doll resting against one of the beautifully-painted walls in the dollhouse living room. I know the boys didn't put that there, and I know I didn't. "Here, Clara, I'll help you," I say, smiling to myself. I sit in front of the dollhouse, and pull a box towards me, beginning to take out each doll and piece of furniture for the house. The fair-haired girl must be Clara.

There's also a dark-haired woman with an apron on and two male dolls. They are wrapped in butcher paper, stained with age. I'm a bit disappointed. I want more newspapers. Almost in answer to my silent wish, at the bottom of the box, the front headline of *The Newport Ledger* stares back at me, dated 1891:

BODIES RISE IN THE JUNIATA: NEWPORT LOCAL FOUND

CHAPTER EIGHTEEN

I shiver, remembering the tranquility of the riverside. I can't imagine the horror of the people who found bodies washing up. Taking the paper out of the box, I re-read the headline and see that the article was published in June 1891: two years after the flood. The decay, the *smell*... I pull my hands into my sleeves and try to shake the image from my mind. I remember from my research that it took years for bodies to be recovered, and some never were. I do my best to decipher the tiny, fading print of the article, though it is illegible in some places from age and wear.

NEWPORT, PENNS. – The bodies of what appear to be two children and four men have been found in and on the banks of the JUNIATA RIVER in NEWPORT, PENNS. since March of this year, following rainstorms that caused flooding and rising water levels in the Juniata River. It is estimated that hundreds more could be found, as the count of those missing after The Great Flood of '89 is still in the hundreds. In the past two years, bodies from the towns surrounding Lake Conemaugh have been accounted for hundreds of miles away, crossing state borders in the sweep of the flood. The deadliest flood in history continues to claim victims. Families' prayers are answered grimly, as answers to questions of various missing persons' whereabouts are made clear through recent discoveries. Amongst the bodies to be identified is a local of Newport, Mr. Jasper Baker, son of Dr. and Mrs. John Baker. He is to be interred in the Newport East Cemetery forthwith.

I PUT the paper down and rush to my bag. I know I've read that name before. I find my notebook and flip through the pages, seeing notes on death tolls, property damages, towns affected, and question marks next to "Front Street" and "Bitting's", but those don't seem relevant now.

Standing in the foyer, I scour my pages again, realizing that for all my scribbles, there's little of import now – my notes are scattered between those useful for ghost hunting and those just curious questions of the local history. I scan for the name Baker, but nothing.

Then I remember. Lynn's papers. The builders of the home.

John Baker. Was this Jasper *our* John Baker's son?

Was this paper saved on purpose? The dolls were nestled together with their dollhouse rugs and butcher paper, so why was this one here?

I hurry to the next boxes filled with glassware and empty the box quickly, unwrapping the oil lamps, decorative dishes, and other Victoriana tchotchkes, checking each wrapping for newsprint. Only butcher paper, stained but blank. The next box yields the same. In desperation, I go to the box of blankets. I pause, then go over to the coffee table and retrieve my gloves first and grab my car keys. Picking up the box, I head outside, closing the front door behind me this time.

It's starting toward sunset, the sky deepening, colors spreading through the clouds. Fortunately, the grass is dry, though there's a smell of snow in the air which I find soothing. I look up across the street at the single streetlight, not yet on. Looking at the sky, I take a deep breath in, then flip the box, emptying it in one fat heap onto the dead grass below.

It's sheets. Faded yellow or maybe even ivory. I use a gloved hand to shake it out, bracing myself for spiders or worse. Sure enough, some dead bug falls out, landing in the grass beside me. I step back onto the walkway and shiver, not from the cold.

I gingerly pluck the other corner from the ground and assess the sheet. It's yellowed in a pattern against the folds it's held for a hundred years. It looks to be an extra tarp from the furniture downstairs. The next item is the same, showing the same yellowing and, blessedly, fewer dead insects.

The third was once red and is heavy like a curtain. I shake it out, spreading it on the railing of the front porch behind me to see the length: nearly nine feet. It has a subtle damask pattern, and with proper cleaning, it could be usable or sellable. The fourth is the same as the third: a second curtain panel, perhaps. I can't find a seam, but I don't want to pull or prod them too much. I kind of hope they're curtains: they seem made for our living room's elegant, tall windows. I set aside three final cloth items – more blankets – before giving the box one last good shake. This box has no papers at all. I sink down beside the blankets, defeated.

I start to stack the blankets back into the box when I stop. The last three cloths I remove from the box surprise me. They're small blankets, hand-knit from rough wool. Baby blankets, perhaps. I open them each and find a finely embroidered AB.

I stand there, looking at one of the baby blankets in my hand, trying to feel its energy, asking it to tell me something.

I feel eyes on me.

The sun is starting to recede behind the houses up Fickes Lane, and I turn toward the still-dark streetlight. Someone is under the light. He's watching me and seems to know he's hidden by the dark as he doesn't flinch or back away at my glance. I continue to look, not sure what else to do.

Then the street light flickers on.

It's Charlie.

Charlie, from Bitting's that day we decided to buy the house. Charlie, crying in his car at the grocery store. Charlie, blushing at the counter of Bitting's just last night. I'm tired of the mystery, and it's awkward not knowing each other in such a small town.

I smile at the figure under the lamplight. At first, Charlie doesn't move. He's at least 100 feet away, and the harshness of the streetlight washes out his features – I can't tell what he's thinking or feeling. I push it a bit further and wave my hand at him to come over.

To my great surprise, he does.

As he approaches, I realize I don't know what to say.

"Hi, I'm Kendra Hill," I start. I extend my hand, and without meeting my eyes, he shakes my hand.

"Charlie," he replies. He swallows audibly.

"Nice to meet you. I feel like we keep running into each other," I say and then hastily add, "at Bitting's. That's twice now I've seen you there with my husband. When I'm there with my husband, I mean, we see you there, too," I laugh nervously.

Charlie thrusts his hands into the pockets of leather jacket, his eyes hidden under his baseball hat. "Did you find all that in the basement?" He nudges a foot toward the blanket box.

"Yeah, how'd you know?" I ask before I realize how snappy that sounds. "It's a small town, I guess," I add quickly.

"Mom and Dad made sure to keep everything down there after the flood," he said. "I grew up here." He nods toward the house, still not looking at me.

I stop, feeling my heartbeat in my ears. "Charlie Harr?" I ask in disbelief.

Charlie nods. "The flood of '72 meant we shacked up in a motel for nigh on six weeks while the whole basement was redone. Mom and Dad used to use the attic for storage, so luckily, nothing was damaged. But when the renovation was done, they put everything in the basement. Got new furniture, put even more of the old stuff down there too over the years. We used nearly everything here and there for parties and such." He pauses in reverie, looking up at the dark windows. "But we tried to keep all the original things the house came with. It was my grandma's promise to Mrs. Baker when they bought it. Nothing leaves the house, and nobody gets hurt." I expect him to laugh, but he doesn't. He clears his throat. "Keeping their things safe is the safe thing to do," he adds, still not looking at me. I feel the urgency in his voice. It's not a threat, but a warning.

I swallow, then sheepishly try to smile. "Charlie, can I ask you something?"

He doesn't say anything, but he lowers his head slightly.

I swallow again, my mouth dry as I think how to word this. "I, well George and I," I begin, and then cut to the chase. "Have you ever seen or heard any ghosts here?"

Charlie looks up, his eyes peering out from under his hat, keeping his hands in his pockets as he brings his shoulders up to his ears. "Yes," he says, strongly, clearly.

"Clara?" I ask.

He meets my eyes for the first time.

"Yes," he says with shocked conviction. "Yes," his voice wavers a little, and I don't know why, but I hear sadness in his voice.

A car is coming down the road, and I know without looking that it is George and Dad. Time slows, and in the few seconds it takes before Charlie hears the car, I feel like I'm trying to befriend a stray cat, fearful that he will dart away, and I'll never see him again. "Charlie, if you want to come inside, if you want to talk to Clara, or if there's any advice you'd give us, we want to respect this house. We love this house. And Clara."

Charlie's expression is unreadable as he lowers his eyes again. He takes a step back, ducking his head so that his eyes once again recede beneath his ball cap. "Thanks, Kendra," he says. He starts to shuffle off, and I hear him say something more, but only catch one word, "... care."

CHAPTER NINETEEN

Over our feast of surprisingly good pizza, I tell Dad and George about Charlie. "Can you believe that's him? He lived here! I bet it kills him. He couldn't buy his own childhood house after it was so suddenly back on the market. I wonder where he lives. I wonder –"

"Ken," George cuts me off. "I hope you didn't badger Charlie with all that. I agree. He should feel comfortable coming here, and I especially agree that he could help us."

"I'd prefer if he came by while I'm here," Dad asserts. "I'm not too keen on the fact that you talked to him alone, Ladybug."

"He's harmless, Dad, just a sad, lonely guy. I wasn't scared. If anything, I was afraid I'd scare him away."

Dad shuffles in his chair and grabs another piece of pizza, looking thoughtful.

While George does the dishes, Dad and I look through some of the glass things from the basement. "I'll dot some of these around the house," I say, holding up an oil lamp to the light. It has a porcelain base with a delicate floral pattern, small yellow flowers along a dark green vine. Something feels very right about leaning into the house's own wants like I'm honoring a request.

George comes in, wiping his hands on his jeans. "I left the gardenia dish set as it is. We'll tackle that in the morning if that's okay," he says. He picks up a wide dish with a bubbled glass pattern around it. "If these are crystal, not glass, they're worth a good bit," he remarks. "I'll ask Mom how to identify it. Are we ready to call them?" he asks.

Dad and I exchange looks and nod. George unlocks his phone, and I hear it dialing through.

"Hey, Georgie!" the Levys say in unison, trying to share the frame. Their phone is constantly moving and positioned closer than necessary to their faces, so we keep getting a nice close-up shot of Mr. Levy's wrinkling, pink nose and graying mustache. Eventually, they seem to have figured out their positioning, and we're now finally able to see Mrs. Levy as well, who is wearing a classic red lipstick, complementing her dark complexion.

"Hi, Mom! Hey, Dad! Kendra and I are here with Mr. Hill, if you'd like to see some of the wares we found here at the house," George says, holding the phone high to show me and Dad at the couch, the lamps and the glass dishes on the table.

"Absolutely. Kendra, how are you, sugar? And Philip, you are looking dashing!" Mrs. Levy has a way of flattering everyone she talks to as if their blushes give her a renewed vigor. Her face spreads in a grin as she speaks, comforting, and it's as if she were on the couch next to us.

"I'm doing fine, Mrs. Levy!" I call.

"Now, Kendra. We've talked about this. Please call me Mom, if you may," she scolds me.

"I'm doing great, and you are as vivid as ever, Margaret," Dad says. "I hope Isaiah is treating you well," he adds.

"Always, Philip, you know that. We've just been to the car show this morning, and we've been taking it easy this afternoon." Mr. Levy shuffles in his seat on the couch, the phone momentarily staring at the ceiling before refocusing on his nostrils. Video calls with parents never get better.

"What have you got there on the table?" Mrs. Levy asks. "If those are crystal, they're worth a good penny," she says, referring to the bowls and containers.

"I was just saying the same." George picks up a port decanter and holds it to the screen. "How can we tell?" he asks.

"Well, you'll need to do the water-on-the-rim test," Mrs. Levy says matter-of-factly. "Like Ben Franklin's instrument. Wet your finger and sound around the opening. Crystal should have a tone."

George snaps his fingers. "I knew it was something like that! Speaking of, we found some other fun things we will keep. I'll give you the whole tour." He turns the screen so that the back camera is showing the dollhouse. "This is Kendra's new toy. Well, new to her. We think all of this is original to the house."

"We met the son of the late owners," I chime in. "He said that they kept all of these things in storage and left them with the house on purpose. He feels like they belong with the home and with this dollhouse, I'm happy to oblige. We're also keeping some dishes in the kitchen," I add and wave goodbye as George takes them around the house on a tour.

Dad and I sit alone on the couch as George moves upstairs. "How are you feeling? Lots of activity this weekend," I ask.

"Good, good. It's good to move these bones," he grins, leaning back into the couch, lacing his fingers.

"You're staying again tonight, right? George has plenty of clothes you can borrow. Shoot, we can even run out to the department store. It's not too far."

"Thank you. I actually stopped at the supercenter next to

the pizza place. That plaza has everything you need. Even a blasted home improvement warehouse," he adds a bit bitterly.

"I'm so glad you'll be here with us for a bit, Dad." I send a quiet burst of love to George, now in the kitchen, it sounds like. I'm glad he insisted and is being so welcoming to Dad.

"I am happy you'll have me. You know, Bug, I miss you at home. The house is too big for just me." He meets my eyes and smiles.

"I miss you too, Dad. I mean it. Stay a week if you'd like. We both are effectively off work: I'm writing, and George is editing photos, but he doesn't have a shoot for a good while yet."

"I'm happy to stay as long as you'd like," he says in a protective tone.

"You know, I'm not scared here," I say. "It's just Clara as far as I can tell, and I'm not bothered about ghosts. It was her house first." I think about the second person I saw, the dark-haired one by the door. And the gray-eyed man. I brush the thoughts away. "And anyway, Charlie grew up here happily. And I think he'll share more knowledge about the house with me."

"I'm sure we'll run into him at the diner. Although, we should do *some* cooking here," Dad lightly snorts.

"Hey, we're just settling in here! But you're right. Eating in does save money."

Dad looks at the floor. I wait for him to say something, but when he doesn't, I continue. "This house was a great deal, for sure, but we don't have a lot left," I say. "George wants me to keep writing, focus on that, and hopefully, this meeting will be favorable." Dad is very interested in the floorboards. "I'm thinking of looking for other writing opportunities, online tutoring, or content writing for blogs or magazines. George has a well-booked spring and summer. It was his idea."

Finally, Dad speaks, without looking at me. "I know you kids are responsible. It's just weird for me. With retiring, I don't have much to offer beyond my own skills. There's not... well." He clears his throat. "Retirement wasn't what I was hoping for, I guess."

I want to ask more, but watching his cheeks redden, I decide not to pry. My intuition tells me this isn't the time.

George is walking up the stairs now. "Want to come refill the heater? We've got enough wood for another few nights before we'll venture out and find some. The last owners left a good stock."

Dad grunts, putting his hands on either side of himself and rising from the couch. "Let's do it."

The kitchen is tidy, but I wince a bit at the pizza box on the table. I don't want Mrs. Levy thinking I don't feed her son as well as she does. There's a tradition of cooking I'm still learning from her. I'm no master at mac and cheese, and I never think to cook collard greens. But George never asks; he's like that, accommodating to a fault. I take out my phone and add collard greens and a block of cheddar to my grocery list. I've got pasta and milk, so maybe that'll be tomorrow's dinner. I unlock my phone again and add rotisserie chicken to the list. Now that's a fine meal.

Dad is already opening the cabinet, inspecting the heating system and the refill mechanism. "This is truly a wonder," he says. "I hope he shows Isaiah. He'll get a kick out of it."

"It's definitely unique. They said there's only a few homes in the state still running on it," I say. "It's as old as the house but upgraded with this ramp feature. It's the warm wood stove heat without the constant tending."

Dad laughs. "What do you know about tending a wood stove?"

I shrug, a bit stung. He's right, though. "We have yet to try the fireplace upstairs," I remind myself. "I'll be learning soon enough about it all."

I pick up one log at a time from the pile to the right of the stove and place a few in the ramp. "That should do us for tonight." I look around and see a silver glimmer on my right. It's bright, bigger, the size of a fist. And this time, I can make eye contact with it. It's hovering at about elbow-height, unmoving. Waiting for me. "I'll see you upstairs. Go join George on the house tour," I say, not taking my eyes off of the glimmer.

Dad agrees, not noticing, and pats my shoulder on his way out. The fairy dust glints to the gardenia plates. When I hear Dad's feet reach the steps, I approach it slowly. As I do, I turn my head, watching it bounce from varying angles, trying to see if there's any dimension. Sure enough, there's a veil, the glitter shining like points on a vector, a constellation on the outline of someone. The thin light through the kitchen window illuminates her like dust motes. I see long hair, a wisp of a gown behind her. She is assessing the plates. I can't read the translucent pixels of her face, but I feel that she is thinking.

Keeping my eyes focused on her, I face my palms outward, toward her. I breathe deeply, in through my nose, and out through my mouth, softly exhaling, feeling my diaphragm contract. I create a protective shield of energy around me – imagining the ethereal light of the universe washing over my body. It falls gently over my head, covering outstretched arms, extending delicately from my crown to my toes, like a soft satin sheet. As the white light envelops me, I feel protected, balanced. A perceptible warmth radiates from my palms. I direct some of this light to her, sending a warm, loving energy. I feel it reach her, and as it does, she turns to me, slowly. I get the same sensation I felt with Charlie like I'm afraid I'll scare her away. I smile, and she doesn't move. Her gown wisps out behind her, the folds visible in the air. I don't speak first this time. I wait.

"Kendra," she says, hollowly, questioningly. She gestures an open hand to a plate, and as she nears it, the shape of her sharpens. As she touches it, I watch her colors fill in, golden hair, bangs, waves. Her eyes are blue, her skin porcelain. She's older than I thought, around fourteen.

"She loved these," she says, low and sad. She picks up a plate. I watch it in the air, as she turns it and takes it in. "She called me her flower," she says.

I smile again, realizing that my mouth is in a wide O of surprise. I send another warm current of energy to her, hoping to keep her with me longer. "Keep them," she says. "I miss her," she adds, delicately placing the plate on the pile.

I don't know what to ask as I try to process what I'm seeing. She doesn't seem scared anymore. "Could you go to her?" I ask after some time.

Clara shakes her head. "She should be in here." She looks around the kitchen. Her face is so sad, her voice quavering as she looks at my eyes. "I thought she'd be here," she says, looking at the floor. "And her room is gone."

"Clara Baker?" I ask. "Is that your name?"

She nods, slowly, as if unsure. Then she nods sharply, decidedly. "Clara Baker," she draws it out like she's trying on an old dress, pleasantly surprised at how well it fits. "Clara Baker," she says again, and I see the corners of her mouth turn up, smiling.

I smile back, gaining confidence to ask another question. "Did you have a brother? Jasper?"

Her eyes squint at me, remembering. And then they widen in slow, realized horror.

She screams.

She screams and screams: a sound that goes on forever.

CHAPTER TWENTY

For the first time in our new home, I am truly scared.

I close my eyes, slamming my hands over my ears. George and Dad come running in, the phone at George's side but Margaret and Isaiah still connected. I open my eyes and see nothing. The plates are still neatly stacked. Clara is gone.

"What? Kendra, why did you scream?" All of a sudden, George is with me, his phone on the table, his hands on either side of my face, looking into my eyes.

I look from him to my dad to the phone on the table. "I thought I saw a mouse. It was huge!" I say. "It must've come out of the box with the plates, or maybe it was in the wood pile. I was going to get a head start on some of these new dishes." I know my voice is still shaking, but I hope they'll buy the mouse story. George, standing closest to me, has his eyes locked on mine. He isn't buying it. I plead with him silently to drop it for now, my eyes darting between his. He gives an almost imperceptible nod, and I sigh with relief.

I pick up his phone. "So sorry about that. I'm a bit dramatic sometimes!" I hope they can't see me blushing. "How was the tour?"

"Excellent. That attic is a bit creepy though! I hope you don't have any ghosts," Mrs. Levy says and chuckles.

I laugh hollowly. "Old houses have lots of stories," I say, proud I avoided a lie. If they visit, we'll get into it, but this is not the time.

"Well, kids, we'll take a look at that basement another time, unfortunately," Mr. Levy says.

"It was too dark down there to get any good insights," George fills me in. I nod, secretly glad they're hanging up. I need to process what just happened with Clara. "Oh, but one more thing, if you have the time, Mom and Dad," George says and hands the phone off to me.

We head into the living room, Dad and I situating ourselves on the couch next to each other while I hold the Levys. George excuses himself while I ask the Levys what they thought of the house. A few minutes later George returns with the old toolbox.

"We found this upstairs. What do you think it is?" he says, sitting between Dad and me. "It seems locked or maybe just rusted."

"Well, if you ask me, it's a butcher's box." My heart sinks. Mr. Levy continues, "In the 1800s there were dentists who, well, weren't really professionals like we might expect today, but they managed a business of tooth removal, capping, replacements. Gruesome work, but better than nothing." Then he adds, "You should see if you can get a rust-removing agent. Don't just pry it open. The box itself is valuable, and if it has the kit all in one piece, it's a real find."

"Thanks, Dad, we'll see what we can do." George fiddles with it, flaking a bit of rust off.

I bat his hand. "Don't tamper with it until we get what we

need," I say good-naturedly. I'm afraid of what we might find, but I don't want to scare his parents. They worry enough, being a seven-hour drive away.

We say our goodbyes and see-you-soons and hang up.

"Mouse, my ass," George says as soon as the line is dead. My Dad looks at me, too. So much for buying it.

I tell them about what I saw, and what Clara told me. "She's afraid of him, I don't know why. I don't like this butcher's box, and I don't think we should open it."

"I agree with Kendra," Dad says. He only calls me Kendra when he's worried or angry. In this case, I think it's the former. "Your mother would have said the same." He turns to me as if that settles the matter.

"Compromise. What if we open it outside? Or somewhere else, like at an antique shop?" George suggests. "Then we can see what's inside and be rid of it in one go."

Dad and I look at each other and then at George. "Good thinking, kid," Dad says. "Okay, we'll put this on the back burner for a bit. Maybe we can have an antique appraiser come for the furniture too. If they like the box, they could haul away any goods themselves and save our aching backs." He says it like it's a joke, but I know he's hopeful.

I sigh and stand, squeezing out of my corner of the couch. I sit in front of the dollhouse for the third night in a row. I pick up the doll in the second-story bedroom. She's blond, blue-eyed, wearing a light blue dress. Like Clara.

For the first time, I really take a look at the pieces. Dusting them as I pick them up, I start with the people. I think back to my dream: sitting on the floor, holding the dark-haired doll. I must have been playing dolls with Clara somewhere. It was a small room. Maybe the dollhouse was in the attic before – but that room was so square, no eaves or windows.

Smoothing the dolls' hair, I find two dolls that could've

been in the dream. Another girl doll with dark hair and a similar style white dress and a motherly doll with her hair styled in a bun, wearing an apron. And then, from a dollhouse carpet, I unroll a man, with a bushy mustache made of real hair – I don't touch it, for fear it'll fall off; and lastly, another male doll, wearing black suspenders and a white button-down under a gray or once-black coat, twice-buttoned. They're all the same height and seem to be of the same porcelain make. The arms and legs don't move, and they don't stand either.

The furniture is almost more impressive. The dining table has a set of six matching chairs, the legs of which all have ornate curvatures and spirals at the top. I place them in the dining room. The bedrooms have wardrobes, beds with perma-nently-made sheets, and there are several rugs. I lay out the rugs, removing and replacing the dining set on top, and I make up the rooms. I have a suspicion that Clara will set this to her liking this evening. I have a sudden urge to look for her, but I don't want to scare Dad and George.

As I sit at the dollhouse, Sherry comes down the stairs. I feel relieved. "Hi, Sherry girl," I coo, inviting her close. She comes over, rubbing her face on the edge of the dollhouse, sniffing at the dolls. She goes over and settles on the chair across from the coffee table, circling, then lying down.

George gets up and walks over to her, petting her behind her ears, then comes over to me, putting his hand on my shoul-der. "It's a great sign she's down here." He gestures to Sherry behind him. "Are you okay, baby?"

"Yes, I'm fine." I pause, and then add, "I just want to settle into a healthy, normal life here. Clara doesn't bother me, but I think something's bothering her."

Dad slams his hands on his knees. I whirl around, George lifting his hand from my shoulder to do the same. "You kids are ridiculous!" He roars. His temper is rare, typically driven by fear and worry, and I jump in surprise. "This isn't funny. This isn't cute. It's terrifying, and it's ridiculous that you think this can be lived with. I want you to get a professional in here, and that's final!" he slams his fist on his knee again, like a judge with a gavel.

I stand. "Dad, this is our house, and we aren't going to make any decisions until we feel we understand what is going on. Besides, it was hard enough for Lynn to sell it. It's not going to be easy to sell it again. On the market three times in as many years?" I put my hands to my temples.

George is silent, Dad's rage pulsing into the room. I can hear my heartbeat, and George's too. We haven't spoken it out loud before, but we are stuck. This has to work.

"Besides, we love this house, and we aren't scared. We want what's best for everyone in it. You're scaring Sherry." I gesture to the sweet girl on the chair, looking wide-eyed at us, her neck and ears pointed back. As he calms down, and we're quiet for a few seconds, she starts licking herself. George lets out a nervous laugh, which I do my best to echo, calming myself and trying to break the tension. Dad sniffs. "I still think this warrants a professional if getting some of this furniture out here doesn't work. Ghosts are sometimes more attracted to *things* rather than the whole house, right?"

I nod, rising to sit next to him. I put my hand on his, and he takes it. "I'm sorry this is stressful. Any house we can afford in this market should've been a red flag," I laugh mirthlessly. "But I'd rather ghosts than flood damage."

He pats my knee, not brushing my hand off the top of his. "Your mother told me that ghosts are more like energy than people."

He says it like a statement, but as he doesn't continue, I take it as a question. "Something like that. There's different kinds of hauntings. A residual haunting is like us finding a chair that then isn't really there. It's more like energy, just an imprint of what once was. Like when people see ghosts moving through walls – it's an imprint of an action often repeated. Usually, a door was once there." Dad nods as I continue, "The other kind, like poltergeists, or people that haven't moved on, are really people. They think they're still alive or at least don't realize they're dead." Dad looks at me a bit confused as I explain. "They might have died suddenly. Like Clara, she's a young girl. She shouldn't be dead so young. That sometimes leads to people sticking around. You know, the 'unfinished business' types. It's not always about revenge."

I smile, and after a pace, Dad smiles back. He shrugs. "What revenge could a little girl want?"

CHAPTER TWENTY-ONE

My mouth is so sore. I can't stop massaging my jawline, trying to sooth the pain. It's worth it, though, knowing she's safe. The front door slams, startling me. I wince as I bite down involuntarily. I rub my jaw again, and rising from in front of the dollhouse, I back up beside it and feel my back against the wall. He walks into the atrium, and I hold my breath, hoping he won't notice me.

"Hello?" he calls up the stairs. When there's no answer, a slimy grin breaks out on his face. He rounds the corner as if he knew I was there all along. "Looks like it's just you and me."

"Don't you have any patients to attend to? Anyone else to bother?" I slide against the wall until I'm against the window.

"Oh, I didn't know you'd changed your mind about that." He is less than a foot away from me, and I can smell alcohol on his breath. "I wouldn't mind torturing someone else if that's what you prefer."

"No! No." I stand, planting my feet firmly. "Never."

"It's for the good of the family, Clara. I'm a professional, you know."

"A butcher," I murmur.

"What was that?" he sneers in my face. Before I can answer, he slaps me. I fall to the ground and hear feet before I see her.

"No!" I shout, blood gurgling out onto the floor as I try to stand, shaking.

Just before he turns on her, he gives me a grin, eyes full of hate as he pulls up his sleeves. I hear her scream as he grabs her arm, dragging her to the stairs.

THE NEXT DAY is sunny and warm for January, nearing the 50s. I wake with my jaw locked tight. Massaging it, I see a flash of the dollhouse. Someone was screaming. I yawn, thinking, trying to remember. When nothing comes, I join George in getting ready. We decide to take a walk, get out of the house, and show Dad the river.

"Smart that they raised the tracks like this," Dad remarks as we make the somewhat-steep climb to the railroad tracks. "It must have helped in case of future floods."

George pulls one side of his jacket further across his chest. "Why not just zip it?" I say as I pull my hands into my sleeves.

"Why not just wear gloves?" He smirks.

"Touché."

We get to the spot where I found the gardenia, and I walk over to it. "Check this out, Dad. It's a gardenia bush," I say, placing a hand on the spiny limbs.

Dad plods over, taking heavy steps. "This whole area has been leveled," he notes. "It must have been a lovely garden. In the spring, you might find more remnants of the past out here, albeit safer and prettier ones." He's in a light-hearted mood today. The fact that the activity from last night hasn't escalated into nightmares for anyone or problems this morning is an unspoken relief for all of us.

George and Dad move to continue on toward the river. "I'll be right there," I call after them. George waves a hand in acknowledgment.

I kneel in the garden, facing the gardenia. I inspect the ground, running my hands over the dead leaves, scurrying them away, like I'm cleaning a grave. I try to picture it blooming. Was it a practical garden of veggies, beans, or herbs? Somehow I know it was a pleasure garden of various blooms, the gardenias stealing the show.

I place my hands in the dirt at the base of the gardenia, sending love to her roots. I close my eyes and try to feel her still growing in the ground beneath us. I imagine a warm pulse spreading from my heart, down my arms, out my hands, and through the dirt, invigorating the roots.

"I'll see you in a couple of months," I grin, opening my eyes, taking in the browned, brittle limbs of the bush. I take a hair from the back of my head and place it over the bush: a traditional offering to the land spirits. I hope it'll help this gardenia to bloom and encourage the land to help her grow.

I rise, wiping the dust from my knees and the back of my jeans. I pull my hands into my sleeves, then plunge them into my pockets, prepared to turn toward the river. I feel eyes on me, but when I turn around, there's no one there. I wait for a few breaths, but no one appears around me. I turn back to the bush, waving my arms across the air around it, checking for cold spots that could denote ghosts; but it's no colder there than in the rest of the area. I wish I had my pendulum.

I face the bush, focusing on Clara. Then I think of the dark-haired woman. "Clara?" I whisper. When there's no answer, I try again: "Clara's friend?" Nothing. "Mrs. Baker?" I listen and wait. No movement. Shrugging, I head towards the river.

Dad and George are at the riverbank, watching it flow. I watch them for a moment, enjoying these brief intervals when they're spiritually grounded. They wouldn't call it that, but taking in the peace of nature is the highest experience of spirituality. Dad looks calm but thoughtful, and George's face is blank.

"What're you thinking about?" I ask, approaching George.

He shrugs. "Just the house, and what we'll do if we remove all that furniture."

"Tiki room," I say with mock decisiveness.

Dad laughs. "You're kidding, but an indoor hot tub isn't a bad idea. Though, I still vote pool table."

Heading back to the house, we don't speak, just enjoy the company of each other and the atmosphere. It feels good to breathe out of doors.

"It's Monday," I say, "and there's an antique store in Millerstown, not even ten minutes from here. We can head over there with the crystalware and the butcher's box–" I shiver a bit, rephrasing, "this dentist's kit, and see what they say about coming out to look at the furniture."

Dad nods. "I do love me some antiques," he says.

"I'll sit this one out if you guys don't mind," George says. "I've got some editing I'd like to finish for my client from a few weeks ago."

I smile at Dad, knowing he's excited for a day to ourselves. "We'll find a nice restaurant for lunch," he grins back.

A Stitch in Time Antique Mall is massive. A 'mall' is the right term for it: it's three stories high and has at least fifty individual vendors, corners that bleed into each other with only the variation of time periods or types of collectibles giving any sense of differentiation. An entire section is dedicated to dolls and accessories, plastic and glass looking at us as we walk the maze. Another section is old soda bottles, canned foods, cobalt glass medicine containers – an elaborate medicine cabinet from antique homes of the last one hundred years. I pick up a jar of pickles marked five cents, looking at the discolored gherkins.

"These have to be eighty years old," I say, slightly disgusted but mostly intrigued. "Who would want these things?"

"You'd be surprised," a croaky voice interjects. A hunched, rigid man comes around an unseen corner – it's impossible to tell in a place like this where he came from. "People hoard these things for generations, and then suddenly, someone wants it. Their value is rarity," he adds. "Some people want the jar of pickles they had as a child or always saw in grandpa's fridge."

"Nostalgia," I nod. "It's powerful, for sure."

"I'm Ray, Ray Hammon," he says, extending a gnarled hand to my dad first and then to me. I roll my eyes internally at his antiquated, sexist manners, but I can't be surprised. Ray seems to be a part of the bizarre antique museum.

"Philip Hill and my daughter, Kendra," my dad says with a grin. "Shopping or selling?"

"Selling, I'm afraid. It's a hit or miss business, and in January, the Purple Hat Club ain't exactly making outings."

I snort a little laugh at that. The little old ladies are the bread and butter of antiquing. "And I suppose there's not a lot of road-tripping retirees, either," I joke.

Ray cracks a smile. "You're a young antiquer," he says, sizing me up.

"Actually, as much as I do love antiques and history, I have some pieces I'd like to sell. My husband and I just bought a house out in Newport, and we have some glassware we're hoping may be crystal. We weren't sure who would be interested in something like that," I add in case this isn't how these things are done. I briefly imagine setting up a vending space here but hope there's an easier solution.

"Well, some people do specialize in that, but it's not going to bring the money you'd expect, I'm afraid. The best move for things like that are individual eBay sales, and even then, it's a waiting game. Old or not, crystal or glass, there's only so much demand for candy dishes and decanters."

"They're Victorian, if that helps at all," I try, but he shakes his head.

"It's not as rare as it sounds."

"We have some oil lamps, too," I add.

Ray looks thoughtful at that. "I wouldn't mind taking a look." He ambles back the way he came. "I'll show you my shop," he says.

'Ray's Corner,' a wooden sign at the top tells us, is a crowded tour of fifties memorabilia. He has everything from baseball cards to lamps, some plugged in, giving the booth a warm, yellow light. "I don't specialize in Victoriana, but I wouldn't mind something like oil lamps. There was a carriage house revival in the fifties that fits my theme a bit." He gestures to the booth. "Many of these things are from my own childhood or my parents' house when they passed. A lot of good memories, but I hope they'll bring more to others." He looks far away as his eyes unfocus toward the baseball cards. "It was a simpler time," he adds.

"That it was." Dad nods slowly. He grew up in the sixties, but I imagine he feels the same.

After some half-hearted poking around, I offer to get the items from the car. Dad nods, and I move off, leaving him and Ray to discuss the past.

I find the box of crystal and add the butcher box on top.

Coming back, I find Dad and Ray speaking to someone else, a portly woman with glasses on a beaded chain. She's wearing a colorful dress with a shawl, and I hear her voice first, a booming alto. "It was a shock, but I couldn't be happier!"

Dad is laughing when he sees me approach. "Kendra, this is

Ms. Wilkins." He gestures to her with an open hand. "She's a Victorian antiquer, and she's very interested in our furniture if you can believe our luck!" He's in a great mood, talking to strangers. I forget sometimes how much of a people person he is. I put my box down on the floor in front of me.

"Yes, little miss, I am," Ms. Wilkins says, thrusting her arm past Dad and toward me. She pumps my hand in hers, telling me about her latest haul at an estate sale. "It was a shock, but I couldn't be happier to find that much furniture on a blind bid!"

I get my hand back and smile broadly. She's infectious. "I brought our crystal and an interesting oddity you might really like," I say, picking up the dentist's box.

"Oooooh ooh ooh," she says, long and expectantly, like she's reached the end of a treasure map. "You haven't opened it yet? Let's do it!" She bustles past me, surprisingly lithe as she skips over the box in front of me. I smell a warm, classic scent of perfume on the air as she passes. She reminds me of a retired dance instructor or an art teacher. She must be over sixty, but she moves much younger. I pick up the crystal and follow her.

Her booth, 'Victoriana, etc.,' is much classier than Ray's, but maybe it's because Victorian trends purposefully engaged with clutter. Every item would look at home in our house. She has several oil lamps with delicate patterning or intricate glass work, some Tiffany-style lamps, candy dishes, and elaborate dining sets under glass in cases forming a wall with the aisleway of the mall, giving the booth structure. She has some elegant dishes, but I don't see any full sets. I won't be leaving our dishes out if she comes by to see our furniture.

I place the box of our wares on the table. Ms. Wilkins empties the box one piece at a time, creating what appears to me as random categories. She moves quickly, here and there, tapping a finger to a piece and holding it to her ear. I didn't think you could detect crystal that way if that's what she's doing, but something about her makes me trust her process. In a few minutes she's done, putting her hands on her hips.

"I'll give you fifty for this pile, ten for this one, and twenty-five for this one," she says, pointing at each in turn.

I look at Dad, who shrugs. "Less than $100 for all of this?" I'm a little crestfallen, and I'm not sure I hide it well.

"Truth be told, sweetheart, these lamps don't even move, despite how rare they are to find intact. And these candy dishes, forget it. You'll see they only go for five or ten bucks maximum on eBay, and they could take years to actually sell." She makes a lot of eye contact, which makes me trust her. She gives me a small smile. "I promise, you won't find a better offer."

She hasn't brought up the dentist's kit which makes me think this is a good-faith offer. I can appreciate a good business-woman. "And the dentist's kit? I know they're rare, especially in original condition," I note.

Her smile broadens. "I won't lie, that will break my bank a bit, but it will be well worth it for all involved. Truth be told, I'd like it for my own collection," Ms. Wilkins smiles greedily, and I like her more already.

"Do you have any WD-40 or something? I think that's what we need," Dad asks.

"Yes, actually. This is a common problem," Ms. Wilkins slides open the glass-topped table, sorting through some things which we can't see. "Here we go. And this isn't the only trick up my sleeve if it doesn't work." She bends down and comes back up with a flathead screwdriver and a hammer.

Setting the box on the top of the table, she applies the WD-40 to the rusted closure. "There. We'll give it ten minutes." She brushes up her sleeve, checking a rhinestone-studded watch face. "So, you folks have some furniture as well, I hear?"

I nod. "It's an old house, and it survived both the 1889 and the 1972 floods," I say. "This furniture is in excellent condition. It's a rare find, I think." I do my best to maintain eye contact, her searching gaze intense.

After a pause, she smiles. "I'm free today. Let's head over," she says. I love her directness. I return her smile, genuinely and widely.

"Excellent. Thank you, Ms. Wilkins," Dad chimes in.

"I'll give George a call," I say, "while we wait."

I walk away to a yet-uncharted section of the antique mall, dialing George.

"Hey, baby."

"Hey, honey. We are about to open the box. Do you want me to video chat?"

"Yes, yes, thank you. I'm curious what we'll find. Did you find an antique dealer interested in anything?"

"George, you won't believe it, but yes! She is a Victorian collector, her booth is adorable, and every item would look great in our house," I laugh. "She bought all of the goods for eighty-five dollars, not including the box."

"Only eighty-five? I thought –" George starts, sounding disappointed.

"I know, but these things are unfortunately so common. Another dealer told us the same before we met her," I explain. "I almost want to just keep everything, but I know we won't use most of it."

"Yeah, I know. We took out the gas lamps you liked, right?"

"Yes, definitely. The only ones here are plain porcelain, simple. We kept the unique ones. That's probably why," I consider. "There's nothing unique about factory-made items which were made in the thousands. Part of me wants to wait and see. The other part of me trusts her. Oh, and she's coming by today to look at the furniture in the basement."

"Hmm, she's a great find," George says. "After you get that

butcher's box opened, I'll do some more research on eBay and see what certain items should be valued at. I don't want to be taken for a ride," he expresses.

"I know, baby. It's a rare opportunity for extra money we certainly didn't anticipate."

"I did some Googling, and there's absolutely nothing like it for sale. I'm not sure how we could sell it. It seems to be priceless," and then he adds, "I don't think we should take less than $2,000 for it." He pauses while I take a deep breath.

"Okay," I agree. "But do you think it could be worth more? I have no idea what the market is. Are dental collectibles very desirable? What do I know?" My head is spinning with this.

"Kendra!" Dad calls down the aisle.

"Okay, well, we'll open it here, and then decide," I say and then I switch the call to video.

"Hi, everyone," he says. "This is exciting! Nice to meet you. I'm George." He smiles at Ms. Wilkins through the screen.

"Ms. May Wilkins. A pleasure, George." She winks at him. "Okay kids, are we ready?" She rubs her hands together.

"Kendra, do the honors," Dad says, taking the phone from me and angling the camera for George to have a good view.

"Wait, wait for me!" Ray calls, lumbering toward us.

When Ray is standing next to Ms. Wilkins and Dad and George are ready, I look at the box. Holding it in both hands, I feel a cold energy, and not only that of metal in a warehouse. Feeling a shiver, I shrug and grip the top of the box.

I pull. I feel it release. I ease the lid up, thinking of the rigid hinges twisting for the first time in decades.

I rest it on its hinges, and as the box opens fully, I smell something strong, stale, rotted. It dissipates nearly as soon as it comes, but I feel a rush of cool air from the inside of the box. I remove my hands and trace a protection sigil, three connecting circles, on the outside of my jeans.

The box has a dark red velvety lining with a removable tray, indented where it holds several pointy and poky dental instruments. I remember the stained butcher paper from the boxes. My stomach turns.

Dad is lowering George toward the box. "Wow," he intones. Suddenly, on his end of the phone, I hear what sounds like something heavy falling behind George. I can't see the screen, but I meet Dad's eyes as they widen at what they see on screen. The line cuts.

Ms. Wilkins looks at us, darting between our eyes, waiting for him to call back. Dad tries the line, and he doesn't answer video or regular phone calls. It's clear weather today, and my phone has a signal otherwise. Logical reasons failing me, I swallow in a dry throat, trying to hide my shaking hands as I close the lid of the box. I pick it up, holding it tightly under my arm as panic sets in.

Ray looks at Ms. Wilkins and excuses himself. "May, I'll see ya," he coughs and avoids our eyes. "Good luck to you all," he says in farewell, raising a gnarled hand in a wave, and heads to the car. I stay behind.

"Well," Ms. Wilkins says. "I hope everything is alright. Are you sure you'd still like me to come by?"

I look at Ms. Wilkins, taking in her motherly presence. "Please," is all I can think of to say. I watch the indecision in her eyes, and without thinking I reach for her hand. When she doesn't withdraw, I continue. "I can't explain it, maybe it's just the nerves talking. But I'd feel better with you there. Another woman to see and feel what we're dealing with. I have my dad and my husband. It's our first house, and-"

May stops me right there. "I think I understand." She gives me a wan grin and squeezes my hand. "I'll be there."

Despite it all, I find myself able to return her grin. I have a feeling she might be helpful: another witness never hurts. This is probably not exactly what Dad had in mind as 'professional help,' but she's certainly a start. "Why don't you follow us? It's less than ten minutes, Front Street in Newport."

My hands white-knuckled on the steering wheel, I lean forward as it'll make us go faster. I'm going a bit further over the speed limit than I should, and it's a testament to dad's own worry that he hasn't complained. We find ourselves home in seven minutes. I rush up the front walk and, as soon as the key clicks, I swing the door wide open.

"George?" I call, stepping inside, crunching something under my boots.

Glass. I look down and realize the mirror shattered.

And behind the mirror is a dark, deep hole.

CHAPTER TWENTY-TWO

Dad and Ms. Wilkins follow me in. "Careful. There's glass here," I warn. They step gingerly into the study while I go to fetch a dustpan. George is in the kitchen holding one when I come in. "What happened?" I ask, a bit breathless.

"I don't know. I was holding the phone watching you open the box, standing in the foyer, then I heard a crash behind me. It made me jump, I dropped my phone, and I went to find a dustpan. I didn't want the cats to step in any glass."

It's then I notice his hand. "Oh no, are you ok?" I gently take his rag-wrapped hand in mine.

"Oh yeah, just the side here. I washed it out right away. A bit of glass nicked me, nothing serious." I unwrap the washcloth slowly and heave a sigh of relief. He's right, nothing serious.

He takes his hand back and wraps it again, though the bleeding seems to have stopped. "Is that Ms. May?" Her sonorous voice comes from the open study door, admiring the antiques and books.

I nod, feeling giddy as the waves of relief continue to wash over me. "She's a character, but I like her, and I think you will too."

While George cleans up the mirror, I jump over the shards and join them in the study. "I'll be honest, we've only been in the house a week or so," I say as I walk into the room, "and there are too many things to contend with in this room." Ms. Wilkins is standing by a bookshelf on the left side of the room, fingering the astrolabe. As I approach her, Dad walks over to the window, stepping behind the desk.

"I'd be happy to purchase this if you're selling," she asserts, pointing at the astrolabe.

"I'll let you know," I grin. "I'm a bit of a history buff myself, so it's hard to part with anything." I pause and then add, "Besides, I feel strongly that this room is a time capsule meant to stay as it is."

Ms. Wilkins looks thoughtful, removing her hand from the astrolabe and regarding me in a new light. "I can certainly respect that. It has a heady energy, almost stuffy."

"I feel the same thing!" I say excitedly. I knew I liked her. "When we first moved in -"

"Kendra, did you know this bench opens?" Dad interjects, calling me over. I sense the tone of reproach in his voice, and I go to him. "Let's not bring up any ghosts here, okay?" He says quietly so only I can hear.

I resist the urge to huff at him and give a tight nod. "These curtains are original to the house. Do you know if they're Victorian?" I call to Ms. Wilkins. She readily comes over to assess them. I'm somewhat testing her, to see if she senses anything in this corner where I had seen the gray eyes.

Sure enough, she slows her pace. "Do you know who lived here?" she asks.

"Yeah, we have a record. Only four sets of owners, the most recent very brief. Built by John Baker, then sold to the same family who had it for three generations; then the last couple didn't last long. We bought it only a couple years after they did. It was a family's home for decades. We've actually been fortunate enough to meet the son who grew up here."

She walks to the corner, a hand loosely on the curtains. "I'd ask about any history this home has. This area was hit badly by the Flood of '89. Same time as the Johnstown Flood. Only the wealthiest families were able to rebuild or had homes strong enough to survive in any capacity. This one is mid-19th century, no?" When I nod, she continues. "This house has history. No doubt about that."

"All cleaned up. Thank you for waiting, Ms. Wilkins," George says, coming toward us.

As they shake hands, Ms. Wilkins says, "Please, call me May."

"May, then. George – it's a pleasure," he says, concluding their introduction before continuing. "The basement is the storage area right now. I'll grab the flashlight, and Kendra, can you get everyone gloves?" I nod as he continues addressing May, "I'm still not sure what kind of dust and danger is in that place, but it's not damp, fortunately. Before the previous owners, the Harrs lived here for almost a hundred years. They redid the basement after the flood of '72. We still can't believe the furniture survived this whole time."

May starts. "Lionel Harr?" she asks.

I stare at her, and Dad does, too. "Yes," is all I can say.

"This is a small town. I taught his son, Charlie," she says. "I haven't seen him in some time. We crossed paths at Bitting's a while back."

I laugh at that. "That's how we first met him, too. He's a bit of a regular, isn't he?"

May gives a warm smile. "He used to work there, back in high school, bussing tables. It was more crowded in those days before the shopping center went up just outside of town. He's in construction now, I think. I always felt like he tethered himself, kept himself from achieving more. But that's a teacher for you. I taught art for twenty-six years," she adds proudly. Then she sighs, crossing her arms. "Charlie was a strange kid, by himself a lot. He had a few friends, sure, but he wasn't a big talker. He was sensitive, though. He had a real gift in his art. He would draw lots of portraits of flowers, and sometimes a waif-thin girl with blonde hair. Hard to forget. He was a bit of a Victorian, I suppose," she winks, but I feel a chill run up my spine.

After we're suited up, we start heading for the basement. Passing the dollhouse, May stops. "Wow! What a find. This is definitely old. I'd place it in the 1880s. Those dolls are all custom, you know. Back then, they were made to order. The houses were rare too. Not everyone could afford such a luxury toy. This is gorgeous – I don't suppose...?" she tries, but I shake my head.

"That is my favorite find," I smile.

May is interested in almost everything we had tagged with a red sticky note, and I'm thrilled and relieved to know they'll sell for a good bit more than the crystal. While in the basement, the energy feels heavier than usual, and the cold is bone-deep. Completing the circuit, we've shown her everything.

"What about that chair?" She asks. She points behind the long, low table we'd found first. Untarped, in the back of the basement against the wall, is the brown leather surgeon's chair from the attic.

CHAPTER TWENTY-THREE

After May leaves, I brew a pot of coffee. Dad and George are sitting at the kitchen table, silently. George is massaging his head, eyes closed. Dad has his hands clasped in front of him. Hearing the percolator drip, I sit in the center, my back to the kitchen sink, a sense of deja vu setting in over me.

None of us have had the courage yet to look in the hole behind the mirror.

Nor to touch the chair. Neither did May.

I look to Dad, then George. Neither notice. Neither makes eye contact. I cough lightly, and they look up, still in a daze. "I say we sell the chair. And I think the sooner some of these items are gone, the better."

Dad and George both nod. "I agree," George says. "The sooner the better. May said she can come by with her truck this Thursday, and I think we'll find ourselves feeling lighter with that chair – I guess we know it's a dentist's chair now – definitively gone."

Dad shakes his head, and as he does, it turns into a gentle

stretch of his neck, wringing out some of the mental exhaustion of this whole situation. "I don't know how that's possible, that the chair was in the attic, then gone, and then it just reappears in the basement. And on the same day we opened that box? I'm really not sure what to say." He picks the cuticle on his thumb. "I want it and that dentist's box gone. Why didn't you let her take it today?"

I swallow. "I don't know. I don't think it's meant to be passed on. The energy is too strong, and the connection with the chair is obvious," I explain. "Charlie said something about keeping all the furniture together, but if generations of holding onto antique furniture didn't help Clara so far, I think it's worth a try to sell it. My research hasn't led to anything much, yet. I was writing the wrong stuff. Details about the flood... but I need details about the people. I think tomorrow I'll go back to the library and do more digging. I'll look for dentists and medical experts of the town, and we'll go from there."

Dad nods, and George pats the table with both hands in a gesture of finality. "I'm going to try to get some editing done," George says and gets up to make his cup of coffee before heading upstairs.

Dad stands to make his coffee, then sits again at the table. "I'm not sure how normal any of this is, even for a haunting, but there's no way this is going to change."

"I'm surprised at you, Dad. You're not one to give up or walk away from a challenge." I try to smile, but it feels disingenuous. "Besides, it's not all bad. Clara can help us, she –"

Dad waves his hands in front of himself. "No, no, no, no. Kendra, this is not rational. They all need to go."

"Dad, you need to trust me, I –"

Dad cuts me off again. "I know you aren't scared. I know you see the other side as 'just another path,' or whatever." I roll my eyes at his finger wiggling. "I don't think death is sinister, but it's not altruistic, either. Death is not sentient." He finishes, taking a sip of his coffee, avoiding my eyes.

I close my eyes, taking a deep breath. I reopen them and look at Dad, drawing his eyes to mine. "Death is energy." Dad moves to protest, but I cut him off. "No, please, let me finish. It's like Mom told you, ghosts are energy, but death itself is, too. Death is not the end, for anyone. We have souls, we are souls, at our core. There's nothing left of us after we die except for that piece. And if our souls were in enough pain on this earth, if the death was so sudden that a soul couldn't process it, or if, to use the cliché, they have unfinished business on this earth, well, that's a ghost. It's just another person. Whoever is doing this was a person just like you or me, but now they're living – well, existing – on another plane from us. If we were more sensitive to the beyond, we might see hundreds of apparitions in any given place. If we were all more aware and in tune, we'd be seeing and feeling even more than we are in this house. It's the strength of those energies that lets us see even what we *have* seen.

For an energy to move a dentist's chair down three stories while somehow making it disappear for a few days, or for an energy to be powerful enough to shatter a mirror, or even to move a doll to a dollhouse, it has a serious back story. And only by uncovering that do I, or any of us, have a chance at helping this person, this lost soul, onto the next phase of their existence. Or, if their existence is to be here, to make that comfortable and safe for all of us." I pause, suddenly feeling a little tired. Dad looks at me with something I think might be respect, or it might just be confusion. "All I know is," I continue, "I feel nothing sinister about Clara. But I've seen a gray-eyed man a few times, and I thought I took care of him when I..." I inhale and take the plunge, testing the waters of Dad's spiritual respect here.

"When I blessed and cleared the house when we first moved in."

Dad raises an eyebrow. "And that means...?"

"I burned sage and banished negative energy from the space, cleansing the house for us to make it our own. He disappeared. I sort of saw it happen – a negative energy shouldn't have been able to stay. But Clara stayed. Dad, when we first moved in, she would hide. She was as afraid of him as anyone would be. I was afraid of him – I saw him in a corn maze before we even closed on the house. He is a powerful enough spirit to leave the house, to move a chair three floors, to break a mirror. I think opening the box is what triggered that. I don't know why, but he is not happy. He is not a good person. I won't let him stay in our house." As I say that, my resolve strengthens. I feel a vibration of energy flow through my body, a commitment to our family – and Clara – to keep us safe here. I feel my mother with me, but I think there's nothing paranormal about the feeling. She would simply be proud. "I will not let him stay in our house," I say again, louder. I am a firm believer in affirmations, and I will use this one.

I get up and make myself a cup of coffee. Dad is drinking his thoughtfully, looking at me as if he has something he wants to say. I lean on the counter, stirring my coffee, and take a few sips. Then I take a big swig. "Do you want to try something with me?"

Dad shrugs. "It's your house, Bug. I'm right behind you."

THE STUDY IS QUIET, of course, and the stuffy heaviness of it feels deeper and darker than I've felt since we moved in. I turn on the lights and head for the desk where I left the box this afternoon.

Looking at the bay window, I see wind in the branches of

the trees around the lane. A storm is coming, snow or rain, depending on the temperature. In true Pennsylvania fashion, I expect a slushy mix, cold enough to freeze but not cold enough to snow.

I sit at the desk, and Dad sits behind me on the bay window. "That corner there," I start, pointing next to where Dad is sitting, "is where I saw him vanish when I banished him. That's the spot I expect he'll reappear if he's still here," I explain. "This feels like the heart of the house, the center."

Dad adjusts himself on the seat, moving to his right a bit. "Good to know," he says warily.

I pull the dentist's box in front of me, and before I lose my nerve, I open it.

I wait.

Nothing. Only the soft and rising sounds of the wind meet my ears. I move my hand toward the instruments, unwillingly. The energy of pain and cruelty is strong, the latter unexpected. Sure, dentists were painful, especially in a time before anesthesia; but the cruelty, the suffering, is stronger than I would have expected. I start to lift out the top tray, and I feel a cool draft start at my ankles. I look down and see Clara. I push my chair away from the desk and make eye contact with her. I hear a gasp and then a soft pat and turn to see Dad with his hand over his mouth, eyes wide, looking at Clara. Her eyes plead with me silently.

I have to, I say with my eyes. I lift the box's tray.

Underneath is a terrible, awful sight.

Pinching claws, round-handled and sharp-toothed, stare up at me. Three sizes of tooth-pulling elements – I don't want to imagine them in use. And what I see next to it, nestled in the corner, makes me recoil.

A jar of teeth, varying sizes, their roots a muddy color. The glass is yellowed, the cork cracked and darkened.

I wretch a bit, swallowing, breathing shallowly. And then, pulling my hand into my sleeve, I remove the jar of teeth. They feel... sad. So sad. So scared. So... tired. I feel myself choke, sobs growing in my chest. Where did these teeth come from? Something nags at the back of my mind.

I hear a sob and turn to look at Dad. He is still wide-eyed, focused on Clara. I look down and see her looking downcast.

I place the jar on the desk next to the box and replace the tray. These teeth... my intuition tells me they're important. I close the box, making sure it latches, and push my chair back, slowly, so as to not startle her. I sit with her, there, on the ground, and get Clara to look at me.

My heart wrenches. Clara's big blue eyes are brimming with spectral tears. She looks at me, with what, to my amazement, looks like embarrassment. "Oh, Clara, Clara," I coo, beckoning her into my arms, flexing my fingertips while holding an open embrace. "Clara, honey, what is it?"

She doesn't come to me. I hear her sniff, a sob growing in my own throat as I watch her. I reach out to her, wanting to wipe a tear, but my hand goes through her face. I cup her face in my hand, anyway, holding my fingers to the outer limits of her form. I am dimly aware of Dad behind me, but I can't worry about what he's thinking right now. Clara sniffs again and meets my eyes. I give her a small smile and try again. "It's ok, sweet girl."

Her mouth wavers, and then she says the last thing I expected to hear from her: "But it isn't. I deserved it." She looks at me, her eyes bright with memory. And opens her mouth. I unintentionally withdraw my hand from her face when I realize what I'm seeing. Gashes and holes, an empty smile. She's missing nearly all of her teeth.

The look of embarrassment returns to her face as she closes her mouth. I raise a shaking hand to my own mouth, subconsciously rubbing my jaw. Just like in the dream. She fades into the back of the desk, leaving behind her only a cold shiver of wind, and a trail of silver, sparkling light.

CHAPTER TWENTY-FOUR

I close the door and sit on the floor in front of my altar table, after saying good night to Dad.

Back there in the study, I hadn't realized I was crying until I stood, and he wrapped me in his arms, tightly, and whispered in my ear as if he didn't want Clara to hear him, "I don't understand it, but I'm so proud of you."

As he hugged me, I looked at the corner. A gray mist was dissipating.

Taking a box of candles from the drawer of the table, I select a white and a black one. I rebuild my altar space, removing my athame, my chalice, and my candles from the drawer. I light the sage and cleanse the space, asking that it be consecrated for my use in healing and protecting. I sage the whole room for good measure, then sit back down. Checking that my space is ready, I light a charcoal and place it in my incense tray. I snuff out the sage and select a pine resin, a protecting and cleansing plant, and sprinkle a couple of beads onto the charcoal. As the smell rises, I breathe deeply and call the quarters.

Facing the eastern corner of the room, I raise my hands to the sky. "Element of the East, Guardians of Air, may your clearing powers be with me today as I seek to purify this space by dispelling all negative energy." The smoke from the incense curls upwards as Air heeds my summons.

Turning towards the window over my altar, I raise my arms to the next element. "Element of the South, Guardians of Fire, may your cleansing flames clear this home of all evil and ill-intent." I watch the fire circle the charcoal puck, igniting the resin droplets.

Turning to the next, facing the door, I call in the western element. "Element of the West, Guardians of Water, may the purification of your healing waters be felt in this home, as all evil and anguish is banished." I picture the strong river, just outside of our property lines – our protector, like the moat around a castle.

My back to my altar, I complete the quarter call. "Element of the North, Guardians of Earth, may your grounding power be with me in the battle of evil as I cleanse and purify my home." As I invite the last element, the stability of the house is tangible beneath my feet.

I let the power of the elements flow through me. I invoke the Goddess to join me and protect me. I pull up a shield of white light, using the ceremonial dagger, my athame, to draw a circle around myself and my altar. I place it on the altar, and feel its metal singing like a tuning fork. The exhaustion seeps from my bones as I feel reinvigorated by the magic.

Using my fingernail, I carve the protection sigil on the white candle: three interlocking circles. Underneath it, I make a mark in the candle, a tally for myself, George, Dad, and Clara – and then a fifth for Charlie. His energy may still be tied here.

I place it on the table and pick up the black candle. I'm stumped for the perfect sigil here, so I draw a simple banishing one, a circle with a large, deeply-carved X running through it. I picture the gray eyes and focus on the fear that Clara felt, the fear I felt in the corn maze; the uncertainty of the encounters with the chair, the negative energies of the basement and the attic spaces, even the study.

Opening my essential oils box, I select juniper, bergamot, and lavender for protection, strength, and calm and begin blessing the white candle. Smoothing the oil over the surface of the candle, using two fingers on each hand to rub the oil to each end, I envision this house free from evil. I see the house, each room clean; I see George and I waking up refreshed and focused each day. I feel joy in writing in the study, picturing myself there, unafraid, the energy lifted. I see Clara as a white light, shining with peace and joy. I see my dad enjoying a nap on the couch, blissful. The real magic is in the visualization of the results. My intention for a safe home is strong. Once I feel the candle pulsing with energy, I place it in a holder and rub my fingers on my jeans to clean them.

I select the strongest banishing oils I have – thyme, peppercorn, and sandalwood – and apply a drop of each to the black candle, picturing the gray eyes dissipating into the ether. I see the form of the man I saw in the corn maze, turning to black smoke and rising into the sky, gone. I can clearly see Clara, open and free, laughing through the house. Behind Clara in my mind's eye is a shadowy figure, the dark-haired woman standing there like Clara's shadow. I watch the shoulders of the shadow release, hearing Clara's tinkling laughter. I take a deep breath, picturing those gray, dead eyes evaporating, vaporizing. I place the candle on the table.

"With this white light, may our home and its inhabitants be protected and cleansed of evil. May George Levy, Kendra Hill, Philip Hill, Clara Baker, and Charlie Harr live in peace, and be protected from all negative energy. May the evil spirit that lives here have no power over us. So mote it be." I light the white candle. It rises to life, a high, solid flame. I watch it settle, feeling the protective energies flood the room.

"May the light of this black candle burn away and banish any negative energies: the dark, evil energies of the gray-eyed man. He is not welcome here." I raise my voice, commandingly repeating, "He is not welcome here! Banish him forth from this home. May he bring no more evil to those who abide within. So mote it be." I light the black candle. It rises and then falls, snuffing itself out as if it were pressed between two fingers. I light it again, watching the flame rise, then sputter, diminishing to nothing. I lift the white candle in my receiving hand, and with my left hand, I hold the black. The flame meets the black candle. I hear a loud crash as if it's coming from the basement. Then another, but this time closer, like it's in the living room. The hand holding the black candle starts to shake nervously as I hear heavy footfalls bounding up the steps.

I jump, spilling wax onto the altar table. I place the candles down and stand, listening. I hear George calling from the top of the steps. Relieved it's only George, I call back, "In a minute!"

I take a deep breath, frustrated but undaunted, and try again. The black candle is still not burning. I dismiss the quarters quickly, thanking each element for their help. I thank the Goddess but leave the white candle burning. My fear fades into anger as I try again and again, this time with a lighter instead of the white candle.

Nothing.

I've never felt powerless in my magic before. Never, not even when I was just starting out. "Please, Goddess, help us," I say, picking up the still-burning white candle, and hold it to the black candle. George calls up again, louder. I hold the white candle desperately to the black, but it fails each time as if the wick is wet.

Resigned, I open the circle with my athame and head out into the hallway.

Immediately I can feel it. The energy is all wrong.

George is downstairs, talking to someone. I hear Dad's voice replying. I rush down to them and see them standing in the living room.

"What's –" I start, and then, stepping between them, I see.

The dollhouse is smashed in, splintered down the middle.

I stare at the dollhouse in disbelief, shaking my head. I wrap my arms around myself, pulling my hands into my sleeves.

"We checked the front door. It's still double-bolted. No windows are open anywhere. The basement is still closed." Dad says.

"The kitchen backdoor is locked as well," George adds. "Where were you?" He says it quickly, not accusatory but concerned. He pulls me in and hugs me, kissing the top of my head.

As he releases me, Dad rubs my shoulder. "Are you okay, Ladybug?"

"Yeah, yes. I'm fine. I was in my Craft room trying to – well, trying to banish the dark energy here, that man with the gray eyes. I don't think he liked that." I kneel down and pick up a doll, Clara's likeness. Her head is cracked, an arm missing. I check the time. The library will already be closed. "I'm going to the library first thing tomorrow."

"I'm coming, too," Dad says.

"Don't leave me here alone," George adds with no hint of humor. I move closer to him and put my arm around him, leaning on his shoulder. This is getting to him more than I'd been willing to accept. Somehow, this realization is more unnerving than anything else we've been through.

We stand like that, unable to move, for what feels like

hours. Looking ahead at the window behind the sofa, I see gray eyes. They're not outside. They're reflecting from in front of the dollhouse. A face fills into the dark reflection. Moppy black hair frames it.

He smiles.

CHAPTER TWENTY-FIVE

My footsteps echo in the silent darkness like cannon fire despite my bare feet. I hold my nightgown's skirt in one hand and a candle in the other, illuminating only a small diameter around and before me as I walk. I can see my breath in front of me, the winter chill creeping in. It's well after midnight, but I can't find her anywhere.

I peek into the living room, checking behind the sofa, under and behind the piano. Nothing. I rustle the long, heavy curtains – no one behind them. The doll house is where it always is, facing the wall that divides the foyer from the living room. Maybe it's the low light, but it looks like it's been shifted out from the wall.

I place my candle on the floor and begin to pull the dollhouse out from the wall, sliding it at a snail's pace to keep it from scraping. It squeaks once, and I flinch, frozen in place. When no movement answers, I push it farther, until I can peer behind it. The section of false wall has been removed from the lower half of the wall, as I expected. I shake my head, smiling slightly in relief.

"Are you in there?" I whisper into the darkness. The space isn't large enough for two of us no matter how close we'd squeeze, so I just peer inside. I reach behind and pick up the candle from the floor, lifting it over the dollhouse. I see small, bare feet recede into the dark corner of the cubby hole.

I can picture her there in the dark, arms around her knees, folded up toward her chest. "Come out now," I whisper gently, waiting for the feet to reappear. I hear the hushed rustle of fabric and sit down, my back to the wall. Still holding the candle, I start to slide into the space. Like I used to when she was scared of thunderstorms, trains, visitors. She's always been fearful.

My shoulder is suddenly whipped back, an unseen hand pulling me to my feet. I gasp loudly, dropping the candle. It goes out, and I hear the candle separate from the holder, rolling to the back of the hole. I can't see who it is as they roughly hold me by both shoulders.

A train whistles, followed by the bright light and jarring sound of the cars rattling past the window, flooding my attacker with strobing yellow light. Gray eyes. In the next split second, as the next car passes, I see his moppy hair, black. Light flashes again, and I take in his suspenders over his white collared shirt. As the cars click past behind us, the final, red light of the caboose illuminates his face one last time. His lip is curled in anger. I try to scream, but he puts his hand over my mouth.

I'm STILL BEING SHAKEN, both shoulders held in place by strong arms. "No, no, stop, stop!" I'm shouting, thrashing in his grip.

"Kendra, honey. Wake up. Wake up now," George says urgently as he shakes me.

"George," I gasp in utter relief, opening my eyes. "George," I say again, his name pulling me back to the present. I pull him in for a hug and then look down at myself. I'm almost surprised to see my Van Halen t-shirt and leggings instead of a white nightgown. I push off the covers and swing out of bed. "Baby, I need to check something."

I head downstairs, George following me. "Good morning, Ladybug. The coffee is – hey, what's wrong?" Dad is already down, holding his mug in the kitchen archway.

Not answering, I rush to the dollhouse. The window is right behind it, just like in the dream. The dollhouse is against the same wall, too. I start to pull the dollhouse aside as George skips over to the other side to help me.

The dollhouse removed, I knock on the wall. It's hollow, thin. I take a deep breath and peer around the wall. The Tiffany lampshade, my first impression of this beautiful, elegant, mysterious house, spreads its warmth over the atrium.

There.

"This is a false wall," I say to Dad and George without turning around. I use my phone flashlight to scan the space behind the hollow wall. Something is in the corner.

"I think there's something back there," I say. There's just enough room for me to step inside. Shining my flashlight across the space, I steady my hand against the false wall on which the dollhouse leaned. I feel the panel shift. This must be how Clara got in here in my dream.

My flashlight lands on a stout, dust-covered cylinder. I reach out and pick it up.

A candle stub.

ENJOYING our coffee in the living room, I tell Dad and George about my dream. "Neither of you had anything like that happen last night?"

They both shake their heads. "It was colder than usual but no dreams," George says.

I sip my coffee thoughtfully, looking at the candle stub on the table. "I've had dreams before. Nearly every night. And now I'm thinking – they've all been memories. She was never hiding from me or whoever's memory that was."

"Definitely a woman, right?" Dad asks me.

I nod. "Every time. I was wearing a yellow dress in the first one, maybe that time I was Clara, I don't know. But then the other times – an apron and then a nightgown. I was in a different room, once, too. I remember moving my hair from my face. Definitely a woman." I pause, thinking. Dad looks at me, and I think he's making the same guess. "Her mom?" I offer. He nods once. "Then who was she hiding from?"

"It's obvious who. The gray-eyed man. But who is that damn bastard?" Dad says, his hand a fist on his knee.

"Hopefully the library will have some answers," George says.

Ms. SHENK IS LESS than enthusiastic to see us. "You're back," she says to me, the warmest welcome I could expect. Her curls are toppled in a similar fashion as before, her bangs thin over her eyes like lace curtains. She peers through them, inspecting us.

"Yes ma'am, and I brought my dad and my husband, George." I think ma'am was a nice touch. You catch more flies with honey.

When she doesn't reply beyond a nod of acknowledgment, I add, "Thank you again for all your help on learning more about the floods of '89 and '72. It's been very enlightening for us. Our new house has a lot of mysteries to it." I smile.

"Pleasure to meet you, Ms. Shenk. I'm Philip Hill, Kendra's

father. Newport is a lovely town." He extends a hand. To my surprise, she takes it, giving Dad a smirk.

"Alva. You can call me Alva," she says. I notice it's only to Dad.

George raises a finger, butting in. "I'm George," he says. Alva gives no opening for a handshake as she comes out from behind the counter.

"We're looking for some information on any doctors or dentists who lived here in Newport in the 1880s. Would that be available somewhere in newspapers or..." I let the question trail, looking at her expression.

She crosses her arms, leaning on the counter behind her. "I'm not too sure. In Newport or surrounding?"

"Living in Newport." Then I add, "Really, it's dentistry we're most interested in. We think a dentist might have lived in our house."

"If you know it's your house you're looking for, look up the home records. We have those here on the microfilm as well."

"We have the list of the owners going back to the building," I start, but she cuts me off.

"If you know the name, see if it's in our files. Here," she goes back behind the counter. I follow her, shrugging to George and Dad.

She puts her hand on the ancient computer next to the microfilm projector. "Turn this on and type it in. If it's listed it should come up." She turns to leave. "Come on in, then," she calls, beckoning George and Dad to follow us.

I turn on the monitor, pressing in the power button forcefully. The static starts, and the screen enlivens, the tickle and buzz of the old computer taking me back. The database is run on a '90s operating system.

I type 'John Baker.'

117 North Front Street comes up as his address. *1865 to 1919.*

John Baker – wife, Althea Baker. Children – Jasper Baker and Clara Baker.

Clara. Our Clara. Althea; could that have been whose memory that was? Is Althea the other woman I saw?

I click the home now, and the records Lynn had given us match the computer's intel.

"Try clicking Clara's record," George suggests. I go back, and the seconds between screens feel like eons.

"Were computers really this slow back then?" I say to Dad.

He snorts. "At least this isn't a dial-up connection."

Clara's page yields no further results. She didn't marry or have children, no new addresses; but we knew that.

I click Jasper's record. The newspaper article I found in the box downstairs comes up – *Newport Ledger – June 1889.* An obituary comes up as well. I turn and Dad wags a hand for me to continue.

JASPER JOHN BAKER, aged 19 years, 6 months, and 3 days, drowned in the Flood. His sister was also presumed drowned; her body has not been recovered. He is survived by his mother, Althea Justine Baker, and his father, John Lucas Baker. Funeral services were held at Meyers Funeral Home, 6 day of June. He has been laid to rest in Newport East Cemetery. Peace to his ashes.

"PEACE TO HIS ASHES," I read again. Goosebumps spread up my arms and down my back. I feel Dad shiver behind me.

"Ms. Shenk?" I start. She's right behind Dad, the curious old bird. "Where is Newport East Cemetery?"

She raises her eyebrows and then wrinkles them, confused. "There is only one cemetery in Newport, and it's to the south."

I look at George. He frowns and nods. "There's another," I say quietly. "You know that old housing development across the river?"

Ms. Shenk nods, then looks at me, her eyes widening. "You mean...?"

"There's a reason they stopped construction. We found a cemetery there."

CHAPTER TWENTY-SIX

I half expected Ms. Shenk to come with us. She almost looked excited when I told her we had found another cemetery. "I thought that was a local legend, building a development on a cemetery," she said and shook her head in disbelief.

George, Dad, and I drive up to the cul-de-sac of abandoned houses. Dad is silent as he watches them pass by in increasing levels of unfinished construction. Pulling up to the curbside, George turns off the car, and all three of us head out to the field.

The grass is drier now, and because we've had weeks without snow, the stones are almost visible without removing grass. I find *Sm– 1893* again, and we fan out, looking for *Baker*.

Gray rectangular stone after gray rectangular stone. I'm jarred by the uniformity. Usually, old cemeteries have varying types of headstones, and typically, they're upright. These were designed to be flat, like they were hidden on purpose, made to be forgotten.

After some time, Dad calls us over. He's about 200 feet from the curbside, and when we reach him, we see he's uncovered a stone similar to every other one I've seen. "This one ends in -er," he says excitedly. A man of action, I can see the life on his face returning with the sense of purpose this morbid treasure hunt is giving him.

"It seems too long to be 'Baker,'" I say, disappointed. I rub away the dirt with my fingertips. "And I think that's '189-', we're looking for 1889."

Dad snaps his fingers and rises from his squatting position. "Dang it, you're right. False alarm, kids!" He goes back to sweeping his section, and George and I separate to our corners.

On my way back, I see what looks like an arrowhead coming out of the ground just fifty feet or so ahead of where Dad is searching. Going over to it, I pry it up. It's a piece of wrought-iron fence. I follow the length of where the fence would be, although most pieces are missing. I shiver at the thought that people may have looted a cemetery.

For six, seven, eight feet, I walk in a straight line, picturing the fence and its flow. This must be a limit of the cemetery. The ground shifts under my feet.

Something flat is under here.

I squat, patting the ground. Sure enough, it's a curving, metal board. I feel for an edge, and securing one in my fingers, I pull with both hands, leaning back on my heels. A sign mucks free of the still-moist topsoil.

Newport East Cemetery is beaten into black iron, the letters still raised though the paint is long faded.

I hold the sign over my head and wave it to Dad and George. They come jogging over. "That settles that, then," George says, rubbing his upper arms.

"Let's change our search pattern. This is the limit of the cemetery, right? So, we can spread out along it and make our way forward. The graves we've found closest to the road were from 1893, or thereabouts. Let's see if these are our flood victims."

"Dad, it's so gruesome to say it like that."

Dad chuckles. A genuine laugh here in a misty, abandoned cemetery. "I'm glad you have your limits to the macabre, Ladybug."

"Kendra's a loyal friend, even to ghosts. She won't talk about them behind their backs," George puts in with a short laugh. "Okay. I'll start to the right. You go to the left, Mr. Hill. Kendra, take this six-foot or so expanse and work your way forward," George directs.

I smile warmly. "Sir, yes, sir." I give a salute with my pointer finger toward George and get to sweeping. It feels so good to take action – I can tell Dad and George feel the same way.

After some time, I come to another stone, marked *Unk–1889*. We're getting closer. "I just hit 1889!" I call back. Dad is on one knee brushing the grass from a stone. George is... what is he doing?

"George!" I call. He doesn't look up. He continues to dig, slowly, rhythmically scraping his fingers hand over hand at the grave in front of him.

Pacing toward him, I look down at the top of his head. Dirt is streaking up his hand, his forehead breaking out in a sweat despite the January cold. "Baby, what are you doing?"

George doesn't respond. I squat down, level with him. His lips are tight together, white; his eyes averted to his work. I look to where he's digging. A headstone. I kneel down in front of him and notice its writing is upside down. He is digging at its base, clearing dirt, then topsoil from the bottom of the tomb-stone. I place my hands on his, and with some effort, he stops. He looks up at me.

His eyes, his brown-as-chocolate eyes, are gone. Gray, piercing, dead eyes look at me. My throat tightens with fear; but it's the anger that spurs me to action. Holding my breath, I raise my right hand.

I slap him.

He closes his eyes, his head turned to the left by my slap. I hear Dad standing behind me and turn: he's gone pale, his mouth open in shock. No time to explain to Dad, I slap George again with my left hand this time.

When George opens his eyes again, he's back. "Kendra? Check it out, this –" he's looking at his hands, the dirt under his nails. He's ripped a nail on his middle finger. Blood is pooling in the corner. "What the –?"

I move around the stone, not answering, and read the headstone. The words are hard to read, like all of the tombstones, but three words and the year are incriminating. *Jas– Jonn B—r, 1889.*

I stare at the tombstone. I run my fingers over it, closing my eyes. Corner to corner, top to bottom, edge to edge. I feel the depth of the section George dug out.

Something is carved on the bottom right. I open my eyes and look. It's three waves.

I go back to the stone I had just seen, *Unk– 1889*. Moving some dirt and grass, sure enough, it has the same marking. "I think this means flood victim," I say.

Dad looks curious for a second, then goes over to the stones he had been looking at. "These are the same," he calls.

George is still in place at Jasper's tombstone, rubbing the dirt from his hands onto his jeans. He sucks the blood from his hurt finger, staring at the stone. He looks shaken, tired.

I go over to him, putting a hand down to help him up. "Come on," I say. "There's nothing we can do here. We know where he is now." I retrieve the cemetery sign, then stick it upright in the ground in front of Jasper's grave. "We will be back," I say to him, giving the sign a final shove with both hands to secure it in place.

ON THE DRIVE HOME, Dad is talkative with theories and ideas. "Maybe we can hold a seance," he suggests. "Hire a medium."

I laugh. "Dad, trust me, you don't need a medium. And that wouldn't help. We've made contact, plenty of it. Seances don't stop contact; they increase it. Like opening a doorway."

He tries again. "What about a cleaner, like a spiritual kind? An exorcism?"

I shake my head. "I don't believe in that stuff. It's all about demons and Catholics."

It's George's turn to laugh. "You draw the line at Catholics, huh?"

"Hey, if it works for them, fine. But this guy is not a demon. He's just an asshole."

When we get home, I bring my notes from the library into the study where Dad and George are waiting. I flip to a new page and add what we know so far.

"John Baker: first owner – wife: Althea, son: Jasper, daughter: Clara." I speak as I write. Dad rubs his chin thoughtfully, sitting at the desk. George is leaning on the desk, his back to Dad, his hand hovering over the dentist's box. "Jasper, buried at Newport East. Clara, body not found. Althea... we don't know when she died. I wonder if she's who I embodied in my dream if it was her memory. I'll write that down too, just in case."

"What is this box's connection to Jasper?" George poses to the room.

"Let's open it again and see those tools," Dad responds.

I give him an impressed eyebrow raise and slow-nod. "I like the boldness, Dad." I pass him the box, and he opens it. No smells, no cold air emit from the box, but I feel a chill down my spine. Turning, I scan the room behind me, my eyes catching on the gaping hole where the mirror had been. I look away and join Dad, sitting behind him on the bay window, a reversal of our places the night we opened the box together. Was that just last night? Two nights ago? It feels like it's been a week, at least. I cross my arms with my notebook against my chest, and remember Lynn for a moment, the way she held her thick folder of paperwork on that first tour of the house. She was pale, and George noticed how "off" she seemed. Ghosts; they have quite the way of making anyone more uptight, even me, at times. Maybe I was too hard on her.

Dad lifts out the tray, placing it on the desk. He picks up one of the thin, long, pick-like tools, then turns around to hold it in the sunlight at the window. He rotates it slowly and then with a sigh returns it to the tray. He picks up a clamp next, doing the same slow inspection in the sun. "Ha!" He exclaims, making George jump. "It's right here, the maker's mark. It looks like a *WJ*. And here, *Boston*."

I'm not going to waste any time. I pull out my phone. 'WJ Boston dentist 1800s' yields limited results. I add 'tools' to the keyword, and find plenty of Williams, Walters, and Wyatts, but none with a last name beginning with J. I tap my finger on the bench beside me, thinking.

"Try eBay," George suggests.

I give him a winning smile and copy my search term into eBay.

Three results for 1800s dental instruments come up. Two of them are like those in the box, rounded clamps of an aged iron color.

"This is them!" I say excitedly, showing them both the picture. "It says made in Boston, circa 1760-80, made by cutler William Jasper."

The name Jasper seems to echo as I say it. Clara's brother. It doesn't feel like a coincidence.

CHAPTER TWENTY-SEVEN

After some more research in the online records, it turns out that William Jasper was a dentist who had trained a John Baker in Boston during the late 1700s. John Baker had moved to Newport in 1813, marrying a wealthy young widow, Mary Bonang. They had a son, John Baker, Jr., born in 1821 according to an announcement in The Newport Herald. Skipping ahead some years, there are no records of John Baker, Jr.'s marriage to Althea, but if she wasn't someone of import in society, there wouldn't have been.

"So, our John Baker is John Baker Jr., born 1821... That makes sense. He would have been in his 40s when they built the house. And he named his son after his dad's mentor?" George asks, leaning over me and my laptop.

"Or at least after the tools he inherited," I muse.

We had a nice dinner together, and now the living room is abuzz with energy. Dad especially is enjoying the relief of answers, leaning over my other shoulder to scroll the article on my laptop. "It says here that John Baker, Sr. moved down to the

Pennsylvania area, starting a dental practice in Philly before coming to Newport. Three generations and three towns of dentistry." Reading further, he adds, "And he invented a tooth powder. Good for him."

"I'm more interested in this inherited dentist's kit. It's even older than we thought and certainly very valuable. You think our ghost is the Dad?" George asks no one in particular.

"I feel like that ghost is much younger. Maybe Jasper was taking over the family business," I suggest. I remember the dream from a few nights ago, just before I learned Clara's teeth were missing. He said he was "a professional." I cross my arms tight over my chest as a chill runs through me.

Dad shrugs. "I say sell the case and be done with it."

I shake my head vigorously. "I couldn't disagree more. It'll be integral in getting rid of this ghost, that much we know. It's definitely tied to him." I pause, thinking. "I think we should bury it at Jasper's grave."

Dad balks. "Kendra, that kit could be worth thousands of dollars. It could cover your first year of taxes in this house! It's your right to sell it, and I think you should."

George interjects. "I'm not sure, either, Kendra. I mean, I want the ghosts gone more than I want the money, but –"

"Then we get rid of it. If we bury it, and it doesn't help, there's no harm done. We'll just go get it back. We don't have to dig six feet deep or anything. The grave is the logical place. Put the whole matter to rest, literally," I say with finality. I notice I don't blush this time.

They're both quiet, thinking it over. "Okay, Ken," George consents.

Dad sighs. "I hope it works. If not, you'd better dig it back up. And don't let May know you're doing that. She might go get it herself."

"Speaking of," I start, closing my laptop, "May is coming

tomorrow morning. We should try to get as much furniture up from the basement as possible before she gets here."

George groans. "Tonight? It's already dark out."

"Hey now, we've got this under control. Don't we, Kendra?" Dad asks, rolling up his sleeves in anticipation. "Let's move some furniture."

As we get our gloves on, I look out the kitchen window. The woods are dark, the air heavy and still. I feel snow coming.

THE BASEMENT IS JUST as we left it. We start with the tables and smaller pieces. As Dad takes up a rocking chair, I look at the baby changing table and remember the family I saw at the diner. Once all of this is behind us, this home would be a great place to raise a family, George and Dad are right about that. Hearing Dad come back down the stairs behind me, I shake my head. Cats are enough for now. I grab a box and head up the stairs.

Once we've taken up nearly all of the easy items, I look around at the basement. I feel warmed up and ready for the big ones, but Dad shakes his head. "We've brought up enough that we've cleared a path through the rest of the junk down here. She can tell us which bigger pieces she's interested in before we lug them up here." I think about it, then nod in agreement.

Taking stock, I see the chair is still choosing to appear to us. The big, flat table is still there, and the piano. "Wait, did you guys open the piano lid again?" I ask, walking over to it.

They both deny it, and I look down at the bench. The lid is open there, too. And the music is missing. "Huh," I intone, quietly to myself. Then a bit louder, for whoever's listening, "Did you want to keep your favorite pieces as a memento?" I ask the shadows.

"Don't do that," Dad scolds me.

Not responding, I wait and listen. No answer. I close the lid of the piano and move to do the same for the bench when something inside catches my eye.

There's a tooth in here.

"Um, George? Dad?" I say, swallowing bile that's slowly rising in my throat. They come over, standing on either side of me. I close my eyes and shake my head, take a deep breath, and open them again.

The tooth is staring up at me, its roots dark brown. I take a gloved hand and pick it up.

George puts his hands on his knees, passing his trusted flashlight to Dad as he turns away from me. Dad shines the light on the tooth.

"It's not damaged, no cavities, no cracks," I say, turning it in the light.

"I remember my dad telling me that people sold teeth from battlefields; or worse, dentists bought them from gravediggers, for people who needed implants," Dad explains. "Maybe this was... a part of someone's new teeth?" he suggests warily, as euphemistically as he can.

I can't contain the shiver down my back. "I wish I could remember if I had seen this in there before. I can't recall the music that was in here either; did he open this just to put it in?"

George is recovering slowly, and he stands upright, looking at me – while carefully avoiding looking at the tooth. "I think it's a message, either way. Whoever our male ghost is, he's a dentist. Or a tooth seller." It's George's turn to shiver.

Still holding the tooth, I'm at an impasse. "Should I add it to the jar of other teeth?" I ask morbidly.

Dad shakes his head. "Let's bury that for sure," he says. "Just put it with the dentist's tools."

As he says that, we hear a heavy *crack*. It hits the walls of the room and our ears louder than it likely is due to the silent closeness of the basement. We whip around in unison, checking the corners, the stairs behind us. There's nothing there.

"That sounded like a shoe falling," Dad remarks.

"Or something clicking into place," suggests George.

Something clicks into place in my mind, as well. "Like a reclined chair," I say.

Going over to the chair where it rests behind the boxes, behind the piano, I see the base of it is no longer reclined. It has snapped back into place, upright. I beckon to Dad without turning around. "Shine the light here."

As he does, the faint mist of a man fades in a millisecond, condensing as he dissipates into a dusty, gray speck. I follow it with my eyes until it leaves the light. Dad must not be able to see it because he doesn't follow it with the flashlight.

I hear a low rumble. I realize it's the echo of laughter, absorbing into the concrete walls, gone in a second.

BACK UPSTAIRS, I'm glad we finished moving what we did. Exhaustion is sinking in as the adrenaline wears off. The living room is unusable until we get some of this furniture out of here. I look down as Dad closes the basement door, and I realize I'm still holding that tooth.

"Kids, I'm pooped. I'll see you bright and early tomorrow," Dad says, heading for the stairs.

Once Dad is gone, George puts his arm around me. "You doing ok?"

I nod and smile tiredly at him, leaning into his shoulder. "Yeah. My body is more tired than my mind – I think I'm going to write for a bit."

"I'll go spend some time with the girls upstairs. Don't stay up too late," he kisses me on the head before going upstairs.

I go into the study and place the tooth next to the jar of teeth on the desk. Standing there for a moment, I scoff silently. So much for writing in here; it's become the office for our investigation instead.

I go around to the other side and start to tidy the desk a bit, everything except for the teeth. I reassemble the dentist's kit – we shouldn't have left it open – and I clear a space big enough for my laptop and a hot drink. It's time to write. Opening the *Bleeding Glory* manuscript, I try to focus on Catherine and her fashion world woes, but there's something more to these stakes. Something bigger. I go back to chapter one where she's telling her mom about choosing to major in fashion, and the conversation isn't not going well. "But maybe that's not all there is," I say under my breath. *Maybe her sister, yes, her mom's sister... Then she moved to France...* Suddenly the writing is flowing. Revisions to this chapter lead into revisions for the next. It's feeling real, now.

I don't know what's changed. Maybe it's the stimulation of this ghostly excitement, maybe the inspiration of Newport and this room. I smile thinking of my dad in the next room. Maybe it's that I'm understanding family a bit more these days. I think of Clara and her family, and my smile fades.

Leaning back, reading over my work, I fiddle with the top drawer of the desk. Opening it, I remember the letters I found on our first house tour.

I grab our investigation notebook and add our tooth encounter in the basement, and at the top with a star on either side, I add, "Notes in the desk????"

Sitting back in my chair, attempting to claim this space as my own, I pull the folder toward me, gripping it like a shield in front of my chest.

I freeze, remembering.

Lynn. The thick folder of papers clutched like a life preserver to her chest. I thought it was the ghosts giving her face that tense, anxious expression – now I'm sure it was something she found in the papers of this desk.

CHAPTER TWENTY-EIGHT

The snow fell steadily through the night. I woke twice, maybe three times, but the flat silence of the snowy night lulled me back under. Now it's nearly eight. I expect May will be here around nine-thirty. Rolling over toward George, I watch him sleep for a minute. We've only been married two years, but we've been together nearly eight. I still love to watch his long, dark eyelashes rest on his cheeks whenever I get the chance. His unruly curls are sticking up from his head, and without his thick-framed glasses, his hair characterizes his appearance. I kiss him gently on the forehead, and as his eyes flutter, he turns his head, facing the ceiling. I kiss him on the cheek. "Good morning, sleepyhead," I say in a quiet whisper.

George lifts his head and peaks out the window. "We got a lot of snow last night," he remarks blearily.

I follow his gaze. We watch the snow together for a beat. "Snow like this reminds me of Alicia and me growing up," George grins. "As soon as Mom gave us the all-clear that school was canceled, we'd grab our sleds and head out. Then she'd make us hot cocoa when we came inside." His smile fades as he looks at me. I blush, internally cursing my face for always showing exactly what I'm thinking. "Sorry, baby, I didn't mean to talk about my mom like that."

I shake my head and force a smile. "I don't mind. Really. When I was six, right around the time mom was really sick, I had a snow day. I went outside to play – I loved making 'potions' with the snow and dead twigs and such. But when I came back in Mom was sitting at the table." I pause, looking down at my hands. "She looked so tired," I start.

I was young, but it was one of those days I remember with perfect clarity. I came bounding inside, rosy-cheeked from the snow. The heat of the house warming my nose, I stripped off my snow pants and headed straight for the kitchen. I stopped short. The energy of the place – at least that's how I'd describe it now – was wrong. Mom was sitting down, a sink full of dishes undone. A rag was on her head as she leaned back over a chair.

I stepped forward, and she looked up, hastily removing the rag and smilingly tiredly at me. "Hi Ladybug," she cooed. "Did you have fun outside?"

I nodded, but in true six-year-old fashion, I asked the question on my mind. "Are you sick, Momma?" I remember the way her face paled. That scared me.

That moment was the first time I realized what that word really meant. There was sick, and then there was *sick*.

And in that moment, Mom's face told me everything I needed to know. I don't remember what her answer was. All I remember about what happened next is sitting on her lap, her holding my head against her heart. I remember every second of me listening to the sound of her, smelling the scent of her. She got so much worse so fast after that day.

Leaning against her, her face resting on the top of my head, she gave me the advice I'd heard in my head ever since. "I'll always love you, whoever you become. Don't be afraid to let others love the real you, too. Come what may."

I shake my head, coming back to myself, and see George's reassuring face. "It was a long time ago, now. I've made my peace. I'm glad her pain has passed," I say as I lean my head on his shoulder, then shake it off and change the subject.

"Are you ready to get this furniture out of here?"

He yawns, stretching his arms out of the covers and reaches for me, pulling me against his chest. "Do you remember our first apartment? Back in college?"

I laugh into him, my face tucked under his arm. "We didn't even have a bedframe, just a mattress on the floor." I shift, our brown eyes meeting with the sloppy smile of early morning. "You used to cook me omelets before every final for good luck."

"I don't know how we did it with four other roommates vying for the kitchen," he chuckles, stretching as he sits up in bed.

"We were always the only ones who cooked." I sit up beside him, raising my arms above my head. "I can't believe that was five years ago. Three years in Harrisburg, and now we own our dream home." I snuggle against him.

"So ready for that pool table," he says with a sarcastic grin. "I hope it's for the best, getting rid of this old furniture."

"It will be," I say. I feel it in my bones. "The hectic energy of this house needs a fresh start to really change. Decluttering is the first step. It's sad, in a way. Ghosts aside, that furniture has been with this house for years and years. But it's the right choice. We can't use any of it, and they're not getting any love down there. They're some gorgeous pieces, just not for us to enjoy."

He kisses the top of my head. "I love how you see the spirit in everything." I can hear the smile in his voice.

"That's animism for you – everything has its energy," I grin, closing my eyes as I listen to his heartbeat.

Shadow jumps up onto the bed, mewing and chirping. Sherry isn't far behind, yawning, ready to take our warm spaces as we rise.

Going to the window, I open the curtains. There's at least a foot of snow on the ground.

"George, did you give May your phone number?" I ask, gesturing to the fresh, unmarred snow.

"I didn't, actually. Your Dad gave his." Pulling on his robe, he goes out to the hallway. I take a minute with the snow, opening the window just a crack to inhale the fresh scent. Without the intermingling of sounds and fumes from cars, as we'd grown accustomed to expecting in Harrisburg, the clean crisp scent tingles my nostrils, and the lack of sound pollution adds a layer of stillness to our surroundings. While the snow is done falling, the larger trees at the border of our yard and those across from us still shed light dustings of white powder. I have a sudden desire to go sledding, to make snow angels, to build snowmen.

George comes back in. "He hasn't heard from her yet. I wonder if they plow out here." He points to our short driveway, invisible beneath a blanket of snow. "I'll be shoveling all morning. I can't believe I didn't consider that it's been... well since I was a kid that I've had to shovel," he muses. "Can't say I've missed it." He starts getting dressed into his thickest pants, rummaging for hats and gloves in his dresser. To both of our relief, he finds them.

Dad has brewed coffee when we come downstairs. I notice he looks a bit tired today. "Did you sleep all right?" I ask him.

Dad smooths a hand down his face and nods once. "Not really. It's the snow. When it's so silent like that, I can't stop myself from thinking." He doesn't say more, and I'm not sure how to ask him anything without seeming pushy. "You'll need a hand out there, George," Dad continues, managing a tired smile. "Do you have a second shovel?"

George takes a sip of his coffee before answering. "To be honest, I don't think we even have one shovel," he laughs a bit nervously, then takes a second sip.

Dad laughs, unapologetically. "Apartment living has made you soft! We'll have to hit the local hardware store one of these days." He's looking more awake at that. Carpenters in hardware shops are like witches at a faerie festival. "But until then, I might have one in my car."

"We can check the basement, too," I chime in. "There's got to be something shovel-like they would've used for the woodstove."

After breakfast, Dad checks his truck and finds a shovel for digging dirt. After digging a thin, jagged path from his car to the house, he comes in, tapping the shovel free of snow and resting it aside the front door. "It'll work, but it's not ideal," he says as he closes the door and comes in. "It'll come in handy later for when we get rid of the dentist's tools later, I guess."

I smile at him as he grimaces, likely thinking of the prospect of digging in a graveyard. "It doesn't count as gravedigging, since we're adding something, not taking anything," I say.

Dad looks at me evenly. "Yeah, but I'm not looking forward to it all the same."

We head down to the basement to look for a better shovel, flashlight in hand. It's much more bare after our excavation, the gray of the concrete floor now dominating our view from the bottom of the steps. "If May can take everything we've already put upstairs, it's only one more trip with the truck for the big things before we're done here," I rub my hands together expectantly.

Scanning the basement's sprawling room, I don't see

anywhere a shovel could be in the main space. "I'll check under the stairs," George says, walking past me with the flashlight.

I go to where the dollhouse sat, a wide rectangular imprint of dust in its place. There's empty metal shelving next to the small window behind it. Definitely not antique, but old, possibly from after the 1970s remodel. I check behind it. There's a wide cardboard box containing something heavy. I shimmy it out from behind the shelving, gently laying it flat on the floor. "Dad, do you have your pocketknife?" I call.

Dad comes over, kneels next to me, and uses his knife to pop out the rusted staples from the corners of the box. The top opens easily, the cardboard brittle after years down here. He pulls something out: a flat, sanded piece of wood. Underneath it are three more pieces like it and two wider, flat pieces. Laying them side by side on the ground, Dad stands and picks up the cardboard box, shaking it out onto the ground. A small, deeply yellowed plastic bag falls out, and a piece of paper equally aged flutters to the ground beside the bag. George comes back empty-handed, shaking his head. Then, observing Dad and me, he stoops to pick up the paper. I grab the plastic bag. It's an allen wrench and screws, with little right-angled metal brackets. "I think it's supposed to make a box," I say.

"Sort of," George says, flipping the paper toward Dad and me. "It's a coffin."

"BEFORE YOU JUMP TO ANY CONCLUSIONS," Dad says, putting his hands up, "these kinds of coffins are for animals, like pets that you want to bury. You probably don't remember, but we had a dog when you were first born. Jesse. She was your mom's when we first met, so she was pretty old. We had a coffin just like this for her when the time came."

"Why would they have it here?" I ask. I don't want to think about Mom right now.

"It was never used, so maybe they bought it in anticipation and then didn't need it or decided to cremate or something. We can't assume the worst here."

I'm zoning out, staring at the floor in front of me as I think. I don't know if it's just the mention of Mom, but I can't shake this unsettled feeling. My intuition is nagging at me – something's not right about this particular find. "That makes sense, Dad," I finally say, refocusing my eyes, coming back to reality. "I'll put this back where I found it for now."

"Bring it upstairs. May might want to look at it. It's got this '70s font. It's kind of cool, might be novelty in an antique shop to have an unused fifty-year-old pet coffin," George says, inspecting the instructions page.

I shrug. "It won't hurt."

We set the coffin by the stairs and continue our search for a shovel. We move along the walls but ultimately can't find anything that even resembles a snow removal tool. As we're about to give up our search and head back upstairs, I observe the basement. It feels vast in its near-emptiness – much less creepy than the first time we came down here. No white sheets: they've been set aside to be washed or have been washed already. No shadowy, tall, mysterious furniture – we've seen it all – pieces like the bookshelves are no longer ominous but are once again gorgeous, even in the dim light. I notice they're pushed out a bit from the wall like something might be behind them. Dad used to keep all sorts of tools in all sorts of nooks and crannies of our garage. "The bookshelves," I say out loud, breaking my own reverie. "Let's just check behind them, no harm in that."

George and Dad on either side, they move the bookshelves out from the wall at an angle, like a door on a hinge, one at a time. "No dice," Dad says. And then he hesitates, "Wait a second."

He shines the flashlight at the wall, and George and I see what he noticed. The floor is uneven here, the concrete rippling in places like it was finished hastily. There are no cinder blocks here. The wall is a solid piece of drywall. Dad raps his knuckles to it. All three of us can hear that it's hollow. Dad turns and looks at us.

As he does, his phone rings, making us all jump out of our skins.

"Hello? Oh, good morning, May. Yes, we are absolutely still thrilled to have you back with the truck, but only if the roads are safe." My Dad has the velvety voice of a 1950s car salesman when he's on the phone with strangers, it never ceases to amaze me. "If you're sure; don't go worrying us, if – okay, alright, that's swell, we'll expect you this afternoon." He closes the line, and George smirks at him.

"Reverse psychology?"

Dad rolls his eyes, exaggeratedly. "No, human decency," he says with a smirk of his own.

"Sure, sure, Mr. Salesman. You've still got it," George says, and I jab Dad in the ribs good-naturedly, his big grin at that compliment warming and tugging at my heart in tandem. In all the craziness lately, we haven't had time to process, much less celebrate, his retirement. I think he prefers it that way, but I also feel he's not sure what he'll do without his work.

I put my arm through his, pushing aside thoughts of our shovel search for the moment. Looking into his eyes, I feel him thinking of his retirement, too. "I think she's sweet on you," I look at him from under my eyebrows, giving them a wiggle as I do.

George laughs, adding, "You made quite the impression on Wanda, too, and maybe even thawed old Ms. Shenk's heart."

He puts his hands on his hips like he's the father scolding his flirtatious son.

It's dim in here, but I swear I see Dad blush. "I wouldn't say... I mean she's a kind woman, they're all lovely, kind women, but, well, but I..." he stammers, withdrawing from my grip and stepping backward onto the uneven concrete toward the wall.

"Dad, be careful!" I reach for his arm. Dad's eyes grow wide as he falters, trying to regain his balance. I try to pull us both away just as he reaches for the wall for support. We both fall, right through the drywall.

CHAPTER TWENTY-NINE

Blinking my eyes as the dust settles, I see a bed, stretched just between the two walls ahead of us. I rub my eyes, suddenly dry from the dust, and when I reopen them, the bed is gone. I see a cinder block wall ahead of us that looks like the other walls of the basement. The floor here is hasty concrete, as well, slightly uneven. It's very dark, unlit. George passes Dad the flashlight, and he shines it on the back wall. George steps through and helps Dad and me up, then we set about investigating.

The room is a perfect square, formed by three cinder block walls of equal length and the wall we fell through. It's familiar, but there's no chance I would have known it was here. Approaching the end of the concrete where I thought I had seen a bed, the floor changes. Stepping onto it, my feet feel grounded in a wet, almost spongy soil. It's not sand but real dirt. The space is colder, maybe from the soil, but it feels – sad. I kneel down, placing my hands to the floor. The sadness increases. A feeling of loss sweeps over me. I feel a sob forming in my throat like it did when I watched Clara cry under the desk just after we opened the dentist's box. Sadness, loss – and shame. Embarrassment. Guilt. And overwhelmingly, pervading it all is the kind of fear only helplessness can create.

Dad and George are silent behind me. I notice they haven't stepped into the dirt themselves but are standing, Dad with his hands in his pockets awkwardly, watching me.

"Anything there?" George asks quietly.

"Do you guys feel that?" I ask without answering. "That heavy sadness? There's trauma here. Something terrible happened." I rise and step over onto the concrete, taking a deep breath, swallowing the sob. I raise a shield of energy around me, from my crown to my root, grounding myself, protecting myself from these feelings. "Something terrible," I say again, trying to process, trying to imagine what it could be. "I think this was a servant's room. I swear I saw a bed in the back – like I've been here before." Something is biting at the back of my mind, but I can't catch it.

"Well, there's nothing down here now. Looks like it's just a room that they walled up and forgot about," Dad says.

George runs his hands through his curls. "I'm not sure unless they buried something they didn't want found. Or found something that was buried. That's the only reason I can think of to hide an entire room," he says.

I look at Dad, and I can tell we're both thinking the same thing. "Should I get the shovel?" He doesn't break eye contact with me, letting me decide.

I hesitate and then shake my head. "Not until May leaves."

Dad nods in agreement, the look of relief on his face unmistakable. We'll keep one more mystery buried for now.

"Let's head back upstairs," George says. "And I'll get to shoveling the snow."

I know he's freaked out when George is excited to do physical labor.

As we turn to leave, I look back at the room. The uneasy sadness is replaced by the nagging sensation that I've been here before. I look toward the wall, recalling the bed I swore I just saw. My dream from the other night flashes in my mind: the dream where Clara handed me a doll. We were sitting on the floor next to a bed in a small room. This room. I rub my hands over my arms, warding off goosebumps rising to the surface.

Back upstairs, George bundles up again, dirt shovel beside him, ready to go back outside, and I think of something Dad and I can do to keep our minds off of the gruesome questions I know we're all pondering. We need a distraction. "Before we let May take all of this out of here, let's see if any of this furniture can work in the attic," I say. "Do you have a tape measure?"

Dad grins slightly and nods. "Of course, I do. I'll be right back." He follows George out, heading to his car.

While I wait for Dad, I take in the furniture haphazardly stacked and arranged across the foyer and living room floors. The dollhouse is almost inaccessible, but I look at it sadly. It's probably beyond repair. I haven't heard much from Clara since the day it was destroyed; I can't imagine how she's feeling. Dad returns and sees me looking at it. He puts a hand on my shoulder. "Don't worry, Bug. I think I can fix it."

I smile at him, then lean my head on his shoulder, wrapping my arm around his. "There's no shortage of ways we need you around here, Dad," I say. After a few beats, I pull away from the embrace and gesture to the furniture. "What do you think? Maybe those side tables? Could we measure them and see if they'd work in the attic? We could make extra guestrooms, or just use them as storage. I don't know," I think aloud.

Dad takes some measurements down in an old notepad. I recognize it as the one he's used for clients for the past few years. I wonder idly at all the jobs he's done, the thousands of hours of experience he has. What must it feel like to put that work behind you?

"Do you know the basic measurements of a full-sized bed?" I ask as we ascend the stairs to the attic. "We can map out some possibilities up there," I add.

"You bet. Got it right here," he smacks the notepad on his hand like a stack of bills.

At the top of the steps, I hesitate and then go to the left room first, half expecting the chair to suddenly have returned. I exhale louder than I intended.

Dad laughs. "I'm relieved, too."

Stepping inside, the small, triangular-framed window has a collection of snow on the outer sill, the eaves growing icicles. It's charming. Dad is fiddling with the light switch. "Did we find any lamps down there? I think this is the switch for this plug, here."

I shake my head. "No, but I have one in my Craft room we can test it with." I head downstairs, worrying for a second about Dad up there alone, and then I shake it off and find the lamp. I take a minute at my altar, visualizing a protective shield of energy rising up and around me, fingering the white candle. I haven't cleaned up the ritual I'd attempted, the spell to banish the dark energy. I go over the components of it in my head again and decide that I'll try it again once we've buried the box. Something personal might be needed to strengthen the magic.

I'm still pondering what the spell was missing when I return to the attic with the lamp. Dad is on one knee in the far corner of the room. I plug in the lamp, grateful there are no sparks or issues with the old plug. I flip the light switch. "It works!" I exclaim excitedly as light from the lamp floods the small room more than adequately. I can see now that the walls are ridged in inch-long vertical stripes. "It's actually a very cute room," I say, noticing the charming slant from the ceiling where Dad is kneeling to the highest point by the door. "Maybe servants were up here." I look at the scrapes on the corner of the hardwood. "Or more likely, the dentist's practice." I don't need to remind Dad that this is where we had seen the dentist's chair first. "This would be a great place for guests," I add, breaking my reverie into the past.

Dad shakes his head, "I wouldn't say that, yet. Sadly, only a twin-sized bed would fit without crowding the room. It'd be great storage, and excellent for a kid's room." He catches himself after he says it, looking toward the wall behind him as if it's suddenly interesting. "Or a nice little area for sewing, maybe, if you feel you want to take that up."

I smile at his efforts to cover himself. Not every parent accepts the reality that they won't be getting grandchildren without a fight. "You know, you're right about us being too young to know just yet," I start. "George's getting all nostalgic for his childhood now that we're in a small town."

"There's no rush, Bug. None at all." He stresses the last sentence. "You're not running out of time."

I feel a sob rising in my throat. It's different than what I felt in the basement: this one is for me. For Mom. I nod, afraid to speak.

"You'd be as great as she was, and better," he puts his hand on my shoulder. I lean my head on his.

After some time, I change the subject, wiping the wetness from beneath my eyes. "We could put little Yule trees in the windows of each room next winter," I approach the window for the left room and look out. I can see George has finished the walkway, wide enough for us to carry the furniture out through. The cars are cleaned off, too, and our parking area is almost done. I'm looking for George when I realize he isn't in our yard.

"Can you see George from up here?" I ask Dad as he comes over to stand behind me.

Squinting down, he shakes his head. "No, maybe he's back inside already?" I shrug and turn back to the room. "I guess we could keep the two side tables that match, one in either room, for now. And get a couple of twin-sized beds with trundles. That way, if we do have guests, they can still move around the room after they wake up in the morning," I say.

Dad crosses his arms and nods, impressed. "You've got your mother's eye for design," he says.

"Are you missing mom lately?" I ask him outright. It's been twenty years since she passed, but there's a sadness in his tone I don't need to be an empath to notice.

"Yeah, something like that. She told me, you know. She knew she wouldn't make it after the cancer came back the second time. She told me to remarry, to find someone to be a role model for you, or at least a feminine influence in your life you could trust. And I never did. Never felt like I could without betraying her. But I felt guilty, too, because maybe there was something I couldn't give you that you needed," I move to interrupt, to assure him that wasn't true, but he puts a hand up to stop me. "No, I know. We had a great time together. I loved raising you. I was selfish, I guess. Didn't want to share you." He smiles at me, memory in his eyes. "But you're good here. You're okay. George is great, and I'm happy you kids found each other. You kids and your new house got me thinking about this next step in my own life, is all." He fiddles his hands together, picking at his thumb's cuticle. "Retirement: it's a sentimental time," he laughs again.

"It's a new beginning, not an ending," I say, forcing his eyes to mine again. "You've had an incredible career, a great life. You've been the best parent and friend a girl could ask for. No shotguns aimed at my boyfriends, no awkward period conversations. You have more than earned this next step." Grinning, I add, "And you seem to have your choice of suitors here in Newport, if you're up for it." I nudge his side.

He laughs, a belly laugh, the laugh I've known my whole life. "I think you kids are really exaggerating that one. I guess I'm a flirt – no harm in that, of course, but I suppose there could be more." He lets out another short laugh, looking at his hands, his fingers intertwined. "We'll see, I suppose." He shrugs, then meets my eyes with a smile. "I appreciate the support." He goes back over to the window, patting my shoulder on his way. "I still don't see George," he says.

I walk over and peer out as well. We can see all the way to the lamppost from here and down the street where I'd met Charlie the other night. The right side of our yard is obscured by the chimney that divides the attic into its two rooms. "Maybe we should go check on him."

Back downstairs, I call for George. There's no answer. Shimmying into my coat, I open the front door.

George is there on the porch, sitting on the stairs.

Sitting next to him is Charlie.

CHAPTER THIRTY

"Charlie! How are you? Keeping warm?" I ask, hopefully not betraying my nervous excitement. I'm reminded again of a stray cat I'm grateful to see again.

"Hi, Kendra," Charlie says, turning but not looking at me.

"This is my dad, Philip," I say, gesturing to Dad as he joins us on the patio. Charlie looks past Dad into the house in an almost imperceptible glance. "Would you like to come in for coffee? I'm sure George could use some," I add, putting a hand on George's shoulder.

Charlie nods and enters last, taking a moment in the door frame before stepping through. His energy changes as he enters. I can feel him relax, but his shoulders don't come down from his ears, as if he's trying to hide how relieved he feels to be inside. The energy of the house changes too. It feels like a deep breath is being released. I see a silver sparkle, dancing a bit quicker than usual out of the study and past Charlie, playfully, behind his back. His eyes take in the furniture. "That's stuff from the basement," he asserts, not asking. Of course, he recognizes it. "We kept these things in the attic then moved them all down after we refinished the basement," he continues.

"Good thing it was safe up there," George says. "Or the flooding would have ruined it all."

Charlie nods. We all wait for him to say more, but when he doesn't, George puts in, "Did the rain bother you all much after the renovation? We don't know what to expect, being this close to the river."

Charlie shakes his head. "No, not really. It's a strong house," he says. I wonder if he's actually thinking about the house itself when he says it.

"I have some bad news though," I say, walking Charlie over to the living room. "The dollhouse was damaged the other night."

Charlie's face falls. "Oh, geez, that's awful. It's original to the house. The Baker family left it for my grandparents when they bought it."

"It was a sad accident," I say, watching Charlie's face. "We've had a fair amount of activity since we moved in."

He shoves his hands in his pockets and looks at the dollhouse with fresh eyes. "Clara loved that house," he says, in a reverie.

"We don't think it was Clara: we brought it up for her, actually." I explain.

"Kendra, please, don't bother him with this." Dad blusters, red in the face. Embarrassed, like I'm airing the family drama.

I ignore him, still looking at Charlie. His face grows red, too.

"Mr. Hill? Would you help me with coffee in the kitchen?" George cuts in through the silence.

I wait, turning to George and then looking at Dad. For a second I don't think he'll go, but then he does. I send silent thanks his way. I sidle through the furniture and sit on the chair across from the couch, holding my arm out toward the couch, indicating for Charlie to sit.

He does and takes his hands out of his pockets. Though balled into nervous fists, he places his hands on his lap, and surprising me, meets my eyes. Then he says the last thing I expected to hear. "It was the gray-eyed one, wasn't it?"

I stare back at him, goosebumps spreading across my shoulders and down my arms. I nod. "Did you ever learn anything about him? Who he was?"

Charlie's eyes unfocus, remembering. "Clara told me. It was her brother, Jasper." He whispers the name, afraid to invoke him here. "He was always messing with my toys. He was jealous, mean."

I almost smile, catching myself just in time. "I have good news for you, then. Well, closure, anyway. You're right. It's Jasper Baker. Clara and J–" I stop, seeing the way his face whitened when I said his name. "Clara and her brother lived here with their parents. Their father was a dentist. We're quite sure of that. We found an old box of his."

Charlie looks at me, eyes widening. "Where?"

"In the guestroom bathroom. At the back, behind a curtain that was there in place of a wall. There's a little cubby hole type of space in the drywall." I explain as thoroughly as I can, feeling the pressure of his gaze.

Charlie's brow furrows. His mouth tightens, his wrinkling lips turning white as he thinks, hard, back to old memories. "Was it dusty, rusted old leather? Brown?"

"Yes," I nod. "It seemed like it had never been opened."

"I think I found that once as a kid. I put it right back, though. Never opened it." He looks thoughtfully at the coffee table. "Forgot about that. What's in it? You open it?" he asks.

"Yes, we found dentist's tools. We were able to find similar kits online, for sale on antiques websites. They are very old, generations old. Jas–" I flinch with Charlie as he reacts to me saying his name – "Clara's brother would've been the third generation of Bakers to use them. They were made in Boston by John Baker senior's mentor, William... Jasper." I whisper the craftsman's last name and look around, half expecting the gray eyes to stare at me in the window like they had when I found the dollhouse destroyed.

I look at Charlie, expecting another question, but when none comes, I continue. "We found something else."

I explain to Charlie about the cemetery, and I find myself telling him the plan to bury the box before I can consider if it's a good idea or not. "I hope you don't mind. I know it's old, and we should maybe even look for a museum but, Charlie, that box." I don't know how to describe the feeling I had, but seeing Charlie's face, I can see he understands.

He nods. "I would, too. I know my grandma said nothing leaves the house, but I think that's worth a try to get rid of him. Free Clara." I notice his hands are relaxing, just resting on his lap. I feel his curiosity is as strong as mine, stronger even than George's. I realize then what the difference is: he cares about Clara, too. Probably more than I do, given their past together.

"Can I ask you about that?" I pose, leaning toward the table. "Why can't anything leave the house?"

Charlie shrugs. "Dad never said, just told me it can't. My grandma... she died in this house, too. When the flood of '72 came through. She said not to, so he said not to, and so, I didn't want to either."

He pauses, looking at his hands. "I was supposed to own the house myself, you know, but the bank, the property values now, the credit scores... I don't rightly understand how I can't live in my own house." He stops then, his face reddening. I smile at him, encourage him. He continues, "But I need the change. I've got my own place now. Small. Ghost-free." He laughs hollowly. "I'm glad you nice folks moved in, instead of that stuffy couple who – well, I won't gossip. I'm just glad Clara likes you." He stops short, his hands coming together in his lap as tight fists.

"Charlie, what is it?"

He looks to his right. I follow his gaze. Silver starlight is glittering on the couch, right next to him. Suddenly he nods, standing.

"Charlie, is everything okay?"

He doesn't answer but walks over to the dollhouse. He looks out the window and then turns back to me. The afternoon light reflects off the snow, brightening his face. He's much younger than I had first thought, no more than mid-40s. "Clara said he did it," he says to me. "He's getting stronger."

I swallow. "I feel it, too. Charlie, I promise I'll do everything I can for her. To get rid of him."

"It's not fair. Over one hundred years she's been tortured by him in this house. How much longer?" He makes a fist, looking down at the floor.

"Is there anyone else here? Did your grandma stick around?" I want to know who that brown-haired woman is. "Or Clara's mom?"

Charlie hesitates, looking over the dollhouse sadly. "I don't think so. Grandma, she loved this house. Never wanted to leave it. But I never felt her. Clara was the only one I got to know." I look at him questioningly. "I didn't see anyone else either. Just the gray-eyed man."

"No one with dark hair?"

He shakes his head. "Just Clara."

There's so much more I want to ask him. The gardenias, the garden by the tracks, the attic, the chair. The walled-off room. I can see he's antsy. "Would you like to see the rest of the house?" I offer. "I know it's been a while. You can see we're keeping it in good order."

He hesitates, then shakes his head. "I'd love to, but I shouldn't. It's just old memories now."

I stand and approach him at the window. I see Clara glittering in the sunlight, hovering by her dollhouse. I smile, glad to see her again, if only for a few seconds. "Charlie," I say. "I have to be honest with you. We are getting rid of some furniture."

Panic flashes in his eyes. His lips whiten as they come together over his teeth. I watch, ready to call for Dad and George. Then his face softens, his eyes turn thoughtful. He nods once, not curtly, but decisively. "It might be best. We did what Grandma asked, and it never fixed or changed anything. Maybe this is the right choice."

I change the subject to something hopefully more uplifting. "You won't believe who's coming to purchase it. Ms. Wilkins, the art teacher."

His face clouds in memory. I swallow, feeling guilty for bringing up high school. It must have been a difficult time. But then his face clears, like the false start of a midwinter storm. "I always liked her class," he says after some time.

I grin. "She's coming today, if you want to stick around," I try, but he's already shaking his head. His hands are back in his pockets. He turns his face away from the window, walking toward the foyer.

"I'd better get back," he says.

"What about coffee? It's nearly ready, I'm sure." More like *I'm sure it's been ready for a quarter of an hour, but Dad and George are listening at either side of the kitchen's entryway.*

He shakes his head again, not meeting my eyes. "I really appreciate this, Kendra. I really do. It's been..."

I hope he'll say more, but I feel that he already has. It's been *hard*.

"I hope you'll come back for that coffee another time," I say as he puts his hand to the doorknob. "I owe you a cup."

Just as he's about to pull it open, he notices the gaping hole where the mirror had been. "What happened here?"

"You-know-who, when we opened the butcher's box. The dentist's kit," I clarify. "Sorry for the morbidity, but Mr. Levy said that's what they're called."

Charlie swallows, then dares to peek inside. "She told me about this hiding space, I always wondered if it was here." I know he means Clara.

"Charlie, did you ever have any dreams?" We're both standing in the atrium, looking over the wall at the little hiding space. "Dreams from back in her time?"

He turns to me, and I realize this is the closest he's ever been to me. I can smell the winter musk of sweat-beneath-cold on his cracked leather jacket mixed with the scent of men's shampoo.

He nods, rubbing a hand on his jaw, just like I did when I woke the other night. "Yes." He pauses before meeting my eyes with the sad, helpless look. The look I saw in Clara's eyes. "Clara has always been scared."

And with that, he turns and leaves the house.

CHAPTER THIRTY-ONE

Dad and George heard everything. After Charlie left, we gathered in the kitchen to take stock over some coffee, as usual. A cup of hot coffee in hand makes any conversation more palatable. Dad starts us off. "He's as weird as I thought he was." He sips his coffee looking at the center of the table.

"Come on, Dad. He's no weirder than I am. Besides, he's validating what we all know to be true, and that's a relief to me. It was good to talk to someone else who knows what's been going on." I look to George for help on this, but he's pensive, silent.

Dad continues sipping his coffee. "I especially dislike that you told him of our plans with the furniture and the dentist's tools. What if he tries to interfere with the sale today? Or he goes and digs up that box?"

I shake my head, frustrated, putting my mug down. "Dad, I don't understand where you're coming from with this. He is a good man with a history in this house. He only wants what's best for it. He's not malicious. He's not going to take the dentist's box. After all that he knows about this house, he's the last one we need to worry about."

"He's a desperate man. Desperate men do desperate, unthinking things," Dad retorts.

"Nothing we can do about it now," George cuts in. "I'm not going to worry about what might happen. Besides, I'm hungry. Let's get something to eat before May gets here. I make a mean grilled cheese," he adds with an eyebrow wiggle at me and Dad.

"Okay, that sounds good," I give George an appreciative smile. "You start on those. I'm going to go check on some things upstairs."

At the top of the stairs, I'm greeted by Shadow. She runs through my legs, following me to my Craft room. I leave the door open in case Sherry wants to join us. Taking a seat at my altar, I close my eyes and do some deep breathing to ground and center myself. I raise a cone of protection around me from the ground upward. When I picture the ground I want to connect to, the gardenia bush pops into my mind's eye – powder covering its brittle, brown limbs, the garden obscured by snow. I roll with it, picturing the space of the woods there, as if instead of cross-legged and warm in my new house, I'm there on the silent, crisp snow, feeling the chill of the unmoving winter air. I move the cone of energy up and around my body, and then bringing it to a point over my crown, I imagine a brilliant white light enveloping me.

As I exhale and open my eyes, I light some incense: a grounding, yet stimulating stick of rosemary. I sit there in lotus pose for a few minutes, not sure what to ask or do. I keep finding my eyes drawn to the white and black candles. Something wasn't quite right last time, something wasn't powerful enough. I felt the magic. I felt my own power working. But the banishment wasn't effective. The black candle wouldn't light.

Something was missing.

I open my drawer and see the bottle of ashes from the sage bundle. I never made my black salt. I take out the bottle, place it on my altar, and reach to the back of the drawer for sea salt. I place them both on the altar and light the white candle again. "Protect the people of this home, George Levy, Philip Hill, Kendra Hill, Clara Baker, and Charlie Harr," I intone, just as before. I pour the salt over the ash in the bottle, then put the lid on it and begin swirling it in a clockwise motion. "I invoke protection and security on our space." When the ash has settled, gray powder coating the glass in a dusty film, I add more salt. I shake and swirl the jar clockwise again. "I invoke the cleansing and purification of salt. May this black salt protect our home and the five souls within it from the negative energies and black soul of Jasper Baker." As I say his name, I feel a charge of resistance beneath me.

A knock at my Craft door makes me jump.

I turn.

Dad is standing in the doorway, his mouth slightly agape as he tries to make sense of what he's seeing.

"Hi, Dad," I don't know what else to say. I feel embarrassed and angry at myself for feeling embarrassed. This is my path, my beliefs. I shouldn't feel embarrassed about that. I force my back to straighten as I turn to him. "Want to come in?"

He nods, and then takes a step inside, not coming all the way toward me. "What are you doing?" He asks, like he's not sure if he's allowed to.

"Meditating, in a way," I say. "I'm just doing a little magic. Drawing a protective shield around all of us, blessing this black salt to protect the home."

He laughs, and when I don't, he asks again. "What?"

"I didn't know how to say it, and then so many years went by and I just, I didn't want you to be disappointed in me. I'm a witch." I spit it out. It's done. I feel like I ripped a bandage from my chest, the tender skin over my heart searing. The sting vibrates through my body as I wait for it to numb, or for the pain to get worse, knowing Dad's next words will determine that.

After interminable seconds he answers, "I didn't know people could be witches," he says with some trepidation. "Is it a religion or something?" We never had much religion in our lives, so I'm not sure if he's upset or just confused.

"I guess you could say that. It's my beliefs, 'my path'; that's how I usually describe it. It's a nature-based religion, of sorts," and then before he can ask the typical question I've come to expect, I shoot it down. "And no, we don't worship nature in the way Christians see Jesus or God as omnipotent. It's about respecting and living in harmony with nature and the energy that we believe is tangible everywhere on this planet, in people, trees, weather, objects. It's called animism, believing everything has a spirit."

When Dad doesn't scream or cry, I continue. "If you have other questions, I'd love to talk about it. George doesn't subscribe to it, but he's cool with it. It's not harmful or anything, and, truth be told, it helps me deal with crises like ghosts a lot more responsibly." I push out a short chuckle, the best I can do with the nervous energy cramping my stomach.

"I don't fully get it, but if that's what gives you the courage to deal with these ghosts the way you have, I can certainly respect that. Your mother, she liked ghosts as a novelty. You understand them." He's not smiling, but he's not angry. I can live with that.

"I was so scared to tell you. I thought you'd be disappointed or have some other idea of what I should believe. I'm always afraid people will think I'm ignorant or just looking for attention or something. But it's personal. It keeps me grounded, calm. I feel more like myself when I'm regularly practicing. It's not just about protection from spirits. It is the most empow-ering thing I've ever done." I pause, swallow, and look at Dad again, trying to read his eyes. He's still thinking; not judging but thinking. "This is my altar. My ritual space." I gesture to the table in front of me. I put the bottle down, watching the white candle burn. "Do you want to sit?"

Dad takes it in, looking at the candle, his hands in his pockets. "Smells nice, anyway," he remarks. Taking his hands out of his pockets, he kneels down.

I force a smile, faking calm. "That it does. We joke some-times that witches are just obsessed with candles and incense and need an excuse to light them all the time." I take a deep breath, summoning courage as much as the Goddess in this moment. "I guess I was afraid of what you'd think. I couldn't risk pushing you away." I don't look at him, but I feel his eyes on me.

"Bug." He pauses, and when I find the courage to meet his eyes, he continues. "Kendra. Nothing you could do could push us apart. I'm glad you found something to... what's that word you used? 'Ground' you." he smiles sadly. "You might not remember it this way, but carpentry became an art for me only after losing your mom. Connecting to the wood, the craft of creating something beautiful and personal out of something so natural and rugged... it gave me solace, a purpose. It showed me that there was some beauty left in this world." His smile bright-ens. "But you are the beauty in my world. Always will be."

I smile broadly, my nerves forgotten. I lean over and hug him awkwardly from our positions on the floor.

When we pull apart, Dad seems to really take in the altar space. He gestures toward the burning candle. "So, you're just sitting here meditating? Like Buddhism?"

"You could say that. We meditate a lot," I laugh again, feeling more relieved that he's asking questions. "And use a lot of herbs, incense, and candles. We celebrate the full moon, the harvests, the changing seasons. It's all about the earth," I say. "I guess that's why it keeps me so *grounded*," I exaggerate, enunciating the pun.

That garners a chuckle.

I stand, lick my fingers, and pinch out the incense. I snuff out the candle, whispering a hushed, 'so mote it be' as I usually do. Dad makes no indication that he's listening, just watching. I pick up the bottle, taking it with me. I should've done this a week ago – making the black salt, but also telling Dad about this elemental part of who I am. "Let's get some grilled cheese," I say as I start toward Dad.

He nods, and we're about to head downstairs when I snap my fingers, remembering. "Hold on, I'll be right back." I run back into my Craft room and grab my pendulum from the top of my altar. Putting it in my pocket, Dad looks at me questioningly. "For good luck," I explain. He asks no further questions.

AFTER GRILLED CHEESE, I do the dishes while Dad and George take the side tables up to the attic. When they come back down, we go over all of the furniture again, making sure we're ready for May. "Should we keep the big, flat table for the dollhouse?" I ask as we sit on the living room couch, Dad in the chair across from George and me.

George is noticeably tired, not nearly the chatty self he usually is. Shoveling, lifting, cooking. Homeownership will kill him. He shrugs, his arms out on either side of the top of the couch as he leans into it, his head back. "I guess so. But let's do it tomorrow. I'm exhausted, and I'll be helping May in –" he checks his watch – "less than two hours."

"I'm with him. Let's watch some TV."

I sigh and from the side table, take up the remote, passing it to George, and pick up my laptop. "You boys enjoy that. I'm going to my study," I say in a mock British accent.

"Enjoy yourself, dahling," Dad says, in his best British as well.

AFTER STOPPING to make myself a cup of tea, the waning, yet still steady afternoon sun is at my back as I settle in. I'm seated at the desk, ready to write. It's been a strange January so far, to say the least. I've missed hours of opportunity to write. I read over my changes to chapter one. Catherine's journey is feeling grounded now, coming from a place of real experiences. My conversation with Dad loosed something in me. I keep going through the chapters, editing dialogue, giving her some personality.

After a couple of chapters, I'm feeling light. This is working. Finishing my now-cold tea, my investigation notebook catches my eye. Reading my research notes – most of it useless information on Newport's developments and changes through the 1800s – I find myself rereading the encounters we've had. The sparkle: who I now know as Clara, seen that first day we toured the house with Lynn. *Lynn* – I've just reminded myself: I need to call on her tomorrow and ask about those missing letters.

I go through our other encounters, expanding our list. The apparitions in the apartment kitchen window before we moved; the basement noises when we toured with Lynn the second time; the corn maze; the chilling sight of George seemingly possessed at Jasper's grave.

I look at the jar of teeth and then under the desk for Clara. No sign of her. I sit back, looking at the bookshelves. I stare at my own boxes, still piled in the corner. I can't face that today, so I get back to my writing.

Another hour goes by. It's working. It feels like a real book. Chapters revised, I'm almost catching up to where I left off – Catherine is gaining confidence in the weeks leading up to her first Fashion Week.

May should be here in the next twenty minutes. The sun is nearly set, the gray of twilight heavy behind me on Fickes Lane. The streetlight hasn't come on yet, and the lane is dim.

Standing up and looking out the window, I see the snow plowed into drifts along the side of the road. The drifts are still white, not gray, nor slushed by constant traffic as we saw last winter in the city. I imagine only a few cars have driven past since the snow fell. I look out at the thin strip of yard just before the bay window. It's so pure, no steps or movement, not even a raccoon has passed through our snow there yet.

Feeling the cold of the glass as I lean on the window, I look out to the right at the yard. It's well shoveled by George, May will have no trouble walking up, and her parking spot is dug out. To the left of the yard, I peek into the dark of the trees, seeing no light, only the dark outline of the spindly forest on a black canvas. I notice the snow is banked up close to the house, and I wonder idly if the little window in the basement has any light coming through it. I try to find where it is, looking around. Then I get the idea to look below, under the bay window.

I can't see the edge of the house, but kneeling on the bench, my head pressed to the glass, I can see an indent in the snow. A strong divot made by what must be human hands is clearly visible. It looks like someone tried to pull snow into the basement.

Or tried to pull themselves up out of it.

CHAPTER THIRTY-TWO

I don't want to worry George and Dad, so I join them silently in the living room. My first instinct is to head outside, spread the black salt, and be done. But I can't – even talking to Dad, I'm not ready to let the whole neighborhood and May know I'm a witch. I'll have to do it in the cover of dark. They're watching a game show light and cheerful enough to take my mind off of the basement. I know no one is down there. Both cats are upstairs. And we'll be down there sooner than I want to be once May gets here.

Twenty minutes or so pass, and the next game show is about to start when Dad's phone rings.

"Ms. May! All right then, May, you got it. Drive safe, then." He hangs up and looks at me and George. "She's on her way. Fifteen minutes tops, she says."

When May arrives, the whole energy of the house shifts from lazy and sleepy to upbeat and energized. Her joy is infectious. I'm glad she's here.

"Hello, hello!" She says, stamping her boots on the porch before stepping inside and taking them off. "I see you've made my job easier; I thank you kindly," she says, regarding the furniture we've brought up from the basement. She smiles at each of us, lingering on Dad. "I hope you're enjoying the first snow in your new home. It's good luck, you know." She taps one side of her nose with her finger, reminding me of Cinderella's fairy godmother.

Dad smiles a bit goofily. "It's very exciting to have you here. I mean, for all of us," he adds that last part in a rush, looking at me and blushing briefly. I give him a smirk.

"We can show you what's in the basement, but if you'd like, we can start loading up your truck with these smaller items first," George offers.

"Let me take stock and see what we'll be taking." She walks around the room, a small clipboard materializing from her massive purse. She writes things here and there, humming and nodding to herself. After some time, she turns back to us, holding her clipboard at her side. "I'll take it all! Let's see what you have downstairs. We might be able to take some more than this today."

Back in the basement, we're careful to start with the wide, main expanse. I'm eager to avoid any conversation about the small room behind the bookshelves. Thankfully, she agrees to take the chair, the piano, and the other tables and storage pieces. She shakes her head at the metal shelf but is intrigued by the coffin. "A true oddity, to be sure. I think the novelty of it will attract some strange tourist," she remarks.

"I told you!" George says, looking chuffed about his newfound eye for antiquing. His parents would be proud.

"Anything else lying around here? An operating table, a dentist's chair, and a piano, and we're not even halfway through!"

My ears perk up. "What did you say? An operating table?"

May nods eagerly. "Oh yes. In the Civil War, these would

have been used on battlefields." She puts her hand on the wooden table we had envisioned for the dollhouse. "If you look underneath, there are removable legs. They slide out of the joists and can be reassembled fairly quickly. It was ingenious in its time. Almost as much as ether, though no one wanted to use that for another forty years. A real shame for those boys in that war," she adds.

I feel a draft of cool air around my ankles and look down and around me for a sparkle to glide by. When none come, I look back at May and force a tight-lipped smile. "Do you think dentists of the 1800s would have, well, just gone in cold? No anesthetic?"

May nods, her mouth in a grimace. "Not until the late 1880s at the earliest, and in country places like this, it's very likely they didn't use anything beyond a leather strap to hold the patients down." She goes over to the chair and puts her hand on its arm. My heart stops, half expecting her hand to go right through it, but it holds, solid. I feel a chill again at my ankles and down my back. "No straps on this one, oddly. It's a strange old chair. So rare to find one from this period, before the 1910s. This is a great find." She marks it on her clipboard, not taking her eyes off of it. "It's unsettling, don't you think?" she looks to us, the three of us forming a crescent at the bottom of the stairs.

We all nod, not saying a word.

You have no idea, May.

Despite the unknowns of the room behind the shelves, I'm feeling a weight off my shoulders. I look to George and see he's really perked up, too, and Dad is grinning like the winning contestant on that game show from earlier. While May is going over her checklist, I lean into George. "This is great, right? She's taking everything so far, pretty much. And the shelves and the couple of dinged-up tables she's not, we'll find use for."

He nods, kissing me on the head. "It's a big relief."

"Anything else you folks want me to check on? This is a great selection; I'm still floored so much of this is here. From so many periods, so many different families."

"What do you mean? I thought it was all late 1800s," Dad puts in. He's usually good with this kind of thing, dating wood furniture and construction styles.

"Oh no," May says, shaking her head slowly. "There are a few small tables from the 1920s, art deco. And a couple of pieces from the Civil War and possibly antebellum – the table I showed you and that baby's changing table seem even older. It's quite the family collection."

"Huh," I say, crossing my arms, thoughtful. Clara and Jasper could have been babies on that table. And Grandma Harr must have bought that newer furniture themselves. It's a relief to know the old biddy was really just a minor hoarder, telling her kids not to get rid of furniture. "Did you investigate the lamps and such I'd given you before? Any crystal?"

May gives a sly smile at that. "I can't lie to you, Kendra. There were two crystal bowls in that collection. And the oil lamp, one was hand painted. Excellent find. But they weren't as old as we thought, most of them. Some even had factory marks, from the '40s."

It's my turn to shake my head slowly. "It's a real museum of the house, then. Only two families before the last owners, you know," I tell her. I'm suddenly conscious that we're only a few feet away from turning the corner and her seeing the hole behind the bookshelves. I shift my weight on my feet.

May notices. "Something wrong, hon?"

I tighten my arms around me. "I can't lie to you, May," I say, echoing her. "We've got one more thing to show you."

She follows me around the corner and takes in the book-shelves first. "Well, I'll be," she says, a bit breathless. "These must be custom made, late Victorian for sure," she starts, and then she sees the hole in the wall. "What in...?" The question hangs in the air for a minute before Dad catches it.

"I'm not sure. We broke through it by accident when we tried to shift the shelves. Heavy, sturdy things, you can tell your buyers that. But it seems to be another storage area, walled off, maybe by accident. Nothing in there, though," he adds quickly. He tries to steer her back upstairs, but May is immovable, looking through the hole.

"It was made when the rest of the basement was finished, back in the '70s I think," Dad continues. "Anyway, should we take the bookshelves up? What do you think? Can you fit it in your truck?"

May doesn't answer. She's looking through the gash in the drywall. From behind her I can only see a ragged outline of the space, the broken drywall irregular enough that I can't see the floor, just a hint of cinder block wall. "What is it, May?" I ask her, concerned at her silence.

"Nothing, I think. I'm just trying to remember, is all," she says cryptically.

"Remember what?" I press. George is behind me now, and Dad to her right. I'm behind her on her left, close enough to hear her breathing.

She takes a deep breath. "Something Charlie had drawn back in grade school," she finally gets out. "It was so strange, even then. He would draw it again and again. I think it was this room. But it was different, the floor was red."

"Red? Like soil? If you go to the back it's covered in dirt, so maybe –"

"No, no," she cuts me off. "There was a red pool, like a bloodstain. Why do you think I remember it so well? And he said it was real. The first assignment he drew was... well what was the assignment, now?" she puts a finger to her lips, thinking. She doesn't take her eyes off of the room or turn to meet mine. She shuts them, her lips turning white as she purses them in thought.

"That's right," she says. "The assignment was, 'paint a place you've seen in your dreams.'" And then she pales and turns to look at Dad. "But like Charlie had said, this is real."

WE GET May upstairs and sit her at the kitchen table with a cup of tea. I make it myself, invoking calm with chamomile and some lavender I dried myself from a festival a year ago and stir in some honey, clockwise, adding sweetness to the tea and her mood. "This is a weird house, Ms. Wilkins. I hope it didn't frighten you," I say, passing her the tea.

She takes it gratefully, inhaling the scent with her eyes closed. When she opens them, she looks tired but not scared anymore. "No, no. Antiquing always comes with strangeness. No wonder poor Charlie was a quiet kid," she muses.

"He was here today," I decide to tell her. "He's doing okay, quiet as ever though. But he had a nice visit." I pause before adding, "I think he misses the house."

"Oh really, now? It's good that he stopped by. I'm glad. He needs friends. His parents have been gone for at least five years now. He's been adrift much longer, though." She takes a sip of her tea, and I see its effect instantly. "I wonder why he didn't stay in the house."

"He said he can't," I say sadly. "He was welcoming and kind to us, though, and I'm grateful for that."

Ms. Wilkins nods, sipping her tea. George and Dad are awfully quiet, so I sit back and look to them to continue the conversation. The tiredness is back in George's eyes, and Dad is a million miles away in thought.

After a few beats, George flutters to life, putting his hands on the table and leaning forward. "Would you like Mr. Hill and I to start loading the truck while you enjoy your tea?"

Dad nods and finds one of his winning customer service smiles. "It'd be our pleasure, May. You enjoy yourself in the warm kitchen."

She smiles warmly, Charlie and the room forgotten. She passes him the keys. "Make the most of the space – I think we can fit it all in there," she says. Dad takes the keys and gives her a wink. She blushes, looking down at her mug demurely. The old flirt's still got it.

"My mother's been gone nearly twenty years," I say when the front door closes behind Dad and George with the first load of tables. "He's grateful to be out of Philly and in the quiet of Newport. He hasn't moved in, but I think he might; or get a place of his own, here, closer to us. I'm an only child," I add, hoping I'm not rambling.

May grins, a bit wistfully. "He's a real character, a gentleman. I lost my husband in '08, a little over a decade now." The 'I'm single' conversation is very different over sixty, I realize.

Dad and George come back in, taking two more pieces with them as they leave again. I feel guilty for not helping, but I'll give George a massage tonight. At least Dad didn't have to help with the shoveling. I keep forgetting he's getting older.

"So," I say, as the door clicks shut again, "do you think the pieces will sell?"

May shrugs, a small smile on her face. "I know they will," she says. "There's a customer for every period, and the Civil War and art deco pieces will fly in the summer when the New Englanders come down." I smile, thinking of George's parents. I'm sad they won't get first dibs on anything, but their house is a museum as it is. It's a blessing in disguise. "My Victoriana obsession is personal, so if those others don't sell, I'm a woman with a sickness who won't mind keeping a few pieces for myself." She raises her eyebrows over her mug, enjoying her tea.

Dad and George return, grabbing the last of the pieces from the foyer. As May finishes her tea, I stand, taking her mug to the sink, then open the cupboard to place the teabag in the trash.

Clara is sitting in the corner, her arms wrapped around her knees.

She puts a finger to her lips. *Shhh.* I hear it, like wind through an old window.

Turning to May, I'm relieved to see that she didn't seem to hear. I sigh inwardly, flash Clara a small smile, and close the cupboard door.

I'm grateful when I hear Dad's booming voice, "There's plenty of room. We'll get the shelves next and then put the old surgeon's table on top."

"It'll be a game of Tetris, but we should be able to take everything but the piano," George says, smiling. "That truck's about as big as our moving van was."

"Will you need any help with it once you get it to your stall?" Dad asks.

May inclines her head in an old-fashioned gesture of thanks. "No, sir, but thank you. Ray and the guys will be around. I'll wait until tomorrow to unload. Friday's the unloading day for most in anticipation of the weekend antiquers."

Thinking back on my impression of him, I almost laugh at the idea of Ray lifting anything, but I'm sure the others will be useful.

As we stand and head to the basement, George reaches for the door. He lurches forward as he tugs the handle. It doesn't budge. "Kendra, did you lock the door when we came up earlier?" he asks.

I shake my head. "I don't even have a key."

Dad moves forward and tries the door himself. Inspecting the gardenia doorknob, he straightens and backs away. "Huh," he says, rubbing his chin.

"What is it?" I ask, a familiar blanket of dread creeping over my shoulders.

"There's not even a keyhole."

CHAPTER THIRTY-THREE

"Let me try," George says. He pulls at the door, jimmying the handle in its socket, twisting then pulling; twisting, pulling, then twisting again; lifting it up and down as he twists. "It's not working."

"It's never stuck before." My eyes stray to the kitchen where Clara is. "Let me go get a butter knife," I add, giving an excuse to go ask her.

I open the cupboard again, and Clara is gone, no hint nor glint of her in sight.

I grab the butter knife and return, passing it to George.

"Someone doesn't want us taking their things," I say loudly.

May, to my great surprise, chuckles. "Houses have their own ideas about who owns what, that's for sure."

George is having no luck with the butterknife, and his movements are getting sharper as he grows frustrated. "Here," I say, putting my hand out. "I'll take over."

I put my hand on the doorknob, cursing myself for not using the black salt before May got here. This will be even more embarrassing. I lean my head against the door, putting my whole weight against it. I push it in, and I swear it feels like another hand is on the doorknob from the other side. Leaning the weight of my body to the door, it feels like another body is doing the same at the top of the stairs. Ignoring the goosebumps on my arms, I keep pushing, focusing on the energy there. I whisper through the door's crack: "Clara, is that you?" A cold breeze through the door answers me. Not as definitive as I'd hoped.

I try something else.

"Jasper?"

The door smacks against me, and I fall backward into George. "Jasper, open up!" I say. "What are you afraid of?" I probably shouldn't be taunting him, but I'm tired, George is tired, and this is getting ridiculous.

"Attached to a table? A couple of bookshelves?" There's no answer, no rattle.

"A piano?" I swear I hear laughter coming from the depths of the basement's corners.

"You don't want to lose your chair, is that it?" The laughter stops.

May is sweating, despite the cool of the foyer from the door opening and closing. I get the feeling this is more than the usual strangeness of antiquing she was talking about. I'll have to explain later.

I turn to Dad. He's looking at me, bewildered. George looks on wearily. "I have an idea," I say to them. I turn back to the door. "Fine," I call to Jasper. "We'll just take the shelves and the table. Deal?"

There's no answer. I try the door again. It opens. I turn and smile at them. May gives me a weary smile in return. Dad and George just gape, but they follow me down the stairs. I notice George brandishing his flashlight like a nightstick. Whatever helps him feel better.

Jasper had the decency to at least leave the lights on, and we shuffle upstairs with the table. I grab the piano bench, then think better of it. We could use the piano in the living room if the dollhouse can't be fixed. Clara might like that.

I look at the chair for a split second, and I see him.

Jasper is sitting there, legs crossed, hands tented, his elbows on the armrests. He gives me a wink, and I feel like I need a shower.

I hurry up after the boys, accompanying them down three more times for the bookshelves while May waits in the living room. I didn't have to invite her to sit.

We all sit in the tidy living room, clear of any unnecessary furniture, though the broken dollhouse feels more ominous than ever.

"May, I'm sorry you had to deal with all this today," Dad apologizes, leaning over the coffee table to look her in her eyes. "It's been a wild ride in this house." May gives him that tired smile again, and then as he smiles back, hers opens up a bit. "Maybe we could treat you to dinner tonight? Bitting's?"

She grins like a schoolgirl. "I'd love that."

Pulling on our coats, we decide to drive separately so May can go straight home from dinner. Dad goes on ahead to help her back out, and George warms up the car. Before locking up, I grab the bottle of black salt from the kitchen. I'm not going back into that house until this is done.

BITTING'S IS QUIET. I'm glad it's open in spite of the snow. Wanda greets us – no need for a host tonight – and she seats us at the same table as last time. "Ms. May, good to see you in town," Wanda says. I smile at that. Small town indeed.

"Wanda, yes, yes, always good to pop over here. I haven't checked in on the Goodwill in a while, else I would've stopped in," May smiles. "I'll take a warm coffee if you have it. I know it's late, but I need a jolt," she says, squeezing her hands into fists at 'jolt,' her energy coming back. I'm glad Jasper didn't scare her too much.

"You got it. Anyone else? Looks like you need a pick me up, honey," Wanda taps her ordering pad at George.

He blinks, and then gives her a smile. "Sure, thanks Wanda," he says.

"Me too," I say, and Dad nods as well.

"Can't hurt. We've had a long day," Dad says.

"What's Ms. May had you up to, then?" Wanda asks, hands on her hips expectantly.

May looks at me, and I give a short permissive nod. "Picking up some antiques they got when they bought their new home," she says. I'm glad she doesn't add more. For all of her charisma, she's blessedly not an oversharer.

"If I know Ms. May, she'll be keeping it for her home collection," Wanda smirks.

May laughs. "Wanda, I haven't been your babysitter for at least twenty years. 'May' will do just fine." Then she adds to us, "I used to live next door to Wanda. She'd come by after school while her mom was working. She used to call my house 'the museum.'" She grins at Wanda.

Wanda's eyes twinkle in nostalgia. "It was a great place to do my history homework," she gives a chuckle. "Do we need any menus here?"

George shakes his head. "I'll have the burger," he says confidently.

"Me, too," Dad and I say at the same time.

"Don't leave me out," May says.

When Wanda leaves, May watches her go, looking around the narrow restaurant. "I'm surprised Charlie isn't here tonight," she says. "I was hoping we might run into him."

After our burgers come, small talk and Newport tidbits tiding us between bites, we rise to settle up at the counter. May doesn't ask more questions, I don't offer more explanation. Partly from exhaustion, partly for privacy. I'm beginning to think George was right about being careful in a small town. "Thank you again, Philip, for a lovely dinner."

"Thank you," Dad says, shaking her hand and placing his other on her shoulder. "You've been a great sport today. It's a weird house as Kendra says. And the kids couldn't be happier to have those pieces off their hands."

"It's my pleasure," May says. I notice she's lingering in Dad's handshake. "I'm grateful to have some new inventory ahead of the summer rush."

Dad helps her back out of her spot again and waves her off. Back in the car, I put my hands on the two front seats, leaning forward toward Dad. "Sweet. On. You," I say, punching each word.

He doesn't blush this time. "I'll come by again and see if I can take her out to lunch if you kids don't mind." He's beaming.

WHEN WE ARRIVE HOME, I hang behind, holding my bottle of black salt. "I'll be inside in a few. I'm just going to lay a protective ring of black salt around the house. Keep anything nasty from coming in and banish any negative energy from inside."

"I'll stay away from any windows," Dad jokes, making me smile. George unlocks the door for Dad and then comes back out to join me.

"I hope you don't mind, but I'll keep an eye out here with you. It's darker than dark here," he says as he kisses me on the head.

"I don't mind at all," I say, turning my head up to his, kissing his lips. "You were a star today. A champion. Cooking, lifting, shoveling. I'm so grateful for you." I kiss him again, longer.

"I'm relieved she took so much," he says, rubbing my shoulders for warmth. "Now let's shield this house and get to bed." He steps back and gestures to the jar.

"'Shield,' yes! You're learning yet," I smirk and open the jar, getting to work.

I sprinkle the black salt out of the bottle, the thinnest trail I can manage to make sure I cover the whole perimeter. When we get to the back of the house by the railroad tracks, I'm glad George is with me. I see the clawed snow under the bay window again. George sees me staring and follows my eyes. "Yikes, what the hell?" he exclaims, not approaching it. "Raccoons?"

I shrug. "I saw it from the study. The cats are both upstairs. There are no footprints coming from it. I swear it's more of Jasper's tricks. I want that bastard gone." I sprinkle a little more black salt in the walk in front of the bay window, focusing my intention on banishing Jasper, his look, his energy. Finishing the circle, I go back over it with the remaining salt and save the last of it for the two doors, back and front. Facing the front of the house, I invoke protection one last time. "Protect this house from negative energies and unwanted spirits. May Jasper John Baker be banished. May his spirit no longer abide here." I wait and feel no shift or change in energy. Shrugging, I step over the salt border, and George follows. Opening the door, we go inside. The basement door is open.

"Dad?" I call. There's no answer.

We check upstairs in the bedrooms and the attic. No lights on, no answer.

We go downstairs to the basement, feeling an overwhelming sense of dread.

Of course, Dad isn't in the main room, under the stairs, or

along the sides. Calling for him again, we turn the corner and see that the wall of the hidden room is removed.

Dad has his shovel, digging in the dirt at the back.

His movements are frantic and fast as he flings dirt over his shoulder. Approaching him slowly, shielding our eyes from the flying dirt, we peer around either side of him.

The hole is almost three feet deep. Suddenly, he stops. Dad drops to his knees, using his hands to pull something out.

It's a thick bone, the length of my arm. A mammal's femur, it looks like.

A small, human leg.

CHAPTER THIRTY-FOUR

Dad drops it, realizing what it is. He curses, backing away from the hole.

He's dug a space nearly four feet long and at least two feet wide. It's a shallow hole, maybe two feet deep, but he clearly dug far enough. George shines his flashlight on it. Without lights in this room, it feels like we're outside in the dark. The cold of the ground is rising from the hole, adding to the shiver down my spine. The smell is dank and wet despite the lack of mold on the walls. I kneel before the hole, and swallowing my fear, I reach a hand in, wishing I had gloves.

I pick up the bone.

The bone looks to be very old. It's dry, definitively decayed. I place it to one side and take the shovel from Dad's limp grip, poking delicately at the walls and floor of the hole. Another bone, and then another. After a few minutes, we have a nearly-full skeleton. I keep poking, digging into the far right of the hole where the head should be.

The shovel hits something solid. I chisel away at it, and a round object rolls into the hole.

It's a skull. Small, like a child's.

I use the shovel to roll it face up. It's missing nearly all of its teeth.

A sob rises in my throat again, and my shield can't hold back the wave of sadness I feel. I remember the dream: Clara's teeth were pulled. Jasper tortured her. "The Harrs should have noticed these during the basement renovations, right? Shouldn't they have alerted the authorities?"

Dad answers, a quaver in his voice I've never heard before. "There's a lot of paperwork involved with human remains found in houses. Lawyers, even. Maybe they didn't want the hassle," he says, then he clears his throat. "I think we should give this body a proper burial."

"What do we do until then? There's snow on the ground, even if we wanted to bury them tomorrow," George asks, always logical.

"You know who it must be, don't you?" George asks me, putting his hand down to help me up. I stand and look at him, thinking.

"Clara," I say, the sob escaping my throat. "It must be. Her body was never found," I pull my hands in my sleeves and cross my arms. George puts his arms around me. I can't stop staring at the bones. Her body. "Clara," I say again, looking at the face, remembering that night at the dollhouse when she smiled at me. She had been missing so many teeth.

I shake my head. "Jasper did this. Her own brother. He was torturing her for some reason."

Dad blanches. "What in God's name... why?" He and George both look at me, imploring.

I explain what I saw in my dreams – the hiding spot behind the dollhouse, the train lights whizzing past. "He was as sinister in life as he is in death. And Jasper died in the flood," I say, thinking. "She must have died then too. Like the newspaper said, she was one of the missing at the time." I pause, thinking. "I think she died right here. The flood came through at forty miles per hour – she could've been crushed and buried in seconds."

George hangs his head, resting his chin on the top of mine. "This is too much for one night," he says, turning me in his arms toward the door.

Suddenly his grip stiffens.

"What?" I say, looking toward the door.

Jasper is standing with Clara in front of him. He has one arm over her chest, the other over her forehead, like a hostage. I break free of George's arms and head over to them.

"You are no longer welcome here, Jasper Baker!" I shout at him, pointing to the window. "Get out, get out, get out!" I realize then that he's not holding Clara to torture her, at least not fully. He's holding her like an anchor to port. He can't stay without clutching onto her energy.

"Clara, give me your hand," I say, reaching for her. He tightens his grip, and her hand can't reach more than a few inches from her body. I don't want to, but I step closer to them, reaching for her fingers. As they make contact, my fingers go right through hers. I hear a whimper, echoing in the small room, and see tears fill her eyes.

"I will get you out of this, Clara, you'll be free," I call, as I run through her and Jasper, heading for the stairs. I swear I see a dark-haired shadow just outside the room in the dim of the basement. The mystery woman. For the first time, we lock eyes. But she's a lot younger than Clara's mother should be.

"Help her." Her whispering voice barely reaches me. I don't have time to think about who this woman is. I watch her recede towards the basement stairs, and I run behind. We're coming, Clara.

I don't stop running until I have the dentist's box and the

car keys. "Wait," Dad says, panting behind me. I didn't even hear him and George running behind me. "Should we bring the bones? Finally end this?"

I don't hesitate as I shake my head. "Clara has suffered in his presence long enough. I won't let them rest together for all of eternity." I look at the dentist's box in my hand, feeling the horrible energy, picturing the endless tortures Jasper enacted with these tools. "Tonight, we're burying Jasper. Once and for all."

I'm opening the front door when I remember I'll need a shovel. Just then, George is behind me, one hand on my shoulder, another carrying the shovel.

George leans the shovel on his shoulder like a rifle. "Let's do this," he says.

THE CEMETERY IS COVERED with snow. I'm not surprised, but I had hoped it would've melted a little throughout the day. Instead, it seems to have slicked it into an ice rink, the moon reflected in the large patches of driven snow. I try to run to the grave, but the slippery ice makes it so difficult that I feel like my movement is in slow motion. We have to break the surface and trudge ahead to get the best traction.

After minutes that feel like hours, we come to the grave with the sign sticking up out of it. I can't stop thinking of Clara, scared and alone with him.

For all these years.

Dad starts shoveling, but I put a hand on his shoulder. "You've done enough today. I want to do this," I say, my face set. He nods and gives me the shovel. In a few strokes, I hit the frozen ground. I put all of my weight into my feet, pressing into the sides of the shovel head, digging deep, using my full strength to pull up a mound of dirt.

"It's okay, Ken, let me take over from here," George tries, but I shake my head, sweat falling into my eyes. I make it for three more heavy scoops before I take a deep breath and lean on the handle, wiping my head with my sleeve. My hands are raw, and for the second time tonight, I wish I had remembered gloves. In the heat of it all, I even forgot a hat. I pull my hands into my sleeves and grip the handle again, grateful George and Dad don't offer to help again – I might've said yes. With three more agonizing scoops, I've made a two-foot hole, deep enough for the box to be unretrievable.

I turn to George, and he offers the dentist's box to me. I place it in the hole, pressing it into the softer earth of the undersoil.

"Jasper Baker, your time on this earth has ended," I say, loudly, not caring who hears. "Jasper Baker, you are banished from 117 North Front Street! It is no longer your home, and your spirit is banished! I bind you to this grave, to this place of rest. May you move on and find peace in the next life. Your time on this earth has ended!" I repeat and start shoveling dirt back into the hole.

With each scoop, as the box is obscured, I feel better, more free, more powerful. "Jasper Baker, you are banished to this grave, bound here in body and to the next plane in soul. You cannot abide on this earth! You are banished from 117 North Front Street! You are banished!" I repeat with each heave of dirt into the hole.

When the hole is filled in, Dad and George help me smooth snow over the top of it, finding the purest white we can to mask the dirt. I take up the sign, throwing it a few feet away.

"Let's cover our tracks," I say, and we trudge in different directions back to the car, disrupting the pure, driven snow of the whole cemetery. Before getting in, I look up at the sky and

entreat the elements for another heavy snow tonight to cover
our tracks – and bury Jasper more fully.

*I'M WOKEN up by the acrid smell of soil. I try to lift my head, but
there's something on top of me, surrounding me. I try to take in
my surroundings, but it's black as pitch, like I'm in a coal mine.*

*I listen, but there's nothing to hear. No voices, no sign of the
train. There's not even a whistle of wind to be heard. I start to
hear my heart beating in my ears as panic rises in my throat. I
try to calm down, taking deep breaths. But the smell of soil, the
horrid stench of dirt makes me think of death.*

Death.

*I try to remember. I close my eyes – not that that changes
anything, the darkness is the same – and remember the train
passing by the window as I held her skinny little neck in my
hands. The shrew. Her weakness makes me chuckle to myself. I
can't believe I wanted her before. Before I knew she was a
degenerate.*

*Good riddance. She's much more fun to torture. She still
cries every time she's in that chair. At least Clara has the
decency to shut up.*

*I grin, remembering the terror in her eyes as I had her in my
grip, the train's light flashing across her face from the window
behind her as she looked around helplessly for Clara. Then
what? I dragged her upstairs... no, wait. She got away this time.*

*A throbbing starts at the back of my head. Clara. She hit me
with something. I got up to follow them. They had run to the
basement. To her musty apartment.*

*I try to move my hand to feel the back of my head, but the
space is so confined. Where am I?*

*I thrash my arms around, hitting walls on all sides. I'm in a
box. Am I... is this a coffin? Clara, that sneaky, disgusting bitch. I*

was running to the basement when something knocked the wind out of me. Something cold, hard, fast... like I was drowning on my feet.

What did those witches do to me? I will kill them both. I've been too lenient on them.

"Let me out, you weaklings! Do you imagine Father won't notice I'm gone?" I shout, but the words are lost in the void.

No one can hear me. No one is coming.

"You little bitches! You ungrateful whores!" Coughing and spitting, I scream until my lungs burn. I shout muffled cries for help again and again, more and more desperate until I don't even recognize my own voice.

I MUST HAVE DOZED off in the car on the ride home because the next thing I remember is George's arms on my shoulders. "Ken, Ken, wake up. It's okay. Wake up," he's repeating over and over again. I open my eyes and look at him, confused and then remember.

I was underground. In a box. I could feel the dirt heaved on top of me, smell the soil that was smothering me.

It was terrifying.

I smile. "I think it worked."

Despite it all, George smiles back. "Can this be over now?"

"We'll have to see. Come on."

We take off our coats and run upstairs. I hesitate in the hall-way, just outside my Craft room.

"Ok, I'll be out soon." I shift my feet a little, and George grins.

"Ok, good luck," and begins to turn back towards the stairs.

Before taking a step, he turns back around. "Be safe," he says as he steps closer to me and leaves a soft kiss on my fore-head. I let the safe feeling of his love wash over me for a second.

I think about the snow day again, remembering Mom's words: let people love the real me.

I draw my hands into my sleeves and take a deep breath. "George," I say, pulling my head back from his embrace and meeting his eyes. "Why don't you join me?" I ask, putting my hands in his. "But only if you want to."

I smile, keeping eye contact. I feel a bit embarrassed. This is the first time he's seen a ritual before. I drop one of his hands and walk him to my altar.

Alright Mom, I'm listening. Come what may.

I kneel in front of my altar table, and gesture for George to join me. He doesn't hesitate. "Can't get much more paranormal than what I've already been through," he smiles back, sitting beside me. He's patient and attentive as I call the quarters, invoke the Goddess for protection, draw my sacred space, and as I light my incense and prepare my candles, I remember something.

The spell will be stronger with something personal.

I grab my athame dagger, using it to open an energetic doorway in the circle by tracing a section to enter and exit the protected energy of the circle. "What are you doing with that knife?" George asks, a bit warily.

I grin. "It's a magickal tool. Athames are daggers but never used for cutting anything except energy. I'm opening a doorway that keeps our spell – and you – safe inside the sacred circle while I go get something. I think I know what'll work to banish Jasper this time."

I step outside of the circle, then use my athame to close it again so Jasper can't enter. Taking the athame with me, I go down to the dollhouse and select the doll that looks like Clara. I also take the doll that looks like Jasper and the candle stub from inside the hiding place behind the mirror.

Creating the doorway, closing it again, and re-entering the

circle, I put the dolls next to their respective candles. Clara's for protection, Jasper to be banished. I take the stub and place it in the dish I had used for the sage clearing. Taking a few moments to ground myself, I feel the energy of the circle humming with my own power. I light a match and hold it to the ancient stub.

Magic *is* real. The hundred-year-old candle lights.

"Spirit of this home, Clara Baker, I entreat you to feel at ease. Join me here, you are welcome. The dark-haired woman, too, is welcome." That moment we made eye contact in the basement has me resisting calling her Clara's mother. She was just too young.

I light the white candle, representing protection and purity. "May the souls of this house, George Levy, Kendra Hill, Philip Hill, Clara Baker, and Charlie Harr, be blessed and welcome here. May all negativity directed toward them and this home be banished, expelled, and bound from returning or entering this space. This house is sacred." I repeat our names and envision the protective white light of the candle spreading throughout the home, up to the attic, down to the basement. I envision the yard, and the gardenia patch under the protection of this white light.

It's time for the black candle. I pick it up and hold it to the original stub. "Jasper Baker, evil spirits of this house, you are banished from here!" In the moment, I feel moved to shout, and as I do, the candle ignites.

It's burning. It's working. I look over at George, and he's watching me intently. He gives me a nod and a small grin. I think he feels it too.

"Jasper Baker, you are banished from this home," I say, and hold the doll over the flames. Its little feet take a moment to blacken, the clothes burning first. I picture Jasper in the basement releasing Clara, releasing the darkness he holds over this home. I hear a man's scream. George looks at me, but I shake my head, staying focused.

"Jasper Baker, you are bound from ever contacting Clara Baker or the dimension of earth ever again. You are banished from this house, 117 North Front Street! You are banished to your grave and to the beyond, you cannot interfere on our plane again. You cannot interfere with Clara Baker! You are banished!" The doll's socks are charred remains, wisping into the air. The porcelain is smoking as the clothes of the doll catch. I turn it counterclockwise. "Jasper Baker, you are banished! Move on from this home. You are bound from returning!"

I turn the doll upside down. The scream comes up the stairs and hits my ears like a siren, unending, sounding like he's right next to me. His last push before defeat, I hope. I don't turn to look. I scream louder. "Jasper Baker, you are finished! Move on. You are bound! Be gone. You are banished!" The scream stops abruptly, my last shout lingering in the air. The doll is charred, the paint of its face melting over the black candle in a grotesque, inhuman way. My altar table is covered in wax and ash. I'm suddenly conscious that the doll is hot all over, and I switch hands.

"Jasper John Baker, be at peace. Be gone from this plane. Find the next realm, and be gone, Jasper Baker," I repeat, over and over, holding the flame to the doll again and again. Finally, the porcelain cracks under the heat. I feel an exhilarated whoosh of air. The black candle is nearly burned down, the white even closer. I close my eyes, and then reopening them, I look at the window in front of me. George has backed up towards the door, his eyes on the window. Then I see what he sees.

Clara's reflection looks back at me. I turn, and there she is, more solid than I've seen her since that day in the dollhouse. I pick up her doll and offer it to her, and for a second, we're both holding the same object. I smile at her, and with my other hand, I place my hand on hers that holds the doll.

I can feel her skin.

I don't know if it's the magic circle she has stepped into or the balancing presence of the doll, but I feel her.

I smile and taste salt. I realize I'm crying.

Not taking her other hand off the doll, Clara lifts her left hand and places it on my cheek. She wipes a tear and then pulls her hand back, inspecting it. She rubs her fingers together, her face unmoving. Then she smiles, her missing teeth tugging at my heart all over again.

She pulls the doll from my hand and backs away, receding into the wall behind her. The shadow of another figure goes with her, nearly imperceptible, but I know it must be the woman. The white candle and the ancient stub sputter out as she disappears. A few moments later, the black candle extinguishes.

I release the quarters of each element, thank the Goddess, and open the circle. Exhausted as I am, I carry the burned husk of Jasper's doll and the ancient candle stub downstairs. I'll take care of it in the morning, but I don't want it in the house. I go outside and place it under the mailbox a safe distance away from the edge of the black salt circle and out of sight to any passersby. It's nearly midnight.

I laugh into the darkness at the irony.

It's the witching hour.

CHAPTER THIRTY-FIVE

I 'm sitting in front of the gardenia bush. It's not growing as fast as I thought it would. It's only a few sprigs, but I swear I see a few buds forming on the ends. I rise and wipe the sweat from my forehead with my apron. She's going to love this.

It's a sunny day, warmer than expected for early spring. The sun overhead peeks down through the trees, their leaves coming back already. I can hear the rush of the river; it's sounding louder and louder today. I pick up my basket of gardening things and step out of the garden, walking back over the tracks and toward the house.

When I get to the house, I go around the dirt lane to the back door. They prefer for me to use that entrance. I feel my face get hot in shame or anger or both. Swinging open the door to the kitchen a little harder than I meant to, I catch it and gently close it. I stand there listening for a moment. It's quiet today. It's a Friday morning, but no one seems to be home. Or awake yet.

I tiptoe into the foyer, listening up the staircase for any sign of activity. I hear the patter of wood on wood from around the corner. Clara's at the dollhouse again, rearranging the dolls for the day.

"When are you going to outgrow such nonsense?" I ask, my arms crossed but smiling.

She smirks at me. "They're not toys, you know. It's a model and figurines, a lady's occupation." She places the doll that looks just like her in the dining room, leaning against a chair. Then she reaches into one of the bedrooms and retrieves the doll that looks like me and puts her next to her doll. I join her, kneeling in front of the house. She has it turned around today. "Why do you turn it to the wall each night?" I ask.

"You know why," she says, turning her head slyly to the staircase. "He's always aiming to ruin anything that brings joy to me." Clara puts her hand on my knee. I place my hand over hers.

Footsteps on the stairs jolt us back to reality, and I stand, preparing to retreat to the kitchen.

I'm not fast enough.

"I should say I'm not surprised to see you up here so early," he sneers, his thumbs through his suspenders. He approaches me, closer than I am comfortable. I can smell bourbon on his breath though it can't yet be eight in the morning. "You're lucky Father will be coming downstairs in a few moments." He lifts a stubby finger to my face, brushing a lock of my dark hair behind my ear. I shiver and fight with all my strength not to back away, but I flinch involuntarily, nonetheless. At that, he grabs my jaw between his thumb and fingers, hard, making my knees buckle as he forces my mouth open, exposing my teeth.

"Jasper, stop it!" Clara says under her breath. "I'll call for Father," she adds, louder.

"You will not," he jerks my face and then releases me. I recoil toward Clara. "If you do, I'll be sure to inform him of your dolls and your little playtime and all the things you get up to while Mother and Father are out. You know I wouldn't lie to you."

Clara reddens, not saying a word. Instead, she takes my hand. And my heart swells as I squeeze hers back.

At that moment, we hear feet hit the landing, and we drop each other's hands, separating. Jasper backs up and straightens himself.

"Father, good morning," he inclines his head in an overt show of respect. Mr. Baker returns the gesture, not looking up from his paper. I grind my jaw in frustration at them, their proprietary dance, and then wince in pain. He took two teeth last week, and the holes aren't healing well. I shiver at the memory, nodding and curtseying to Mr. Baker as I retreat to the kitchen. As if I'm a shadow, he doesn't even acknowledge me.

"Jasper, you've two clients coming this morning and the afternoon available for walk-ins," I overhear Mr. Baker's booming voice as I knead bread in the kitchen. "I'll be out with Mrs. Baker most of the day."

I don't hear his reply, but I hear Mr. Baker's study door open and close and then Jasper's feet on the steps back up to the attic office. I roll my eyes as I start tossing together the flour and water for today's bread. If he's not in Philadelphia on business for weeks on end, he's in that study. It's none of my business – except in how it affects Clara.

A few minutes later, as I'm placing a cloth over the dough in a bowl to rise, Clara comes in. I dust my hands on my apron. She watches me fill the woodstove, her hand under her chin. We don't say a word, but we don't have to. Silence is comfortable between us.

Sometimes it's easy to forget the class difference or our family backgrounds; the wall society has between us in so many ways. But ever since I came here two years ago to help in the kitchens, I've felt that wall melt away more and more.

Several minutes later we both look up as Mrs. Baker comes down the stairs, humming to herself. Clara heads into the foyer, starting to say goodbye to her mother. She walks right past her without saying a word. She doesn't even knock on the study door to address Mr. Baker. She just opens her parasol and steps outside, dressed for another Society meeting. She's always cared more for garden parties than mothering. Clara's wave goes unnoticed.

As the door closes, Clara looks at me like she does every morning: crestfallen. "It's like I'm a ghost," she says, coming back into the kitchen.

"Come with me to the woods," I tell her, and I smile mischievously. "I have something to show you."

As MY DREAM hand turns the knob to open the back door, I awaken, eyebrows furrowed. Whose memory was that? Why did Clara show me that last night? I look around for a sign or shimmer, feel for a cold spot, call for Clara. There's no answer. Maybe it wasn't Clara. I go over the dream again and again. I wasn't Clara. I was the dark-haired woman. Like before, with the candle. She's not Mrs. Baker; she's a servant. Was she a friend of Clara's?

As I wake up and get ready, I head into my Craft room for my morning ritual, placing my pendulum in my pocket as usual. I can feel that the whole energy of the house has shifted. No dreams, no nightmares for Dad or George. The room stayed warm, and the cats even came down to breakfast with us.

Dad and I went up to the attic while George did the dishes. Nothing malicious. I used my pendulum to see if I could reach Jasper. No response, at all. The sunlight seems to be coming in brighter than ever in the attic rooms.

I sit in the study and begin writing flashbacks for

Catherine and placing in new scenes that come to me as if I'm channeling them. Instead of feeling tired from the dream or the spell from last night, I feel invigorated, my head clear. The study, too, feels less heavy. At the end of three hours, I've rounded out the chapters I had written before moving here – over this week I've improved the first half of *Bleeding Glory* more than I knew it needed to be. I'm almost caught up to where I left off, now. Tomorrow I'll be writing new scenes for Catherine as she makes it through Fashion Week, the climax of the novel. I smile at that. I feel like I'm beyond the climax of our story, too.

Around eleven, I close my laptop and survey my study. The morning light is bright, the sun warm through the bay window at my back. I don't feel any pressure on me. No eyes watching me. My boxes beckon to me from the corner.

There are answers here, I know it. I open every drawer, scouring it for clues. The search comes up empty, although I do find some fountain pens that might be of interest to May. I'll keep one for good luck on my writing – the others can be a gesture of goodwill for Dad when he visits May next. The old journals stare at me, and I try to flip through and discern what I can until I have a headache. The papers remaining in the drawers are all receipts, administrative; and none too old. Nothing dates back to the Bakers' time.

It's time to call on Lynn.

George and Dad stay behind. Dad is starting to tinker with the dollhouse, and George is back to work on photography. It's only Friday, but our excursion to the antique store on Monday feels like it was a decade ago. Dad's only been here six days. We've only lived here for eight. I pull my hands in my sleeves and grab the car keys, marveling at the illusion of time.

When I get to Lynn's office just a few blocks away, I pause before swinging the door open. She's at the back on her laptop, oblivious to me standing here. Is she from Newport? It's a small town. Did she know Charlie? His parents?

I take a deep breath and dive in. "Lynn! Hey, I wanted to chat with you about the house. We're settling in great," I add, seeing the deer-in-the-headlights look growing on her face. She relaxes a bit at that, and I sit at her desk without waiting to be asked.

"Kendra, great, great. I'm so glad." I believe her. I don't think she wants to sell this house again.

"We've been unpacked for a bit now, and we're really loving the space, but I wanted to ask you about something I noticed on the tour that's gone now. We can't find them since we moved in," I start. I don't know if it's my imagination, but Lynn seems to sit straighter. "There were a lot of old papers, old letters it seemed, in the desk. They were much older than the previous owners' time; I'm sure they were original to the home. I wanted to ask if you could return them to me," I finish strong, keeping eye contact, even when she darts her eyes to her left and quickly back again as if hoping I wouldn't notice.

She puts her hands on her lap, hesitating. I look to where her eyes were pointed. A filing cabinet.

"I'm not sure what you mean," she says, that tight-lipped smile unwavering. I don't return it but maintain eye contact. She finally relents. "Okay, look, I'm sorry, Kendra. I just didn't want you to back out. I know you're cool with the occult and all, but I've heard it all before. The last lady sold essential oils and thought that qualified her," she says with a huff, "and I thought you might be the same. I just didn't want to keep trying with that place. I'm sorry," she repeats. She looks at the filing cabinet again.

I smile encouragingly. "They're all I'm here for; no surprises or tricks from me. I love this house, and I'm trying to find out more about the history," I explain. "We've learned a lot from the local records, but there's much more to it. I know there is."

Lynn surprises me with a raise of the eyebrows. "You don't know the half of it," she says, leaning toward the cabinet and opening the bottom drawer. She draws out a thick manila envelope, unlatches it, and pours the letters onto the table.

"These were all in the top drawer," she starts. "And these," she pulls out a second one, passing it to me, "were in the side drawers. They're not all from the same period, I think, but I couldn't believe that even after three owners, these were still in the desk. I couldn't throw them away; knowing their age, it just felt wrong." She scoops the letters back into the folder, and I lean over to help her, making sure she doesn't miss any.

"I couldn't be more grateful, Lynn. Thank you so much. I completely understand your unethical business practices," I wink. I'm not sure I can pull it off like George can, but she smirks, so I must have done alright.

I don't rise from my chair, and she looks at me questioningly. "Anything else, Mrs. Levy?"

"Kendra Hill, Lynn, and no, not about the desk or anything else missing. But I was wondering. We've met some locals now, and it's hard not to notice that everyone knows each other around here," I chuckle, leaning back in my seat. "Did you know Charlie Harr?"

I must have taken her aback. She blinks fast a few times, her lips pursed in confusion. Her brows knit together, and she speaks. No smile. "Yes, and do you?"

"We ate at Bitting's a couple of times, and I ran into him on a walk," I put in vaguely. "I'm asking because he mentioned he wasn't able to buy his house after his parents died. You must have been working here then, it was only..." I reach for what May had said, and thankfully it comes to me, "five years ago, right?"

She folds her hands on her desk again, ever the business-woman. "The Harrs had a second mortgage he could not assume due to his credit score and employment record. But that is already saying too much. It's personal information."

"Where does he live now, if you don't mind?"

She shrugs, and I'm stung by her apathy. "He rents, that's for sure. Not many people do, here. Must be one of the newer duplexes, or more likely the mobile homes down on 4th Street." The way she says 'mobile homes' makes my temple twitch. Now that I'm not a customer, I think I'm seeing the real Lynn.

"Thank you, Lynn, I appreciate your help," I say, in my best customer service voice. Dad would be proud.

I clutch my manila envelopes to my heart as I leave and head straight to 4th Street.

CHAPTER THIRTY-SIX

I thought it would be near 2nd where Lynn's office is, but 4th is hidden, a maze of turns before the valley of motor homes is visible. It feels intentional, snobby. The change is abrupt from historic and colonial homes to small, uniform rectangles. I don't know how I'm going to find Charlie in the labyrinth of homes, but I start driving around. After the third or fourth turn, I see his truck, recognizing it from the supermarket last week. I turn in next to it and take in the home it's parked in front of. Charlie's trailer is modest, a simple walkup with a small porch. Red vinyl, well kept. No embellishments, no wreaths, or signs on the door, but clean.

I walk up the stairs, and opening the storm door, I knock. There's no answer at first, and I start to wonder if I'm doing the right thing. Clutching the envelopes across my chest, I hold my breath and knock a second time. Thank the Gods, he opens it this time. I would have lost my nerve on a third try.

"Charlie! I'm so sorry if I'm bothering you, I just wanted to show you something, give you some updates," I smile. I notice he's wearing his usual attire, a flannel over faded jeans. He's in his socks, classic white with gray toes. I raise my eyes to his. "Hey, you shaved! You look great," I say, and then my face reddens as I remember we're probably not there yet in our burgeoning friendship. To my relief, he grins and rubs a hand on his chin. "Anyway," I continue, "if you're busy it's not a problem, I just got some old things from the house I wanted to look over with you."

"Oh, no. Sure thing. I've got time," he says, backing away and opening the door for me. "Have a seat," he gestures to a small dining table with four chairs.

As soon as we're seated, I fill him in on last night's successful banishment. His eyes widen, but he doesn't interrupt, his attention rapt. "I think it worked," I say, "but I want to see what more we can do for Clara." Then I take the plunge. "When your family was remodeling the basement, did you find anything suspicious?"

He stares at me blankly. "Anything... that maybe should have been reported to the police?" I say bluntly.

His brow knits together, and then he starts picking at his thumb again under the table. "I don't know. I remember helping Dad down there a lot, and then one day he made me stop helping him. Said it was finished enough and that he had to do the rest. I thought it was something I did. He continued to work down there, mostly at night, and it was weeks before he was done. I sometimes wonder if I went into construction just to show him I could finish the job." He gives a nervous chuckle.

"When we were moving some furniture down in the basement, Dad and I fell through some drywall," I begin, and Charlie leans closer. "There was a room your dad had sealed off. A secret room."

He puts his elbows on the table, looking at the letters. "A perfect square? Cinder blocks and dirt flooring..." he murmurs, his eyes unfocusing as remembers. "I had so many dreams about that place. I started to think it wasn't real."

"Do you remember that room, Charlie?"

"There was always red, coming up like sewage from the floor." I see him shiver as he rolls his shoulders to cover it. "Clara was showing me, I thought. She did that sometimes, visited me in dreams. I didn't think it was actually still there, though." He trails off.

"We dug in the dirt, Charlie, and..." I wait for him to meet my eyes. "We found *Clara* down there," I pause, letting it sink in. "We think she was crushed when the flood came through. It was so fast. So many people were washed away, entire foundations of homes destroyed, basements unable to be excavated."

He pales. His eyes are much more visible now, both beardless and without a hat. So much pain and empathy are in them I have to look away.

We don't say anything for several dragging seconds. Charlie speaks first. "The ghosts of the past. They never stopped haunting me."

I nod. "I'm sorry if I shouldn't have involved you in this," I start, but Charlie cuts me off with a wave of his hand.

"I'm glad you did. And for the first time, I'm glad I'm not the one living in that house anymore. You were able to help her when I couldn't. Maybe I didn't want to let her go," he gives a hollow chuckle, but I know he's serious.

"I understand, Charlie." I smile softly. "Loss isn't easy." I think of my mom and how hard it's been without her on both Dad and me. "But they're never really gone when we keep them alive in our memories."

I look at the letters. "Speaking of memories, I'm hoping these letters will have more answers in Clara's life. They were in the desk in the study."

He swallows and then nods, waiting. I open the first envelope. It's filled with letters, some sealed with wax, some folded into themselves. We split them up and start reading. I start with the unsealed ones. The first one is short, simple, cryptic:

Come to the woods? – T.

The next are all similar:

C, your hair is like golden starlight on a new moon – the brightest light in the sky – T.

Raisins in the dinner rolls please, if you really love me. – C.

See you tonight? – C.

"Happiness, not in another place but this place... not for another hour, but this hour." – W.W. – C.

I missed you last night. It is cold down there without you. – T.

"I think these are love letters. Did Clara have a boyfriend?" I ask.

Charlie passes me the notes he's opened, and I pass him mine. His were all wax-sealed, though previously opened by the presumed recipient. They're written receipts for dental work, requests for dental services, and a few letters of updates from past patients.

"Why would Clara's notes be in her father's office desk drawer?"

Charlie shrugs. "Maybe she wanted to tell her father about him in a subtle way?"

"Or maybe he found them and never made sense of them." If this mystery drew me in, a complete stranger, imagine how this could have affected her own father – her own absent father, at that. "I don't get the impression her parents were around very much; nor very interested in Clara." I shuffle through the letters. "They're signed T. and C., the love letters. Never more detail. It must have been a secret. She was young, right?" I ask him.

Charlie nods. "I always figured maybe thirteen, fourteen at

the oldest. Small for her age, but maybe back then, people were smaller," he considers.

"Let's look at the other pile."

The other envelope is filled with newer paperwork, most of it written on a typewriter. There are several pages of letters that seem to be from the original Harrs' correspondence – conversations on the Wall Street crisis, asking after business investments. These must be from the '30s.

I look through the oldest documents again, sorting them. Dental paperwork and love letters – only two piles.

I drum my fingers on the gardenia tablecloth, thinking. "This might sound crazy," I say, and he looks at me with a raised eyebrow. "Listen, I had a dream last night. I was a woman, for sure. And I wasn't Mrs. Baker. I'd had dreams before, and I always figured I was Mrs. Baker, but this time, for certain, I definitely wasn't. I was someone else. A young woman. And I was good friends with Clara." It clicks. What Jasper mentioned in that dream: Clara's "playtime" ... the things she got up to when she was home alone...

"Oh, my Gods. All this time. My dreams: it was never Mrs. Baker..." I pause, putting it together, remembering the back door comment from last night's dream. "She was the cook or the maid or something." I shuffle to the last love letter: "'It's cold down there' signed, 'T,'" I read aloud. "Her room was in the basement."

"Who?"

"Clara's girlfriend."

CHAPTER THIRTY-SEVEN

Before rushing off, I give Charlie my phone number. He texts me so I have his, and despite it all, we share a smile. "Thank you for including me in this, Kendra," he says.

"Of course, Charlie," I say. And then turn back to him, passing him the folders. "Keep these letters. They're your family's, or Clara's, and she was like family." Still smiling, he pushes them back to me. "No, I think I'm ready to move on. To lay her to rest, for real."

I smile broader. "Then come by later today if you're free. That's exactly what we're doing. The sun is warming the ground, and we are going to have a bit of a wake. I'm thinking we'll bury Clara by the gardenia in the woods."

He smiles broadly, the beard no longer hiding his warmth. "That's a swell idea."

WHEN I GET HOME, George and Dad aren't upstairs. They don't answer my call, so I head to the basement and see that the lights are on.

I go straight to the back room where I find them hunched over the hole. There are two boxes beside them with bones in them. "What are you guys doing?" They both jump, Dad, placing a hand on his heart.

"Don't scare us like that, Bug! Where have you been all morning?" Dad asks.

Georges rises and comes over to me, kissing me on the cheek. "Did you get what you wanted from Lynn?"

I nod exuberantly and show them the manila envelopes. "You won't believe what I figured out," I start. Then I look past George at the two boxes. "Why are the bones in two boxes?" I ask.

"Well, we've made some discoveries of our own today. As we were preparing Clara for her burial. There are two skeletons. We found two skulls," he says. I notice he's not lowering his voice anymore. The energy here is still sad but settled. Easier to ignore.

"I think I have an answer for that," I say, and tell them about the love letters and my dream, the theory of Jasper's blackmail.

Dad whistles, low. "How do we know it's real? Dreams aren't exactly evidence."

I cross my arms and look at him. "I found the candle stub based on a dream. Clara showed me that. Or someone did. The other girl. I thought it was her mom in those dreams, but it wasn't. It was her girlfriend."

George smiles and puts his arm around me, looking at Dad. "Trust me. She is right. Clara would tell us if we got it wrong, anyway."

I approach the boxes slowly, reverently. Squatting down in front of them, I reach into the first box where a skull rests on top of a femur and what must be ribs. George and Dad look on, their attention off the sorting for a minute. They don't say anything, but I feel their eyes on me as I gingerly touch the skull.

"STOP JASPER, LEAVE HER ALONE!" *I yell, again and again, trying to see past the entrance to the cubbyhole. I shriek as someone grabs my arm, pulling me up off the floor and out of my hiding place. "Tabitha?" She pulls me along, not answering. We make a run for the basement, seeking refuge in her apartment.*

Jasper is right on our heels. "Get back here, you whores!" I hear his shoe skid on the floor, just inches behind us. I feel my heart thumping through my skull. "I'll kill you!" His voice is shrill. I've never heard him this angry.

I jump, nearly losing my balance on the top step as Tabitha slams the basement door behind us. We stride down the stairs, two at a time, and hook the corner to her room in the back.

I shove the door closed with everything I've got, looking around for a table, a chair, anything. "Why isn't there a lock on this door?" I grunt, out of breath. Tabitha comes up behind me with a pipe. "I took this from beneath the house, in case something like this were to happen," she says, pushing it under the doorknob, bracing it against the ground.

Just as she does, Jasper heaves his body against the door. I throw my arms around Tabitha, half protecting her, half begging she will protect me. "It's alright, T, it's going to be ok," I say breathlessly, gripping her shoulders with my hands. Locked in her embrace, I can feel her heart against my own, racing in tandem.

"Ha!" Jasper's shrill voice cuts through me like a cold wind. "You will both die today." He throws himself once more at the door. "I should have told everyone about you, Clara," he kicks at the door, and we see the pipe shift backward, a deep divot in the dirt floor. "I should have ruined you. But you ruined yourself," I

feel the anger of his next kick in my chest as if he were kicking me. The pipe slides again. "You ruined her too! She should've been mine!"

Tabitha and I back up as one, still holding each other tightly. Getting to the bed, we sit down in unison. I withdraw from Tabitha's embrace and look at her. I feel my heart swell with pure love as she meets my eyes. "I'd choose you every time, you know," I say, taking her hands in mine.

She smiles, and for that small moment, I can feel the fear seep away from me until only my love for her remains. "I know, Clara." She leans forward and kisses me. I pull her closer.

"You witches, you disgusting hags!" Jasper shouts, bringing us back to reality as his body makes contact with the door again. The pipe slides further.

My heart in my throat, I place my hand in Tabitha's and press my forehead to hers. "Don't let him see fear," I intone gently, and kiss her, softly. Tabitha forces a grin, steeling herself.

Keeping my hand in her right, she makes a fist with her left hand. "I'm ready," she whispers. And then louder, to Jasper, she calls, "We're ready!"

"To hell you are!" We watch the doorknob jiggle as he tries it again. I jump involuntarily as he runs at the door again. "You won't get away with this, ingrates. I'll be back with my tools!" He yells.

We both sit looking at each other, then to the door. For seconds dragging into minutes, we strain our ears for any sound of his return. I stand, and Tabitha stands with me. "Should we adjust the pipe? Move the bed in front of the door too?"

"Wait," she cuts me off. "Do you hear that?"

A rainstorm must have started. "It sounds like the gutters rushing," I remark, but even as I say it I hear the sound getting louder. "I swear it sounds like..." I let my sentence drift as my eyes spot the water coming under the door.

Tabitha grabs me, and I close my eyes as the door slams into us.

It's Jasper, he's back, he's gotten us.... Wait, where is he?

I can't feel his hands at my throat. But why can't I breathe?

"KEN, YOU OK?" George is kneeling next to me.

I open my eyes. I didn't realize they'd been shut. And then I inhale, loudly, strongly, mouth open wide. I touch my neck, expecting to feel bruising, but there's nothing there. "Yeah," I answer absently, trying to shake the feeling of what I just saw.

I look again at the piles of bones, the last solid remnants of a girl I've come to care for and the girl she cared for most. "They were hiding down here from Jasper when the flood hit. They'd just fought back. They were fighting back." Suddenly I feel very tired. Is that how Clara and Tabitha have felt all these years?

"If he had been down here, his body wouldn't have been recovered," I start, then pause. "I guess in a way, it's a good thing they were never found. They died together, their secret safe; and he never found them. Until the afterlife." I pause, shivering with the realization of her reality this past century. "They should have been freer than ever – free to be together. The torture of that – your tormentor stuck with you in death as in life. Keeping your lover from you. An inescapable existence of fear." I reach over to the skull again. I remember that night, cupping her ghostly face in my hand as she cried. The way she held mine last night.

As I contemplate this, my grief turns to anger; my anger turns to resolve. We're not done helping these girls yet. Leaving the boys to continue sorting, I head out of the room and up to the study. As I round the corner of the stairs to step up, my eyes are drawn to the piano.

A girl with dark brown hair is staring at me. She's not quite solid, not quite transparent, but she's wearing an apron over a plain-colored dress, a light brown or a dark cream. I smile at her. "It's safe to come out now, Tabitha," I say. She looks at me but doesn't return my smile. One of her hands is on her lap, the other on the keys. "Have you been the one leaving clues for us down here?" I grin, putting a hand on the steps. She hesitates and then nods. "Thank you," I say. She puts her other hand on the keys and presses down. The keys barely move, but I hear a note sounding low and sad. She, too, can't be more than fourteen.

I look and see the chair is still there. "Let's get that out of there, shall we?" She smiles at me and nods exuberantly.

"George?" I call. He comes around the corner and sees the girl. To my joy, he smiles at her. I put my hand on his arm lovingly. "This is her: Tabitha. Clara's girlfriend," I say, introducing them. "She and I both think it's time to take care of Jasper's chair."

We head toward the chair: I'm at the head, George at the feet. We both pause before touching it as if it might burn us. A quick tap tells me it's solid, and I place my hands on the back. "One, two, three," I say, and George and I both lift at the same time.

In an instant, the head comes away from the seat, the arms drop to the floor, the base falls from George's hands, and upon meeting the air, the stuffing turns to dust. I look at him, bewildered, and we both share a hearty laugh. "That settles that, then." It takes a few trips, but we take the remnants upstairs and straight out to the garbage can. On each return to the basement, the girl is still there at the piano. She's so shy; no wonder Charlie never knew she was here.

When we're finished, Dad stays in the basement to help George, but I put an arm on his, turning to the girl. "Would you and Clara like to be buried together?" She looks at me, confused. I turn to George. "Hold off on sorting. I don't think we'll need to." As the words leave my mouth, a silver sparkle descends the stairs. I think I see a smile spreading on the dark-haired girl's face as the sparkle becomes Clara, standing at her side. Clara takes her hand. "Come on, Tabitha."

I EXPLAINED my plan to Dad and George after Tabitha and Clara disappeared back into the house. Now we're only a few hours from sunset. They bring up the box of bones from the basement and ready themselves. It's a cardboard box due to the short notice; we didn't know how to ask for the wooden one back from May, but Clara and Tabitha don't seem to mind. Before sealing it up, I place the love letters on top. It feels like the right end for their love story – at least on this plane.

It's time for them to move on, together.

They don't materialize again, but I see a shining glitter around the window by the dollhouse and feel the occasional drafts at my ankles throughout the afternoon. George seems to as well, but he just shakes his head or breathes a short chuckle every so often as they pass us.

We're carrying the box out the back door when a knock sounds from the front. Dad takes my space as pallbearer, and I jog to the door, swinging it open. "Charlie," I beam. "I'm so glad you came." He's standing at the porch, wearing a suit jacket over a buttoned-down gray shirt. Still in jeans, but his hair is combed back, too.

And in his hands, he holds a big bouquet of gardenias.

I bring him through the house, brushing off his murmur about his boots on the clean floors – "my mother would've had my head" – and ushering him out the back door.

The sun now setting, a peach-pink and golden oil painting

across the sky, the homes on the lane are reduced to shadows in the foreground. Charlie nearly bumps into me as I stop at the line of trees to take it in. "A beautiful night for them," I say, nodding to the sky. As we head out to catch up to Dad and George, I fill Charlie in on Tabitha and our conversation about burying them together. "You never heard from Tabitha then, in all your years?"

He shakes his head and shrugs. "Clara would disappear and reappear when she wanted. I didn't ask questions."

I want to add, 'Not much has changed,' but instead, I say, "I'm sure she was a great friend to grow up with. Not every kid has a ghost girl for a best friend. She's a real sweetheart."

Charlie smiles at that. "Sometimes I wonder if I should've believed Dad who said she was just imaginary. But I always knew." I want to ask more questions, but I don't. I just keep walking. I place my hand in my pocket and feel the jar of teeth there. When we get close to the garden, Charlie seems to know where he's going. Reading my mind, he says, "I always came here in the spring and summer, especially when they were in full bloom." He inhales, remembering. "I could talk to Clara openly here, no one wondering who I was talking to or what I was doing. It's peaceful."

"You should come out here on walks more often."

"Maybe I will. I believe you mentioned having me in for a cup of coffee sometime, anyway." He grins.

When we come up to the garden, Dad is digging while George looks on, leaning back on his heels in a squat. We still only have one shovel. Charlie goes over to Dad and takes over for him, giving him one of his newfound smiles. Dad smiles back, and I can tell he's seeing Charlie in a whole new light, cleaned up, beardless in a buttoned-up shirt and jacket. George claps him on the back and shakes his hand, and I hear them chatting together about something, but I hang back.

"I'll be right back," I say. "There's one more thing to put to rest first."

As I get closer to the river, I hear the rush of the water before I see it. I try to imagine what it must have sounded like that day the river rose in seconds to claim Clara, Tabitha, Jasper, and so many others.

Standing at the edge, I take the jar of teeth from my pocket and the single tooth from the piano. I roll the tooth in my hand, feeling familiar with Tabitha now, and close my eyes. I grip the tooth in a fist, and in the other hand, the bottle of teeth. I take some deep breaths and focus on Clara's bright, sweet energy, her smile, her kindness. I picture Tabitha as I've seen her so far. Dark hair hanging over an eye as she coyly looks past Clara. Sitting on the piano bench, her hands delicately on the keys. Her gentle spirit and strong resilience.

Suddenly I feel a presence near each of my hands, and I open my eyes. Tabitha is on my left, cupping my hand with the single tooth. Clara is on my right, her hand on mine where I hold the jar. They each smile, and I realize Tabitha is missing one tooth in front, her upper right canine. I open my fist and look – it matches the size. I look at Clara's mouth and the jar filled with at least a dozen teeth of all sizes.

"You protected her," I say, a sob rising in my throat once again at the thought. Jasper found the letters. He blackmailed Clara; she didn't want Tabitha to know, so she let Jasper take tooth after tooth for who knows how long. Until Tabitha found out and tried to take the fall. "You protected each other," I turn to Tabitha. I smile at each of them, swallowing the sob and sniffing. "You don't have to anymore," I say. I open my hands, and the ghosts each pick up their respective teeth, hurling them into the river. Tabitha's tooth disappears as it hits the water, but I watch the jar float for a second before sinking into the depths, rushing down with the current. I turn to the girls, but they're gone. I see a glittering, silver sparkle float up and through the boughs of the leafless trees, merging with the waning sunlight.

We bury the girls in quiet ceremony. Charlie doesn't want to speak and neither do Dad or George. I've had my moment with them. We each shovel some dirt over their grave. Charlie takes a gardenia out of the bouquet for each of us, handing them around. We place them one by one on the grave, Charlie, me, then George. As Dad places his flower, he pauses and grins, holding up the gardenia and looking at us. "Secret love, remember?"

I smile at Dad, then explain to Charlie the Victorian Language of Flowers. "Purity and gentleness, too." He nods and turns away for a moment. I pretend not to notice the tears welling in his eyes. We stand in silence for some time before heading back to the house.

It's completely dark by the time we finish, and we watch our breath as we cross the tracks and sidle down the hill, heading for the back door. I invite Charlie in for coffee, and this time, he accepts.

After coffee, Charlie moves to leave, and I hold up a hand, requesting he stay one more second. I open the cupboard and bring down the plates with gardenias on them. "You should have these. She would've wanted you to," I say. He graciously accepts the dishes, and Dad goes to get him a box to carry them. I decided I'll keep the oil lamp; it'll rest in my Craft room, forever reminding me of Clara.

George puts his arm around me as we walk Charlie to the door. "I think she's finally at rest, Charlie," I say. "I haven't felt her all night."

"Don't speak so soon," he replies, a sparkle of hope glinting in his eye. "She has a mind of her own."

"Don't be a stranger, Charlie," George says, shaking his hand as Charlie opens the front door.

"We'll see you around, kid," Dad says, passing Charlie the box. He takes it and smiles, nodding farewell to each of us.

When Charlie leaves, we sit around the living room, not turning on the TV, but instead take in a peaceful moment. The house is quiet, the energy clean.

"I guess I'll be heading back up to Philly then this week," Dad says, picking at the cuticle on his thumb.

I look at George. We haven't had a chance to talk about it, but I know what we're both thinking. "Dad, why don't you move in here with us? Sell the house in Philly and enjoy your retirement out here in the countryside."

Dad raises his eyes to meet mine, a grin spreading wide on his face. "You mean it? You kids won't mind an old fart like me waking up early every morning?"

I laugh. "You can even use the attic as a workshop. Or the basement," I smile.

"You won't be in the way, Dad. You know that," George says, elbowing him.

Dad smiles wider. George hasn't called him Dad before.

"We can go back up to Philly this week and get your tools and some more clothes. But I've been thinking," I say. "Let's not repair the dollhouse." I can almost hear Tabitha laughing that it took over 100 years for Clara to outgrow her dolls. "We'll keep the furniture and the dolls and make a little scene on top of the piano." A bit of both of their worlds – I think they'd like that.

George kisses me on the head. "That's a cute idea, especially for a Yuletide display," he says.

"If you want," Dad begins, "I can take this dollhouse to May as it is, see what she can get for it from a hobbyist," he clears his throat, putting his thumbs in his belt, but his crush on May is written all over his face.

George looks at me, raising his eyebrows. Then we all laugh, louder and longer than the moment calls for.

I pull my hands into my sleeves and inhale a deep breath of relief. Looking out the window, it's hard to remember this is the same one from my dreams. The energy of the home now feels clear. Clean. Fresh. Like our own.

I look towards the study and feel a deep knowing swell in my chest. I'll write a bestseller in that room. The feeling of knowing I'm an author with an impending book deal no longer fills my heart with anxiety – I know I've earned this.

I made all of this happen. I solved the mystery. I saved Clara and Tabitha. I banished a powerful spirit from this house.

I look around, half expecting a silver sparkle, but there's no one but the living among us now. And thanks to Clara's mystery, Dad is with us, too.

Something is over, for sure. But something bigger and better is just beginning.

I feel completely and utterly at peace in my own home. For the first time, I am not afraid to be the person I was meant to become.

ABOUT THE AUTHOR

Initiated in the eclectic Faery Tradition of witchcraft & holding an MA with a focus in spiritual studies, Elyse Welles is a practicing witch and High Priestess of her coven in Havre de Grace, Maryland. She is a teacher of the lost Earth Priestess Arts of the Mediterranean where she hails from, facilitating retreats in Greece, in Havre de Grace, and online containers. She hosts the Magick Kitchen Podcast, a top 20 show in the US all about witchcraft, as well as Seeking Numina: the Sacred Places Podcast and the Cosmic Theater Mystery School, a podcast bridging the paranormal with the spiritual.

* * *

Selected as a best poet of 2022 by Free Verse Revolution, her essays, poetry, and articles are featured in several anthologies. Her nonfiction book, 'Sacred Wild: An Invitation to Connect with Spirits of the Land', releases with Llewellyn November 2025. "What the Water Remembers" is her first novel. She writes for Witchology, Witch Way Magazine, and is the Greece correspondent for the Wild Hunt. She has spoken at several conferences including Hekatefest and the Water Priestess Confluence. Learn more at seekingnumina.com or @seekingnumina on Instagram.

ACKNOWLEDGMENTS

A big thank you first and foremost to those who read this book in its roughest, earliest forms. To Lauren M, for her unending motivational push by editing my first draft and getting this story ready for publication. To Megan and Kore for being moved by my characters enough to read this book to completion in that early stage. To my husband Brooks, you live in every beat of George's heart. Thank you to my parents for facilitating the right creative space in which to write this book. To my editor Aimee, your attention to detail made all the difference in telling Kendra's story, thank you.

To my patrons on Patreon, your support has enabled me not only to have a book tour through your financial contributions, but in your emotional support in the beautiful community we're a part of you've given me the motivation and energy to get this book out to the world. Thank you.

And a shout out to Julia Cameron. The journey of writing this book began in Week 6 of the Artist Way in 2021, and I likely never would've begun writing without it.

About RIZE Press

RIZE publishes great stories and great writing across genres written by People of Color and other underrepresented groups. Our team consists of:

Lisa Diane Kastner, Founder and Executive Editor
Cody Sisco, Acquisitions Editor, RIZE
Benjamin White, Acquisition Editor, Running Wild
Peter A. Wright, Acquisition Editor, Running Wild
Resa Alboher, Editor
Angela Andrews, Editor
Sandra Bush, Editor
Ashley Crantas, Editor
Rebecca Dimyan, Editor
Abigail Efird, Editor
Aimee Hardy, Editor
Henry L. Herz, Editor
Cecilia Kennedy, Editor
Barbara Lockwood, Editor
Scott Schultz, Editor
Rod Gilley, Editor

Evangeline Estropia, Product Manager
Kimberly Ligutan, Product Manager
Lara Macaione, Marketing Director
Joelle Mitchell, Licensing and Strategy Lead
Pulp Art Studios, Cover Design
Standout Books, Interior Design
Polgarus Studios, Interior Design